Captain's Choice

Praise for VK Powell

Side Effects

"[A] touching contemporary tale of two wounded souls hoping to find lasting love and redemption together…Powell ably plots a plausible and suspenseful story, leading readers to fall in love with the characters she's created."—*Publishers Weekly*

To Protect and Serve

"If you like cop novels, or even television cop shows with women as full partners with male officers…this is the book for you. It's got drama, excitement, conflict, and even some fairly hot lesbian sex. The writer is a retired cop, so she really writes from a place of authenticity. As a result, you have a realistic quality to the writing that puts me in mind of early Joseph Wambaugh."—Teresa DeCrescenzo, *Lesbian News*

"*To Protect and Serve* drew me in from the very first page with characters that captivated in their complexity. Powell writes with authority using the lingo and capturing the thoughts of the law enforcers who make the ultimate sacrifice in the fight against crime. What's more impressive is the command this debut author has of portraying a full gamut of emotion, from angst to elation, through dialogue and narrative. The images are vivid, the action is believable, and the police procedurals are authentic…VK Powell had me invested in the story of these women, heart, mind, body and soul. Along with danger and tension, Powell's well-developed erotic scenes sizzle and sate." —*Story Circle Book Reviews*

Suspect Passions

"From the first chapter of *Suspect Passions* Powell builds erotic scenes which sear the page. She definitely takes her readers for a walk on the wild side! Her characters, however, are also women we care about. They are bright, witty, and strong. The combination of great sex and great characters make *Suspect Passions* a must read." —*Just About Write*

Fever

"VK Powell has given her fans an exciting read. The plot of *Fever* is filled with twists, turns, and 'seat of your pants' danger…*Fever* gives readers both great characters and erotic scenes along with insight into life in the African bush."—*Just About Write*

Justifiable Risk

"This story takes some unusual twists and at one point, I was convinced that I knew 'who did it' only to find out that I was wrong. VK Powell knows crime drama, she kept me guessing until the end, and I was not disappointed at the outcome. And that's not to slight VK Powell's knack for romance…Readers who appreciate mysteries with a touch of drama and intense erotic moments will enjoy *Justifiable Risk*." —*Queer Magazine*

Exit Wounds

"Powell's prose is no-nonsense and all business. It gets in and gets the job done, a few well-placed phrases sparkling in your memory and some trenchant observations about life in general and a cop's life in particular sticking to your psyche long after they've gone. After five books, Powell knows what her audience wants, and she delivers those goods with solid assurance. But be careful you don't get hooked. You only get six hits, then the supply's gone, and you'll be jonesin' for the next installment. It never pays to be at the mercy of a cop." —*Out in Print*

"Fascinating and complicated characters materialize, morph, and sometimes disappear testing the passionate yet nascent love of the book's focal pair. I was so totally glued to and amazed by the intricate layers that continued to materialize like an active volcano…dangerous and deadly until the last mystery is revealed. This book goes into my super special category. Please don't miss it."—*Rainbow Book Reviews*

About Face

"Powell excels at depicting complex, emotionally vulnerable characters who connect in a believable fashion and enjoy some genuinely hot erotic moments."—*Publishers Weekly*

By the Author

To Protect and Serve

Suspect Passions

Fever

Justifiable Risk

Haunting Whispers

Exit Wounds

About Face

Side Effects

Deception

Lone Ranger

Captain's Choice

CAPTAIN'S CHOICE

by

VK Powell

2017

CAPTAIN'S CHOICE

ISBN 13: 978-1-62639-997-6

This Trade Paperback Original Is Published By
Bold Strokes Books, Inc.
P.O. Box 249
Valley Falls, NY 12185

First Edition: December 2017

Credits
Editor: Shelley Thrasher
Production Design: Stacia Seaman
Cover Design by Sheri (graphicartist2020@hotmail.com)

Acknowledgments

I've been blessed to pursue two careers that brought me great satisfaction. The first allowed me to help people and promote advancement for women in a profession that often overlooked them. In the second, I parlayed that career into stories of survival, the struggle to balance love and livelihood, and the fight between good and evil. To Len Barot and all the wonderful folks at Bold Strokes Books—thank you for giving me the chance to tell my stories.

My deepest gratitude and admiration to Dr. Shelley Thrasher for your guidance, suggestions, and kindness. Working with you is a learning experience and a pleasure. I'm so proud of our collaborations and of your success as a Bold Strokes author.

For BSB sister author, D. Jackson Leigh, and friends Jenny Harmon and Mary Margret Daughtridge—thank you for taking time out of your busy lives to provide priceless feedback. This book is so much better for your efforts. I am truly grateful.

To all the readers who support and encourage my writing, thank you for buying my work, sending emails, and showing up for events. You make my "job" so much fun!

Chapter One

Kerstin Anthony paused beside the bronze sculpture of police officer and boy outside the Melvin Municipal Office Building in downtown Greensboro and pulled her suit jacket tighter against the brisk fall breeze. She'd been here often—over seventeen years ago—with a friend in high school, whose father was a cop. She shivered from a pang of unexpected sadness, a reminder that period of her life hadn't been entirely pleasant. She pushed the unwanted memories aside and focused on her purpose.

She'd taken over the architectural project for the first Greensboro Police substation from a coworker who'd been removed under embarrassing circumstances. Her boss was counting on her to redeem the firm's reputation, but more importantly, she needed this project to secure her own future and her mother's. If she was honest, her ego was also wrapped up in showing Leonard Parrish she could handle any messed-up assignment he shuffled her way. She climbed the stairs of the entrance and followed the hallway to the chief's complex.

The chief had obviously not asked his admin to come in for the emergency Sunday meeting, so she waited in the small conference room adjacent to his office. She rolled her architectural plans out on the large conference table and smoothed the front of her favorite red power suit. The butterflies in her stomach accompanied every meeting in which she had to sell herself, actually any situation in which she was not totally in charge. Taking on someone else's project, fraught with pitfalls and problems not of her making, could become a nightmare. But she'd reviewed the drawings and was prepared. She'd simply offer a brief overview to a police officer who knew nothing about architecture, get his signature on the contract, and carry on with the work she loved. The meeting was only a formality. Raised voices from the chief's office, one male and one female, returned her attention to the present.

"Are you kidding, Chief? I'm a street cop. The manager's office should oversee a project this size."

Kerstin considered stepping out of the room, or at least making her presence known, but instead eased closer to the door, curiosity winning out. The disagreement was probably about *her* project, and she hated being left in the dark about anything.

"This is your first assignment. Comes with the promotion. Take it or leave it, Captain." The voices quieted, and a few seconds later the door connecting the chief's office and the conference room swung open.

Kerstin inhaled sharply as a tall, lean woman with observant whiskey-brown eyes and plump lips that evoked memories walked toward her. Kerstin backed away as if distance would change the situation.

"Kerstin Anthony?" the woman asked.

She pressed her fingertips on the tabletop to steady herself. "Ben… Bennett Carlyle?"

"Hi, Kerst." Bennett openly stared her up and down with no hint of subtlety before settling on her lips. "What are you doing here?"

The last time she'd seen Bennett, her eyes and intentions were full of mischief and teenage rebellion, and Kerstin had been terrified. "It's Kerstin." Formality and structure kept her grounded and in control, and right now she needed those traits desperately.

"Okay, Kerstin." Bennett offered a slight smile, and the dimples on either side of her mouth blossomed. "How have you been? Where have you been? What are you doing in Greensboro? At the police station? That didn't sound right. You're just…unexpected."

The sociable Bennett, who'd been so popular in school, babbled nervously, and Kerstin just wanted to escape. She couldn't pretend they were old friends picking up where they'd left off. Too much had happened. Her face heated, and the strong coffee she'd had for breakfast churned in her stomach. She gathered her drawings, willing her hands to steady. Sliding the plans to the edge of the table, she reached for her bag, but the pages fell and scattered across the floor.

"I'll get them." Bennett stooped beside her, and Kerstin inhaled the vivid musk scent she'd always associated with Bennett.

Kerstin stood quickly, pulling for a breath not filled with Bennett's scent and the past. "I won't waste your time or mine. This isn't going to work." Her carefully constructed façade quivered. Her life was already complicated enough.

Bennett rolled the drawings and offered them to her. "What's not going to work?"

"The project. Us. Together." She was a professional and worked with a variety of difficult and challenging people on assignments. She could handle the situation, if she wanted. The question tumbled over and over in her mind. Did she want to? Any person or thing from years ago controlling any aspect of her life rankled.

Bennett's lips tightened slightly at the comment, and she glanced from Kerstin to the rolled pages she held. "You're from the architectural firm?"

"Of course. Why else would I be here? And why is that so surprising?"

"I'm not surprised you're an architect. You always had the smarts to be anything you wanted. I'm shocked you're here."

"Parrish Designs, the firm I work for, had the original contract. It makes sense, economically and design wise." Kerstin reached for the plans Bennett held, careful to avoid touching her, but changed her mind. "Keep those." She refused to explain anything about her life, past or present. "And you're a cop. Didn't see that one coming."

A flicker of sadness crossed Bennett's face, followed by a weighty silence. "It's the family business, but you're right." She waved her hand down the front of the black uniform that hugged her body and added height to her already lanky figure. "Military dress, shiny synthetic shoes, and a twenty-pound utility belt. Not really me. Is it?"

"Certainly not the Bennett Carlyle I remember, but that was a long time ago." And not a time she cared to remember. She schooled her expression and carefully delivered her next statement. "One of us should withdraw from the project. The job is massive, and a personality conflict will only complicate matters further."

"I don't have a personality conflict. As a matter of fact, I've been told I have a pretty decent personality." Her full lips curved into a stunning smile, and dimples again flanked her mouth.

Of course, cool, confident Bennett Carlyle got along with everyone, so she was implying Kerstin obviously had the problem.

Bennett appraised her silently for several seconds. “And, in the interest of full disclosure, I’ll be overseeing the project. Can you say awkward?”

She was supposed to work with a woman she could barely make eye contact with and accept her daily scrutiny? This was so not happening. Her boss might fire her if she didn’t at least make an attempt, but right now she wanted out of this uncomfortable situation. She had other projects waiting for her expertise. “I’ll find a suitable replacement from the firm, someone I think you’ll get along with better.” She turned to leave.

“Wait. What? This job is a big deal, as you said, and I’d hate for you to miss out.” Bennett took two long strides and stopped, towering over her.

Kerstin had forgotten how tall Bennett was, and the difference, once comforting, made her uneasy. And Bennett stood so close, Kerstin smelled her distinctive fragrance again.

“Why don’t we go for a walk and catch up before you make a definite decision? We could cut through the parking lot to Green Bean.”

“No, thanks. I’m here for a business meeting, not a reunion. And trust me, Parrish Designs has other qualified architects who can handle the job.” She almost added that a walk and a cup of coffee wouldn’t come close to catching them up. If she were any other woman, Kerstin would jump at the offer because Bennett was charming and totally hot. As it was, she couldn’t imagine spending more time with Bennett on purpose. Her energy was vibrant and compelling, which terrified and intrigued Kerstin, and she did not want to be intrigued by Bennett Carlyle.

“Okay. How about the canteen down the hall? Coffee’s not bad and a little socializing couldn’t hurt.”

“Again, thank you, but no.” Kerstin released the door handle and turned her head to breathe deeply and avoid those brown eyes. The pinnacle of her portfolio, the project to virtually guarantee the first contract in her own firm, was on the line, but she’d survive. “I need to go.”

“At least think about the job. Your coworker started the renovation, and we need everything to continue seamlessly. The department is in a time crunch." Bennett's tone was soft and obliging, the timbre of a woman negotiating for something important. Was she only concerned about her promotion? "I'm sure we can work together."

"I'm not." Bennett was probably right. They were professionals, so why did Kerstin want to run? She reached for the door handle again, but Bennett beat her to it.

"Let me." She opened the door and waited for Kerstin to walk through. "Nice to see you again, Kerst—Kerstin. I wish you'd reconsider. This project could help both of us."

Was Bennett waving a white flag about their past or speaking professionally? Either way, it didn't matter. She'd simply ask her boss to assign another architect. After all, she'd taken over from Gilbert Early, who'd been pulled from the job without much explanation. Collaborating with Bennett Carlyle was not an option, even if it set back her future plans.

❖

Bennett watched Kerstin until she disappeared down the hallway and then collapsed in the nearest chair. She'd seen Kerstin standing in the chief's conference room and locked her knees. She didn't shock easily, but her heart rate trebled, and a heavy sensation settled in her stomach. She'd read the chief's notes about the meeting, but nowhere did he mention the name of the architect. How had her greatest professional accomplishment and her worst heartbreak collided?

Kerstin looked good. Damn it, better than good. Her sun-kissed blond hair had darkened a shade and lightly brushed the tops of her shoulders instead of cascading down her back. The steel-blue eyes still deepened when she was upset, and she'd definitely been upset at the sight of Bennett. The most dramatic change—a skinny schoolgirl had morphed into a fully developed woman. She transformed a red, tailored business suit from only clothing into a statement that said powerful, sexy woman, don't mess with me. Excitement curled through Bennett, followed closely by a sense of regret and dread. The optimistic, adventurous girl from high school had vanished, or was at least buried beneath a veneer of caution.

Had it really been seventeen years since they'd seen each other? She still ached to know why. She'd rehearsed exactly what she'd say at their reunion, but after her disagreement with the chief and Kerstin's unexpected appearance, Bennett reverted to humor and charm to offset the tension. Face-to-face with her childhood dream, she completely lost her nerve. Surreal to be thrown together again, but Kerstin was clear the reunion wouldn't last. Maybe for the best. Important things had been left unsaid far too long.

No time to reminisce about old emotions. If Kerstin stayed on board, she'd appeal to the chief one final time about withdrawing from the project. Bennett didn't really want to manage the substation renovation anyway. Her new position required focus and dedication far beyond just showing up every day like her predecessor. Pete Ashton was a reasonable man, and she'd convince him she could better serve the department in the field. She'd save face and make Kerstin happy at the same time, unsure why the latter was even a consideration.

She had scribbled her talking points on a Post-it, preparing to leave, when her cell rang.

"Sis, are you at the house yet?" Her brother's deep James Earl Jones voice, so much like their father's, boomed over the phone, always making her smile.

"Hey, Paul Simon." She loved to kid him about his namesake because he couldn't sing a note, and it annoyed him. "You mean you're not there either?"

"Mama and G-ma are going to be pissed, but I got called to the firehouse on a personnel matter. Guess we're both in the doghouse."

"Are Stephanie and the kids there?"

"Yeah. I dropped them off on my way in but didn't have the nerve to face Mama."

"All I can say is you better hurry. I'd hate to see my older brother whipped in front of his wife and kids."

"Very funny. Stall them if you can. I'll be quick."

❖

Bennett rolled down her car window and breathed in the crisp fall air as she drove home for the family's customary Sunday brunch. Like the mature oak trees in Fisher Park, her family had endured the storms of decades, and she and her siblings had climbed many of them growing up. She parked in front of their sprawling two-story home, grinning when Simon's twins, Ryan and Riley, called out, "She's here," in unison. She raced up the steps of the wraparound porch to grab them, but the eleven-year-olds were quicker than they'd been a few years ago and got away.

She followed them through the screen door and stopped in the foyer, always humbled by the massive traditional family home and the memories filling every room. She and Jazz had walked down the wide, creaky staircase on graduation day into the arms of their parents. What she'd give to feel her father's arms around her again. She'd kissed her first girlfriend at the age of fifteen on the old Mission-style sofa in the lounge, while her little sister Dylan spied on them through the stair rails. During her grandfather and father's wakes, the house overflowed with cops, friends, and distant family. The walls made eerie sounds for months after, mourning the loss of each patriarch, so many good memories interwoven with bad. The shock of seeing Kerstin and the stress of possibly working with her drained away in the familiar surroundings of home and family.

The layout was perfect for the large family, with two lounges, a half bath, huge kitchen, and combination dining and sunroom occupying the first floor. Five bedrooms and three baths located upstairs provided for the immediate family who still lived here—G-ma, Mama, Jazz, and Dylan. She'd occupied the fourth single bedroom until two years ago. She and her partner had moved to the carriage house behind the garden, but their relationship ended when her partner left her and the country for a job opportunity. Bennett also suspected she found being so close to the family intrusive. Jazz, her adopted sister, would occupy the smaller residence next, if Bennett ever found the right woman. And she wanted that more than almost anything—a partner to build and share a home with, and maybe even start a family.

Soft piano music drifted from the sitting room on her right, and Bennett peeped in. Surrounded by traditional furnishings and rich colors, her younger sister, Dylan, long hair pulled back in a ponytail and dressed in a white blouse and jeans, undulated with each delicate keystroke, and Bennett marveled at her ability to urge such beautiful sounds from an instrument she'd always found arduous. Dylan's musical interest would serve as a great stress reliever during her challenging medical career.

"Look at you getting all Bob Dylan." Bennett knelt behind Dylan and wrapped her in a bear hug. Bennett loved her little sister, and not just because she was a mirror image of her, but for her intelligence and compassion. She'd stepped out of the family mold and surpassed all their expectations.

"Hey, sis." Dylan rested her head back against Bennett's shoulder for a few seconds, and Bennett traced the patch of freckles across her upturned nose. "You realize Bob Dylan played predominantly guitar and harmonica, right? But somebody has to represent our family of musically-named-but-talentless siblings."

"Paul Simon Carlyle and Toni Bennett Carlyle bow to your superiority. Speaking of our big brother, he's going to be late, so we have to stall G-ma and Mama. You know how he hates to miss a meal."

"That won't be easy. They're already fired up about having to wait for you and Jazz."

Bennett started to ask where Jazz was, but Stephanie, Simon's petite and perfectly turned-out wife, interrupted. "Have either of you heard from Simon?" Her expression relayed that she was thinking the same thing they were—if Simon didn't hurry, they'd start brunch without him.

"Mom, I'm hungry." Riley and Ryan, smaller versions of their strawberry-blond mother with hazel eyes, flanked Stephanie. The children also vibrated with Stephanie's seemingly endless energy, always on the move, always doing something. The only features marking them as laid-back Simon's offspring were cleft chins and their above-average height.

Stephanie patted their heads. "We're waiting for your father."

"Where the blue blazes is everybody?" G-ma called from the kitchen.

"Uh-oh, play something, Dylan." Bennett motioned Stephanie and the kids to her side, and they sang as Dylan played "Itsy Bitsy Spider." G-ma and Mama couldn't resist a good sing-along, and soon everyone was belting out the words in discordant joy.

During the third round, Simon slipped in and added his bass voice to the party, giving Bennett an appreciative wink. When G-ma saw him, she clapped her hands and ushered everybody into the dining area.

Bennett gave Dylan a quick conspiratorial squeeze and sprinted around back to the cottage to change out of her uniform. When she entered the sunroom, her family stood around the long refectory table her grandparents had rescued from a doomed monastery during one of their first trips as a married couple. She and her siblings had carved their names and dates of birth on the underside when her dad determined they were old enough to wield a sharp knife. Chafing dishes rested in hollows worn into the dark walnut wood and kept the food warm.

"You didn't have to wait," Jazz said as she rushed in the back door and washed her hands in the kitchen sink.

"Yeah, we've been waiting hours. I'm starving." Simon waved an impatient greeting.

"The day my big brother isn't hungry, we'll know for sure you're sick," Bennett said.

Simon shrugged. "You know Mama won't let anything interfere with Sunday brunch, not even a call from the chief of police."

"Bennett and Jazz, cell phones in the basket along with the others. I don't want any more interruptions." Her mother kissed them on the cheek and motioned for the family to sit.

"Hurry up," G-ma said as she settled at one end of the table with Simon at the other. "We got us some celebrating to do, times two."

"What?" Her mind was still on the untimely reunion with Kerstin that overshadowed her promotion to captain. "Two?" She noticed the bottle of champagne chilling in the center of the table. "Is Stephanie pregnant again?"

Simon shook his head. "Second guess?"

Bennett scanned the faces around the table until she landed on Jazz. She was normally quiet but wouldn't even look up, her fingers stroking the streak of white hair near her left ear. She was hiding something. "Jazz?"

Dylan sighed heavily to Bennett's left. "I told you Jazz couldn't keep anything from Ben. They're like twins separated at birth."

Jasmine Perry grinned, and her pearly teeth glistened against olive skin as she stretched her arm across the table and opened her hand. A pair of lieutenant's bars rested in her palm.

"No shit?"

"Language," Stephanie said, covering an ear of the twin on either side of her.

"Sorry." Bennett rushed around the table to Jazz. She almost picked her up, but stopped at the last minute. Jazz shied away from unexpected or long embraces, so Bennett settled for a quick squeeze. “Congrats, sis.”

“Thanks, you too.”

“Did you know about this before I got the call?”

Jazz shook her head. “Got mine after you.”

“Where are you assigned?”

“Still in District One. Just moving up a notch.”

“No shi—kidding? Working together, sweet, but my job won’t be as much fun.” Jazz gave her a questioning look. “We’ll talk later.”

They fist-bumped and sat back down.

“Now that’s settled, Riley, say grace, please,” G-ma said.

Riley put her hands together and looked toward the ceiling. “If anybody’s really up there, thank you for this food, for Mommy and Daddy, G-ma, Mama, Aunties Bennett, Jazz, and Dylan. Oh yeah, and my irritating brother, Ryan. Amen.”

G-ma patted her on the arm. “Well done. Somebody pass the damn eggs before they get colder than Garrett’s tomb.”

“G-ma!” Dylan sounded genuinely shocked, but when G-ma and Mama laughed, the rest of the table joined in. Hearing Grandma Carlyle curse wasn’t new, but hearing it at a sacred Sunday brunch was different.

“You all right, G-ma?” Mama touched her mother-in-law’s forearm.

“Of course I’m all right, Gayle, but hungry as hell. Now pass the eggs. Only one thing on earth worse than cold eggs.”

“Don’t leave us hanging.” Stephanie passed the egg platter. “I’m sure it’ll be a doozy.”

“The empty side of anyone’s bed who has lost or doesn’t have a loving partner.”

The clatter of utensils and dishes abruptly ended. Bennett’s Grandpa Garrett and her father, Bryce, had been police officers and were both killed in the line of duty. The family didn’t speak of the incidents often because no one wanted to jinx her or Jazz, the only children who’d followed in their footsteps. Though Simon had chosen an equally proud but dangerous profession, nobody ever brought up how many firefighters were killed in fires.

"Amen, G-ma." Simon smiled at Stephanie with the kind of love Bennett hoped she'd share with a partner one day.

"Can I eat now?" Ryan waved a piece of bacon in the air with the impatience of youth.

"Of course you can, darling," G-ma spooned grits onto her plate. "Everybody eat up."

Mama handed the champagne bottle to Simon. "Do the honors, son?" While he peeled the top and set about popping the cork, she asked, "So, why did Pete Ashton need to promote my two girls on Sunday morning? What's the urgency?"

Bennett plucked a couple of pieces of bacon from the platter before moving it to the right. "My predecessor, Arthur Warren, and his architect got drunk and injured some folks in an accident on the way home last night. Warren flunked the Breathalyzer and resigned on the spot."

"Lucky break," Simon said. "You deserved that promotion a long time ago."

Simon lived the Carlyle edicts to support and uphold the family name, and serve the community. Bennett probably hadn't contributed enough. "Thanks, bro." She'd screwed off for nineteen years, and her father hadn't lived to see her change. She glanced across the table.

Jazz gave a faint headshake as if to say, don't go there. She'd come to the family from foster care when they were both eight, after being passed around a few different homes, and knew all about not feeling good enough. She and Bennett were best friends and confidantes. Bennett was the fire to Jazz's ice, the storm to her calm. Now they'd be running a district, and Bennett couldn't wait.

"Is Ma Rolls ready for business again tomorrow, G-ma?" Simon asked.

"Ready and rearing to go. The police officers on Fairview Street and the other places we serve would starve without our food truck. And I'd seize up and wither away without my weekly doses of town gossip."

Mama glanced over at G-ma and chuckled. "That's for sure, and we'd be bored senseless."

The rest of the meal passed quickly, with each family member talking about whatever he or she wanted, as long as they phrased their comments in a positive manner. G-ma always said there was enough negativity in the world without them contributing. The practice kept the family strong and involved in each other's lives. Bennett wanted the same for her own family one day. Conversation finally lulled, and G-ma pushed away from the table, ending the meal.

Simon poured a cup of coffee and headed toward the lounge. "I think Ben and Jazz should do the dishes since they made us wait so long to eat. Do I hear a second?"

The rest of the family voiced their agreement and ran from the kitchen.

"Democracy's alive and well in the Carlyle home," Bennett said as she transferred dishes from the table to the dishwasher. "Are you okay moving up from sergeant to lieutenant in the same command?"

Jazz nodded. "Everybody knows me."

"And they respect you, but they'll still test you. Comes with any promotion, especially for a woman. I'll be there, if you need me." She wasn't worried about Jazz's professional abilities because she'd moved up quickly in the department despite being five years behind Bennett in seniority, but her introversion was sometimes interpreted as aloofness or lack of concern. Jazz didn't have an arrogant or apathetic cell in her body. If anything, she cared too deeply at times.

"Thanks." Jazz's deep-brown eyes glistened with gratitude she didn't need to verbalize. She dried her hands and looped the cloth through the oven handle. "I'll walk you out."

Jazz wasn't the social type, more comfortable with her own company, so she obviously had something on her mind. As they cut through the garden to the cottage, Bennett's quicker steps caused Jazz to fall behind.

"What's the hurry, Ben?"

"Keep up, slowpoke." She gave the conversation a nudge. "What's on your mind, sis?"

Jazz stopped and faced her. "I was going to ask you the same thing."

They never made each other work too hard for the truth, sensing when the other needed to talk. "The chief wants me to oversee the renovation of the Cone Building for our new District One substation."

"Captain Warren's assignment before he quit. That's a good thing, right?"

"It would be if…" Bennett scuffed her sneaker in the grass, feeling self-conscious.

"If what?"

At five-eleven, Bennett towered over Jazz by three inches, but Jazz wasn't intimidated by the difference. Bennett couldn't bullshit her either, her dark eyes a better lie detector than any mechanical device.

"Kerstin Anthony is the architect." She finally looked at Jazz.

Her eyes opened wide and she said, "*The* Kerstin Anthony from high school?"

Bennett nodded. "And she doesn't want to work with me. If she refuses, the project is delayed again while a new architect gets up to speed and possibly redraws the whole plan. What if the chief thinks it's my fault? What if it is?"

"Did you do something to upset her?"

"I said I was glad to see her and tried to convince her we could work together. Even offered to buy her coffee."

"That sounds harmless enough," Jazz said.

"She's probably still upset about what happened in high school."

"You're both adults now. That's so in the past."

"I didn't quite measure up to her standards then, so she likely expects the same now."

"Don't go there, Ben. You've always been enough. The problem was, and still is sometimes, you don't really believe it." Jazz dropped onto a bench by the koi pond and motioned for Bennett to sit. "You've both moved on. You're professionals with a job to do. What happened is in the past. Leave it there."

Bennett rubbed her hands over her face and through her hair. Seeing Kerstin again had unearthed old feelings like unfinished sentences with no purpose.

"Can you do that, Ben?"

"If you'd asked me this morning, I'd have said definitely. Now I'm not so sure. I really want to understand what happened between us."

Jazz shook her head.

"Say it, sis."

"You're a new captain with a great assignment. You can't let Kerstin Anthony or anyone else interfere with your future. I saw the look on your face when Simon said you deserved the promotion. You're already afraid of screwing up. Don't let this woman be your excuse."

Jazz had hit the nail squarely on the head. Bennett feared being an embarrassment or disappointment to her family and especially to the memory of her father. She'd struggled for years to cement her place in the department. This was her chance to silence all doubters on her way up the promotional ladder.

Jazz rose and placed her hand on Bennett's shoulder. "Do what you need to do. I've always got your back, no matter what."

"Thanks, and congratulations again. I'm very proud of you, Lieutenant Perry." She gave Jazz a playful shove. "But don't think I'll take it easy on you because you're my sister."

Jazz mock saluted before walking back toward the house.

Bennett loved her sister as much as her own life, but Jazz had been hurt too badly in childhood to completely trust anyone with her heart. She'd understand Bennett's unresolved feelings for Kerstin when she faced her own feelings about her mother's death.

Bennett watched the koi jump for insects on the surface of the pond and willed the unsettled feelings for Kerstin back to their hiding place, but they no longer fit. How could she reconcile the need to prove herself professionally with the emotional call to heal her heart? Both tasks deserved her full attention.

Chapter Two

Kerstin texted her aunt Valerie from outside her mother's Central Park high-rise as the streetlights around her flickered on.

Can you meet me in the lobby?

She was exhausted from ping-ponging between New York and Greensboro and the emotional challenges at either end, and today was only the first round. Her phone beeped with Valerie's response.

Excellent timing. She's napping.

Kerstin scanned the height of the building with its imposing steel, granite, and glass façade. When she'd moved here as a teenager, the building served as her prison; the huge panels of glass were her windows on the world, the steel dividers her bars. Central Park, just across the street, provided a personal hideaway with wooded areas, grass, lakes, and playgrounds, basically a giant oasis in a city too chaotic for her small-town upbringing. She shook off the conflicting feelings that often accompanied her return and walked toward the entrance.

The concierge offered to assist with her small overnight bag, but she waved him off as Valerie emerged from the elevator. Her petite stature belied her ability to deal with a physically and emotionally difficult patient. Valerie had been a godsend, especially when Kerstin was away on business or needed a break. Their arrangement allowed Valerie to live in the condo free and receive compensation denied her by the family matriarch because of Valerie's unorthodox lifestyle—lesbian out and proud.

"How are you?" Valerie gathered her in a warm hug, and Kerstin settled into the comfort. Val was often more like another mother than an aunt, nurturing and supportive, while also attending to the demanding job of caring for her older sister.

"Good. You?"

"Very well. Let's sit." Valerie motioned toward a grouping of leather chairs surrounded by plants near the floor-to-ceiling window. "You look tired."

"I'm okay. How's Mother?"

"Elizabeth Anthony. What can I say about that woman you don't already know?"

Kerstin recoiled at the question before she realized Valerie was kidding, and then she burst into laughter. "Thank you. I needed that. Mother definitely defies description."

"She still has a hard time when you're out of town. It's the short-term memory adjustment we talked about. She's better with long-term recall. I suggested she keep a daily journal to help with day-to-day events."

If her mother could forget the past and remember details about the present, their lives would be happier, but that wasn't the hand she'd been dealt from her stroke seven months ago. "Is she using a journal and does it help?"

"Yes. I believe so. She sneaks glances at the notebook because she doesn't want to admit she needs one, and that's fine as long as it works. She's made a lot of progress since the stroke, but she wants to be fully recovered yesterday."

"Sounds like her. Your experience in geriatrics is a lifesaver. I'm so grateful, Val."

"It keeps me close to my sister, whether she likes it or not. I should be paying her…well, not really." She stood and pulled Kerstin with her. "We better go up. She doesn't sleep long this late in the day."

Kerstin released Valerie's hand and suppressed an urge to run. Her relationship with her mother had been challenging before the stroke, with good-intentioned but constant attempts to direct Kerstin's life and set her up with eligible bachelors, and living together complicated things, but running wouldn't help. Her father's gruff counsel and limited attempts at parenting always revolved around dealing with her mother. *"Always have the courage to fight for what you want, especially where your mother's concerned."* Did his advice still apply in light of her stroke and diminished faculties? Kerstin found it easier to go along to get along. She'd need more courage than she'd ever shown to take on her mother for any reason now.

She shuffled behind Valerie across the gray-marble-floored lobby and onto the private elevator servicing her mother's penthouse. She checked her phone, praying her boss could meet with her this evening instead of tomorrow, and immediately winced, feeling guilty. She wanted to help her mother and had tried since the stroke, but it wasn't easy. Elizabeth Anthony didn't make anything easy—not her own privileged life, not her marriage, and definitely not motherhood. Her parents had struggled after their divorce, each using her as a pawn in their settlement negotiations. And her mother's sudden dependence had rubbed Elizabeth and Kerstin raw in previously chafed places.

Valerie unlocked the tall metal door and stood aside to let her enter first. Kerstin stopped for a second, acclimating once again to the stark contrast of her mother's Queen Anne furniture with its curves, cushioned seats, and wing-backed chairs in the lofty-contemporary space. Elizabeth managed to make the setting feel welcoming and comfortable to the hundreds of guests she entertained annually for various charities, but it never quite seemed like a home to Kerstin.

"How nice to see you, Kerstin." Elizabeth Anthony stood in the open-plan kitchen clinging to the large granite island with her right hand. The slight paralysis to her left leg and arm were concealed beneath silk lounging pajamas she insisted on wearing for the length.

Kerstin crossed the loft and kissed her on the cheek. "How are you, Mother?"

"As well as can be expected. It's been a while since you visited."

She'd left this morning, but reminding her mother would probably only irritate her. "I'm sorry. Would you like some tea?" Valerie disappeared with her bag to give them some privacy, and she wished their buffer would hurry back.

"Valerie can do it. Sit. Tell me where you've been."

"Val's busy. Besides, I'd like to make it for you." She'd learned at a young age not to boil her mother's Earl Grey and to pour the milk in before the tea. If Elizabeth knew British aristocracy had used the "milk in first" phrase to refer to working-class folks, she would've changed her preference. But since tea preparation was one of the few things Kerstin did well enough to please her mother, she kept the trivia to herself.

"I prefer Valerie's." She motioned for Kerstin to precede her to the sitting area, a social faux pas before the stroke.

Though the comment stung, Kerstin acquiesced and pretended to enjoy the view from the windows overlooking the park while surreptitiously observing her mother. Elizabeth secreted her slender walking cane behind her leg and moved slowly, posture upright, head high. She'd fought since the day of her stroke, determined to regain complete use of her limbs and total memory recall. She was making progress, but some of the damage couldn't be undone. One thing would never change—her mother's pride and determination—and Kerstin loved her for it. She was the reason Kerstin worked to secure a stable future no one could take from them.

"Anyone care for tea?" Valerie asked as she entered the living area.

"Yes, please," her mother answered.

"None for me, Val."

"Kerstin, don't be petulant because I prefer Valerie's tea." Her mother gave her the chastising look she'd used since Kerstin was a child and settled in a wing-backed chair that gave her a slight height advantage.

She shook her head at Valerie. "I haven't slept well for a couple of nights, and I really need to be rested tomorrow."

"Look at the park. I can't wait for everything to bloom again." With Kerstin's attention ostensibly diverted, Elizabeth slid a maroon notebook from the side of her chair cushion, glanced inside, and then replaced it. She smoothed the front of her silk pajamas and asked, "How was your trip to Greensboro? Remind me why you went *there*."

The implication being she could go anywhere but the place she was born. Her mother detested Greensboro, and her constant complaints had torn their family apart.

"Parrish Designs has a new project there, but I'm thinking of turning it down. I'll meet with Leonard tomorrow morning to discuss my options."

"You mean Mr. Parrish, don't you?"

"Of course." Parrish might be her mother's friend, but Kerstin gritted her teeth every day she had to work for the unpleasant man. He reminded her of Ebenezer Scrooge, tight with money and absolutely no compassion.

Valerie situated Elizabeth's tea on a table to her right and moved it closer. "Do you need anything else before dinner?"

"No, thank you, dear."

"I'll be in my room while you two catch up."

Kerstin gave her a pleading look she hoped would convince her to stay. The shock of running into Bennett Carlyle this morning had already frayed her nerves. Valerie shrugged and retreated. "Coward," Kerstin mumbled and almost laughed at her transference.

"When are you going to move in and help Valerie take care of me? She can't do everything. After all, I'm your mother."

The words were needles, jabbing into wounds that never quite healed. Her insides clenched, and she fought back a pained response. The doctor's explanation of Elizabeth's difficulty retaining new information and her need to have things repeated didn't make the critical tone hurt less.

"I've lived here for seven months, Mother, but I still have to travel for work."

Elizabeth's blue eyes registered momentary shock before she glanced toward the notebook resting at her side. "I know that. It just seems you aren't here when I need you."

Another needle. Kerstin's eyes burned and she blinked back tears. How could she get through to a woman who couldn't remember the past seven months? Elizabeth wasn't a bad parent. She had specific ideas of what her daughter should and shouldn't do and who she should be. Her idea of a fulfilling life included a crowded social schedule, charitable events, and a successful trophy husband on her arm. Children hadn't been a priority. Kerstin didn't have the necessary nurturing skills either, or the time now that the tables had been turned, but she wouldn't stop trying. All she could do was hold on, try not to irritate Elizabeth, and pray Valerie didn't quit. They sat in silence until daylight drained from the sky and the city hummed with nocturnal activities and light.

Valerie returned looking refreshed and asked, "Who's ready for dinner?"

Kerstin's shoulders relaxed. She should probably feel ashamed or guilty, but registered only a sense of relief as she kissed her mother on the cheek and started toward her bedroom. "I'm really tired. I'll skip dinner and see you both tomorrow, though it might be late afternoon."

Her mother's long, disappointed breath was her only response.

Kerstin prayed for sleep as she got into bed, but thoughts of Bennett Carlyle returned. Seeing her had transformed Kerstin from orderly, efficient architect to love-struck teenager as old feelings mocked and injured her again. Kerstin's ultimatum about the project had been a purely emotional one, totally out of character.

She considered sneaking out of the condo and going to the club to let off some steam and regain her sense of stability. Taking two steps toward her closet, she stopped. If a willing partner presented herself at this moment, Kerstin wouldn't turn her down, but she didn't have energy for the hunt. She flopped onto her extra-firm mattress again and stared at the ceiling. What if Leonard sent her back to Greensboro? She couldn't afford a distraction, especially not one like Bennett. Her future depended on her focused creativity and precision.

Kerstin stood at her mother's bedroom door watching her sleep. She debated waking her before she left for work, then decided against it. She wasn't up for a confrontation at home before the one she anticipated at work, even though she understood Elizabeth's fear and frustration. Kerstin would battle for control of her world if the same thing happened to her, but at some point their relationship had to even out in their new reality. While she was away or commuting on an irregular schedule, they'd have to manage.

"She's a challenge." Valerie handed Kerstin a travel mug full of steaming coffee.

"She certainly is." Kerstin inhaled the strong scent of java and hazelnut while searching for something more generous to say about her mother. "I can't imagine how difficult these limitations are for her, but I don't know how else I can help."

Valerie nodded back toward the kitchen. "Let's chat before you leave."

"Thank you again for everything you do." She took a sip and

placed her cup on the bar. "I'm not sure if I'll be back today or if I'll have to fly to Greensboro again."

"Either way, I've got this, Kerstin. Don't worry, and for God's sake don't feel guilty. You're doing everything she'll let you and more she doesn't even know about."

"I keep hoping for something to make a real difference."

"Seriously? Let's recap. You sublet your condo for a year, and if Elizabeth threw you out tomorrow, you couldn't go home for at least five months. Right?"

Kerstin shrugged.

"You took six weeks' family medical leave for caregiving, handled everything yourself until it became overwhelming, and eventually hired me, which I have to say is probably the smartest thing you've done in seven months. Elizabeth responds to me. I'm not a threat. She gave up rehabilitating me years ago. She still hopes you'll suddenly flower into the perfect debutante, join the Junior League, and produce adorable clones of her. She's trying, but she hasn't fully accepted that we're lesbians. Besides, you needed to get back to work for your sanity, and I'd guess to build a nest egg for Elizabeth's future. The family money won't last forever, contrary to her fantasies. Did I miss anything?"

Kerstin fiddled with the handle of her coffee cup, avoiding Valerie's stare.

"That's what I thought." She motioned toward the stove. "Let me fix you a quick breakfast before you go."

"I'm not hungry."

"A piece of toast for the road?"

She shook her head and waved as she hit the lift button. "I love you, Val. Thanks for everything." The door closed, and the mournful symphony music her mother preferred blared from overhead speakers, encouraging Kerstin to search for the escape hatch. The elevator opened, and she rushed out as if shoved.

Kerstin fast-walked to the subway station, found a seat, and rehearsed her speech on the ride. She was as prepared as she'd ever be when she knocked and opened the door to her boss's office. She shelved the subject of Elizabeth and pulled the situation with Bennett Carlyle to the forefront. She disliked conflict, but she couldn't avoid this particular problem.

"I was surprised to get your call yesterday, Kerstin." Leonard Parrish tugged at the tie choking his thick neck. His balding head shone with a customary film of perspiration, and the books and papers stacked haphazardly everywhere reeked with the sour smell of it. "Is there a problem already?"

"You should probably ask Gilbert Early that question. I haven't made a complete evaluation yet." Kerstin tempered the disdain in her voice, but her boss's slight coloring signaled that she'd failed. She'd suffered from Leonard's lack of integrity and willingness to take the easy way out of difficult situations.

Leonard fumbled around on his desk, located a pen, and twirled it, the incessant clicking another indication of his discomfort.

"Perhaps I'm not the right person for this job. My style and vision differ greatly from Gil's." Leonard's expression glazed over. He wasn't buying her pitch. "The bottom line is we're losing money with the delays." Appealing to his pecuniary interests always did the trick and avoided a serious confrontation.

He stroked his chin, an attempt at concentration. "I see. Just carry on with the current design. It's perfect for the project, and so are you."

A knot tightened in her stomach, her foolproof bullshit detector. "What do you mean?" She wasn't getting the whole story about Gil or the project.

"You're a good architect, and this project needs to proceed without any further interruptions. As you said, we're losing money every day the builders aren't on site."

Leonard never complimented her, but the money angle was definitely a motivator. "If time is so important, why did you replace Gilbert?"

He pushed back from the oak desk and stood, his sizeable girth straining the buttons of his discount suit. "The Greensboro Police Department is using some federal money for this build, and you know what the feds are like. If we're delayed further, they'll pull the funding. I thought you'd be happy about the job. It'll look great in your portfolio, if you ever decide to leave Parrish Designs."

Leaving couldn't come soon enough, but telling Leonard would only make her life more difficult in the interim. "I do appreciate the opportunity, but I think someone else might be a better fit." Truthfully, she wanted to dodge the undercurrent of trouble Bennett Carlyle represented.

"I'm sorry, Kerstin, but I must insist you see the project through." The comment was almost shocking in its finality. He dodged a stack of drawings on his way to the door, signaling the end of their meeting.

She hated losing to Parrish, but she'd run out of professional excuses and wasn't about to admit any personal motivation. He'd forge any weakness into a spear and gut her at every opportunity. No camaraderie or organizational support in this company. "I'll do my best."

"You always do." He slammed the door behind her, and she walked to the elevator, baffled. Everything about their meeting seemed wrong, even the final result. She had no choice, but why should she choose between career advancement and dredging up the past? She just wouldn't discuss their history with Bennett. Her work on the substation project needed to come first for so many reasons.

She stepped into the hectic flow of foot traffic and the cacophony of smells on the street, jittery and unsettled. Normally, she would bury herself in work or blow off steam with a willing companion, but work was part of the current problem, and the club didn't open until later. Damn Bennett Carlyle for barging into her life at the most inopportune time and screwing up her carefully choreographed plans. Without making a conscious decision, she automatically joined the frantic pace of commuters and shoppers, elbowing her way forward step after step toward no specific destination. Maybe Bennett would secure a replacement on her end so they could avoid this whole unpleasant predicament.

If not, then what? She'd held her own against the most meticulous clients. Ms. Carlyle would be putty in her experienced hands. Kerstin stumbled at the thought. What was happening to her? She never walked unless absolutely necessary and then only with an endpoint and a goal. Walking served only three possible purposes in her opinion—idle thinking, wasting time, or making her late—none of which ever appeared on Kerstin's agenda. She hailed a taxi, and when the driver stopped in front of her building, her mood and situation remained unchanged. Thank you, Bennett Carlyle. Her life had twisted awkwardly back on itself and bumped into the past.

Chapter Three

Bennett stared at her image in the full-length bedroom mirror the next morning and searched for an internal shift in her feelings. Nothing. The silver double bars positioned midway on her collar sparkled in the morning sun like her lieutenant's bars, but these carried more weight and responsibility and a far greater chance of failure. Her stomach churned uncomfortably, and she pressed a hand against her midsection. She could handle police work, but overseeing an architectural project filled her with dread, and not just because of Kerstin. She'd pitch another reassignment appeal to the chief this morning and hope for the best. She finished dressing and started toward the living room.

She paused at the cottage door and glanced back. Only a couple of sweatshirts and a pizza box littered the otherwise clean space. Not bad for her. Mama, Stephanie, and Dylan, the women in the family with style sense, had redecorated in Bennett's preferred mid-century modern style before she moved in two years ago. The living area was just large enough for her favorite Eames chair and ottoman, a sofa, one side chair, and two barstools at the peninsula slash dining room. She loved the cottage and the proximity to her family, but looked forward to sharing her life with someone else long-term in a home large enough for her own family.

On the way to her police cruiser, she waved at Mama and G-ma restocking the food truck for today's run.

"The new bars look good, honey," Mama called and blew her a kiss.

"You need some help?"

"We're fine, taking our time. You run along. Have a good day."

She drove slowly toward the downtown municipal building, second-guessing her decision about talking with the chief at every turn. She'd known Pete Ashton since she was a kid and rode with Mama to pick up her father after a shift. Pete had worked with her dad, eaten meals in their home, and stood with the family when her father was killed. Pete had earned the reputation as a fair and respected chief, so why was she worried? Perhaps because she took orders and performed every assignment without question no matter how unpleasant or dangerous, until this one.

Walking slowly toward the chief's office, she considered whether her unusual case of nerves resulted from a desire to surrender or retain the project. Work was work, but this job obviously contained an emotional element beyond fear of failure or she wouldn't be questioning her motives. She took a deep breath and knocked on the chief's open door.

Pete Ashton waved her in as he ended a phone conversation. "Have a seat, Captain Carlyle. I like how that sounds, don't you?"

"Yes, sir."

"The railroad tracks are a nice addition to your collar. Your father and grandfather would be very proud."

A hitch in her breathing delayed Bennett's response. "Thank you, sir. I sure hope so. And I hope you still feel the same after I have my say."

He motioned her to a chair in front of his old seventies-era desk, gray metal with Formica top, which he boasted working at since he was a sergeant. "The substation assignment revisited?"

She wiped her sweaty hands down the legs of her uniform pants and nodded. "I'm a street cop, Chief, and you need an experienced administrator for the renovation. The project is too important to leave to chance, and I need time with my new command, to find out what's working in the district and what isn't."

"I'll tell you what's not working, the cramped space at the Parks and Recreation building. You've got no place for temporary detention or interrogation and no weapons security. The list goes on and on. We have federal forfeiture money to remodel a building into our first district station, your station. This is a big opportunity, Ben." He scratched his graying mustache as if considering another possibility. "Are you afraid you can't handle the job?"

Was she so transparent, first Jazz and now the chief? Did she simply want to follow the safe, traditional path of a new captain's command, or was she trying to honor Kerstin's wishes? Maybe she wanted to avoid resurrecting old feelings by working with Kerstin. More likely, her hesitation was a combination of all those reasons. No point denying what seemed obvious to the chief. "Maybe that's part of it, sir, if I'm totally honest."

"If I didn't think you were capable, I wouldn't have promoted you. I have confidence in you, Ben. The project is a joint effort, so I'm not throwing you to the wolves. You'll have city planners, finance, and public-works guys on the committee." He stood. "And I support your recommendation of architect."

Resigned to beginning her promotion with an unorthodox assignment, she replied, "I'd like one final conversation with her, if that's okay."

"Of course. She'll be back in town sometime tomorrow."

Bennett followed him toward the door. "Back in town, sir?" She wanted to ask where Kerstin had been, where she lived, but those questions were extraneous to the job. And maybe he was referring to Kerstin's replacement.

"Don't you know this young lady? She went to school here. I remember her vaguely. What's her name? Kerry? Kelly?"

"Kerstin? Kerstin Anthony."

"You two hung around together in high school. Happy reunion."

"Yes, happy," Bennett murmured. So, definitely Kerstin. Bennett had mixed feelings about working with Kerstin, but she'd just have to deal with them.

"My admin will contact you about your next meeting. If I don't hear otherwise, we'll sign the papers in the finance department, and then I'll send her over to you. If I can help grease the wheels, don't hesitate. And thanks for your service, Ben."

She straightened and shook his hand, feeling both proud and nervous. She'd be plowing uncharted territory because she knew absolutely nothing about architecture or remodeling buildings. The Carlyle name and her reputation depended on her learning quickly. An image of Kerstin's disappointed face flashed through Bennett's mind. At least she'd attempted to honor Kerstin's wishes.

Bennett drove to the Parks and Recreation building that served as the district's temporary station to attend a few lineups and introduce herself to the troops. As she pulled into the employee parking lot, she spotted Jazz getting out of her blue Crown Vic.

"Thought you'd beat me here on the first day?" She slapped Jazz on the back as they walked together toward the police entrance at the side of the building.

"Making a good impression on my new captain. I hear she's a real hard-ass." Jazz grinned and held the door open for her. "Turn left. Lineups are in the big room near the end of the hallway."

"Thanks, Jazz. Give me the full tour after?"

Jazz nodded and again held the door for Bennett to precede her into the midsized office that served as the assembly room for daily troop lineups.

"Squad, attention-huh!" The day-shift sergeant brought his troops from the relaxed parade-rest position to full attention and then joined them in formation.

"As you were," Bennett said. "Carry on, Sergeant. I'll address the squad at the end of your briefing."

While the sergeant read alerts from overnight, a list of new warrants active in the district, and the zone and vehicle assignments, Bennett rehearsed her prepared speech and then dismissed it as too formal.

"Now, I'll turn it over to our new commanding officer, Captain Bennett Carlyle."

"Thank you, Sergeant." Bennett scanned the officers' faces, registering expectation from the rookies and indifference from the veterans. Promotions challenged everyone, especially women, but it was her responsibility to set the tone and be an example for her district. The old adage *Do as I say, not as I do* wasn't how she operated.

"I'm humbled and excited to be your new district captain. Some of you know me and how I operate, and the rest of you will learn. The short version, I say what I mean, support my troops, and don't mind getting my hands dirty. I come from a family of cops and can't imagine not working the street. That being said, the chief has other plans for me at the moment, but it's all good." She motioned Jazz closer to her side. "Most of you know Jazz Perry, a sergeant in the district for several years and now your new lieutenant. She's one of the most dedicated and knowledgeable officers I've ever worked with. Lieutenant Perry will manage the operational side of things while I work on building a new substation for our district right across the street."

A collective yelp went up from the officers along with a few comments.

"It's about time."

"We need locker rooms."

"Weapons storage."

"How about showers, Cap?"

She nodded and waved for them to continue. "What else?" For the next several minutes, they fired off suggestions, and she made mental notes. The officers had strong feelings about the substation and wanted to be proud of their new headquarters.

"Thanks, guys. I'll look at the building plans and compare it to your list of demands." The squad chuckled. "I hope our new place will have everything you want and more. The chief wants our first station to be a showpiece, so it'll be fully outfitted. Any questions for me?"

The room was quiet for a few seconds before one of the veterans asked, "Is it true Captain Warren was driving drunk, caused a personal injury accident, and resigned?"

His sergeant shot him a scathing glance.

"It's fine, Sergeant. I prefer facts to rumors. If you have questions or concerns, feel free to ask. I won't hold it against you." She turned her attention to the questioner. "Yes, that's true, and my quick promotion assures continuity of the substation project. Any more questions?"

No one else spoke.

She looked at Jazz. "Anything to add, Lieutenant?"

"Only that I look forward to continuing to serve District One with all of you."

"Lieutenant Perry and I will be in close contact about operations and the building project. If you need anything or have questions, let her know." She nodded to the sergeant, and on the way out, she said, "I'll see you in the field."

As the door closed behind them, Bennett heard someone remark, "That'll be different."

Once in the hallway, Jazz directed Bennett to the right. "I'd much rather have my job than yours."

"Seriously. I understand cops and crooks, but that's about it."

"You'll be great. Stand here for the tour." Jazz indicated a spot halfway between the assembly room and the door they'd entered and pointed to the left. "That small office at the end of the hall is yours and mine. Pretty tight, but it's adequate." She slid her finger in the air along a series of partitions. "And those are the sergeants' cubicles. Three, sometimes four, sergeants share each unit, and before you ask, yes, it's too cramped."

Bennett looked from Jazz down the long hallway past each cubicle and back to her sister while mentally reviewing the district roster she'd studied last night. "This is an awfully small space for—"

"Don't bother doing the math. It doesn't add up no matter how you cut it. We're like sardines, and tempers sometimes flare from lack of usable space."

"And this is all?" She couldn't believe the confined quarters these officers had endured for the better part of two years.

"Actually, we have one more room." Jazz walked down the hallway past the assembly area to a door across from the captain's office. "This was Captain Warren's conference room, which he always locked unless he was using it."

Bennett tried the doorknob, and a flash of anger caught her off guard. "Okay, this ends now. Your first official duty as my second in command is to send a memo to the sergeants offering this room for immediate use, twenty-four seven. Get a simple Velcro sign for the door we can flip to indicate it's in use or available. If we leave this vacant when our guys desperately need private space, we're being callous and irresponsible."

"Aye, aye, Captain. Warren was nothing if not irresponsible." Jazz rattled her keychain but didn't look at Bennett until she located the right key to unlock the door.

"Something you need to tell me?"

"You won't have to work hard to be a better captain than Warren, but you'll have a lot to make up for."

"That bad?"

"I'm afraid so."

"Why didn't you say anything to Pete?" The question was reflex. Jazz followed the rules and didn't violate the blue wall of silence or ask for favors. When Mama and Pa adopted her, she kept her last name out of respect for her mother and to avoid any preferential treatment as a member of the Carlyle family. She'd fought hard to overcome her childhood in foster care, challenging teenage years, and being female in the police department. "Sorry, Jazz. Dumb question. I know how the game's played."

Jazz shrugged. "Buy me a sandwich? Ma Rolls should be in the parking lot by now. I didn't get breakfast, and G-ma shot me a killer look."

"Least I can do." Bennett's phone vibrated, and she glanced at the text from the chief's secretary.

Meeting with architect scheduled 1000 tomorrow, your office.

"How about I buy and you fly?"

"I'll meet you in the break area in ten minutes, or as fast as G-ma turns me loose. She's on one of her 'all my grandbabies should be settled down' rants today."

"Thanks for the warning. I'll steer clear."

Jazz grinned, and Bennett handed her a twenty. "I expect change."

After a quick sandwich and further logistical discussions with Jazz, Bennett slowly opened the door to her new office. The space seemed harmless enough, but over the threshold lay potential booby traps she couldn't imagine until she stepped into them. She scanned the room, expecting an ambush or possibly someone with an answer to the recurring question. Was she ready?

The office walls were stripped bare; not even a district map adorned the gray surfaces. A large calendar occupied the center of a dark wooden desk, and a black leather chair rested on its side behind it. She calculated the time of Warren's arrest Sunday morning with the arrival of first shift. He'd vacated in a hurry before anyone got wind of his situation. All the desk drawers were empty, nothing to indicate the status of the district, pending disciplinary issues, mood of the troops, or even current crime statistics. Warren hadn't been much of a team player, and she was glad the department was rid of him.

She righted the overturned chair, sat, and breathed deeply for a few minutes, thinking about her father and grandfather. At each new phase of her career, she took time to express gratitude for those who'd sacrificed for the life she was blessed to live. She dug into her shirt pocket and retrieved the .380 shell casing from her father's murder. The full metal jacket shone from hours of rubbing between her thumb and fingers. The firing pin indention in the primer seemed so small to have caused so much damage—a good man's life ended, a family torn apart, the police community shocked and grieving, and her own life still impacted by the consequences. She looked toward the ceiling. "Help me not screw this up." She rolled the casing between her palms one final time and returned it to her pocket.

Pulling a blank notepad from the bottom supply cabinet, Bennett listed the few things she needed to claim this place as her own. She'd bring family pictures, an inspirational saying to motivate the troops and herself occasionally, and her father's badge encased in Lucite. She ripped the edge off the paper, slid it into her pocket, and idly scribbled on the pad. Thoughts of her pending meeting with Kerstin returned, and she bore down on the pen.

Her real job as a district commander was so different from Kerstin's work. Policing required hands-on, person-to-person, interactive, and often physically and emotionally challenging skills. Kerstin's more solitary career dealt with figures, numbers, and creative ideas. Maybe Kerstin's career choice accounted for the more cautious and ordered approach Bennett detected. She couldn't help wondering how else Kerstin might've changed.

What could they possibly have in common after all these years? Some aspects of Bennett's job could be creative—figuring out how to reach a mentally challenged individual and talking him off a ledge; motivating an experienced officer to embrace new community-oriented concepts; balancing a demanding and dangerous career with an equally demanding and loving family. Maybe somewhere in between they'd find common ground. She looked down at the page she'd been doodling on and the initials *KA* were surrounded by *X*s and *O*s.

"Seriously, Carlyle?" She ripped the paper off the pad and tossed it into the trash on her way out. She needed to be in the field answering calls, interacting with the officers, and getting the lay of the land in her new district, not mooning over a woman she'd crushed on as a teenager.

Chapter Four

Kerstin rolled over and hugged the long body pillow tighter. The firm mattress suited her, and she didn't intend to leave any time soon. She nudged her nose from under the covers and barely opened one eye—still dark and the air was slightly nippy—perfect sleeping weather. Snuggling back into the covers, she drifted off again.

Avicci's voice rumbled through Kerstin's head, asking someone to wake him when it was over, a theme of hers at the moment. If only. The snappy ringtone repeated over and over until it registered that she needed to get up. Some meeting undoubtedly waited in Manhattan after a long and crowded subway ride. Why hadn't her mother been in to scold her out of bed and into the kitchen for their usual morning coffee?

She threw back the covers, opened her eyes, and nearly tumbled out of bed. Not home, but Proximity Hotel, over five hundred miles away. The last-minute flights between New York and Greensboro just two days ago were taking their toll, disorienting her to time and place. Plush drapes covering the floor-to-ceiling windows of her corner king loft room couldn't entirely block the bright sunlight. She tapped off her phone alarm and stared at the time in horror. *Nine fifteen.* She had a meeting with her police liaison in forty-five minutes on the other side of town.

She turned on the coffeemaker as she headed toward the huge terrazzo shower. She stood under the pounding hot water for several minutes, the tension in her shoulders easing, and then rushed to get dressed. Being late wasn't an option. She gave the coffee pot a longing glance on her way out and prayed Bennett had been successful in finding a replacement for the substation project. If not, this meeting would be the longest of her life, even if it lasted only two minutes. She refused to dwell on the negative and instead dialed a cab on her way down in the elevator.

When she reached the front door, her taxi was waiting. She'd be on time if he knew where he was going. Greensboro wasn't New York City, after all. The cabbie arrived in the area quickly but circled the block several times before Kerstin finally called the chief's office for better directions and a physical description of the temporary District One offices. They stopped in front of a building that looked like an industrial facility at ten thirty. She wouldn't have chosen this simple redbrick structure as a police substation. She paid the cab driver, hurried through the front door, and wasted more time getting directions to the correct office from a part-time receptionist.

Kerstin stopped short of the entrance to the office and regained her composure. Her stomach knotted, and she regretted skipping breakfast. She smoothed the front of her bespoke suit and was about to knock but heard Bennett's slightly raised voice.

"The architect is late. Are you sure this is the right day? I know, but we all make mistakes. Okay. I'll wait a few more minutes, but if she's not here soon, I'm going to work."

Kerstin stepped into the room as Bennett hung up. "Sorry to disappoint, but I'm still your architect." She paused, trying to read Bennett's expression. "I was hoping you'd had more luck getting reassigned."

Bennett shook her head, her eyes roaming over her body and lingering in places where her suit fit snugly. "Guess it's my turn to apologize. We're stuck with each other."

Bennett wasn't really sorry. The kidding tone she'd used so often in high school oozed sarcasm. She rose and came toward her, and Kerstin tingled all over, floundering for an appropriate reply. "Guess… we'll have to manage." And managing Bennett was exactly what Kerstin had in mind, along with keeping the project moving. "Sorry I was late. I hate tardiness. It shows lack of respect. I don't want you to think I'm—"

"Kerstin, you're here now." Bennett's tone was calm and soothing as she motioned toward two chairs in front of her desk.

She certainly was and wished she could be anywhere else.

Kerstin took a seat and scanned the sterile surroundings, searching for something to define who Bennett was now, how she'd changed, and what she valued, which could prove beneficial in the managing-Bennett effort. The stark walls offered no clues, requiring her to rely on the past and speculation, very dangerous territory.

"I know it's not much to look at. I only got the job and the office two days ago."

Tension weighted the air between them, and though Kerstin's body was on alert, she had to find a way to focus on the job. "Where do we begin?" Why was she asking Bennett? The substation project belonged to her. She reached for the rolled plans in her tote. "Let's review the current drawings and confirm you're okay with everything."

"Actually, could we clear the air first?"

Bennett moved closer, and Kerstin flinched. Her skin heated as she recalled the last time they'd touched and the exhilaration and potential the moment held. Bennett's eagerness and proximity reminded Kerstin of feelings she'd buried long ago, hope and promise, now blunted by age and experience. Emotion was fleeting and unreliable, and in this case, very dangerous. She had to stay connected to her goals or she'd lose everything.

"What do you mean, clear the air?" Brown eyes settled on her, and Kerstin momentarily wanted to be as honest as she'd always been when Bennett pinned her with a stare. She mentally shook herself and reverted to business. "You mean the project."

"We both asked to be reassigned. You must be disappointed. I'm sorry…for you."

The spark in Bennett's eyes and a mischievous grin relayed more than her words, but Kerstin needed to be clear. "What are you saying?"

"I'm not really sorry we'll be working together. I've waited a long time to find out—"

"Bennett, don't." She could barely catch her breath. In spite of her protest and better judgment, part of her wanted Bennett to continue, but another part silently pleaded with her to remain silent. Kerstin clutched the straps of her tote until her fist ached.

Bennett scooted her chair closer and reached for Kerstin's hands, but she withdrew. "We should probably talk about what happened."

"No, we shouldn't," she snapped, her angry tone a bit too loud.

She'd almost convinced herself nothing had happened between them. Bennett's reminder poked the old wound still tender with scar tissue. "If we're going to work together, what we *really* need is to focus on the job, not ancient history." Damn Bennett Carlyle for being so casual and emotionally reckless.

"Okay. If that's the way you want it," Bennett said.

Kerstin couldn't look at Bennett, afraid of what she might discover or reveal. She pulled her first drafting pen from her bag to distract her from the memories. If she allowed those images to emerge, she'd be paralyzed. "Why is it so important to talk about the past? Nothing really happened, and we both moved on."

"Of course, but I'd still like to know what happened when—"

Kerstin placed her fingers over Bennett's lips, felt their silky softness, and immediately regretted the touch. She stared for several seconds as the corners of Bennett's mouth curled up, and then she removed her hand.

"What are you thinking right now?"

"Ben…Bennett, please don't do this. We need to focus on the project. It's apparently important to both of us. Let's not mess it up with history."

"I need to know—"

"Actually, you don't." Was Bennett the brave, mature one, hoping to resolve their issues, or was she totally irresponsible for trying to renew a connection that shouldn't have happened? Maybe she really had no idea how much their irresponsible teenage actions had cost Kerstin.

Bennett's eyebrows scrunched together, and the playful smile at the edges of her mouth vanished. "What am I missing?"

Kerstin couldn't look into those pleading eyes again. She held the ends of her drafting pen in each hand and willed her insides to calm. She mustered a vision of her mother's current situation to remind her what was important. "The only thing you're missing is the significance of this job. Are we working together or not?"

Bennett visibly recoiled. "Well, yeah, but it might be easier if we—"

"It won't."

"How do you do that?"

"What?"

"Make me feel like I'm behind the eight ball, not quite measuring up."

The hurt in Bennett's eyes was old and deep, and she hated that she might have contributed to it. "I certainly don't mean to, and I apologize if I upset you, but our professions are on the line with this project."

"What happened to you?"

"I don't know what you mean."

"You used to be so open and optimistic. Remember the time—"

"Life happened." Why had she become so circumspect and logical? She shook the question away, not caring to examine it too closely. Bennett Carlyle didn't get to question her or her choices. "I don't mean to be rude, but could we get back to the task at hand?" Could she trust Bennett to forget the past for the sake of the project? Could she trust herself? She waited for Bennett to agree and, after a slight nod, proceeded in full work mode. "Why don't you move back to your desk, and we'll review the initial list of requirements?"

"The what?" Bennett rose but looked at her like she'd spoken a foreign language.

"Your brief? Your program? The department's specs for the renovation?" Bennett's blank stare concerned her.

"I wasn't on the original team. My predecessor, Captain Warren, worked with your firm initially, and I have no idea what he listed as our requirements, but it probably didn't have anything to do with real police work."

Now she was really worried. "Don't you have a copy of his file on the project?"

"He cleaned out everything in the office except a useless calendar." She ran her fingers through her hair, an old and practiced sign of discomfort. "Sorry. How do I get up to speed?"

Kerstin hadn't brought the initial brief, assuming they'd be further along in the process. "I have the original documents at my hotel. Maybe we should reschedule, and I'll bring you a copy tomorrow. Ten o'clock?"

Bennett nodded, and Kerstin gathered her materials to leave.

"I'm sorry, Kerstin. I'm pretty good at my job, but this kind of stuff is out of my wheelhouse. I'll catch up."

"We'll get there. May I use your phone to call a cab? I forgot to plug in my cell."

"Why don't I give you a ride?"

The offer sent Kerstin's insides into another dive. "That's not necessary. I'm sure you have things to do."

"It's almost lunchtime, so no bother. Let me. Please."

Coming from Bennett, *please* was a word Kerstin couldn't refuse easily. She had to put distance between them, to settle back into her rhythm, but instead heard herself say, "Thanks."

❖

"I'll give you the nickel tour of the area around the station on our way out." Bennett waited for Kerstin's response before leaving the parking lot.

"Okay. I'm not familiar with the area, and a tour might help me blend the exterior components with the neighborhood."

"I had a high school friend who lived down the street, so we hung out on Summit Avenue, Bessemer Avenue, and the old mall. You were probably busy in Sunset Hills and Irving Park, the rich folks' communities."

"That's not true. I—" Kerstin squinted and seemed to be reconsidering her answer. "Maybe you're right. I was a bit of a snob back then."

"No comment." Bennett grinned, then drove across the street and stopped in front of their future site. "Can you picture our sign out front? Fairview Station District One."

"That's the substation?"

"It will be." Bennett heard the pride in her voice, aware maybe for the first time how much this flagship facility would mean to everyone involved.

"It's different from the pictures. This looks like an old office building or a…"

"A factory?"

Kerstin nodded. "Maybe from the 1950s."

"Exactly. It used to be a laboratory for a clothing company. In fact, a large section of my district is what they called a mill village back in the day. Cone Mills ran several textile factories along the creek on Yanceyville Street."

"Guess I thought it would be bigger."

"We wish," Bennett said, driving away from the curb. She pointed out the recent changes in the Fairview community as she navigated the longest possible route back to Kerstin's hotel. "Once the substation opens, the community will have a place to meet, and the officers will feel more connected to them and their issues. I'm really excited about the prospects." Kerstin gave her a sideways glance Bennett couldn't quite decipher. "What's that look?"

"I'm still adjusting to the older, more responsible Bennett Carlyle, who happens to be a police captain now. How did you end up on the force?"

"Well—"

"I'm sorry. None of my business, and it's unfair to declare part of our past off-limits and quiz you about another."

"Why? People do it all the time. Ask questions. Please." At least Kerstin was interested, a very good start.

"I shouldn't." Her tone said she wanted to ask but wasn't happy about it.

Bennett volunteered. "I guess my dad gave me the bug. He snuck me into his squad car after his shift and rode me around the parking lot, like Grandpa did with him. If no one was around, he'd crank up the lights and siren. At that age, I enjoyed the noise, the color, and the excitement most. But the whole time he talked about the importance of family, community, and service, and the noble profession of law enforcement. Pretty heady stuff for a kid, but some of what he said sank in, eventually."

"But not right away?" Kerstin turned toward her in the seat, her eyes full of interest.

"Oh no. The responsible part came much later."

"More important things to do or—"

"Wait. Somebody's in trouble." Bennett turned the police radio up.

"Car 126, I need a supervisor at 2135 Brighton Street ASAP for a barricaded suspect. Notify the watch commander."

Bennett checked her side mirrors, made a U-turn, and activated her blue lights and siren. "I have to respond. I'll have someone at the scene take you back to the hotel."

"I…I'm…okay."

Bennett cupped Kerstin's hand to reassure her and was surprised she didn't withdraw. "You're pale, but don't worry. I won't let anything happen to you."

The minutes slowed as Bennett checked intersections and raced through one after the other. George McIntyre, a retired cop and one of her father's old partners, lived at the address on Brighton Street. She needed to get to the scene before response escalated. Once special teams and detectives arrived, her chances of mitigating the incident reduced dramatically. Whatever was going on with George, she owed him a chance to come out of it with some dignity intact.

She slid her car to a stop at the police roadblock close to George's house, beside Jazz's Crown Vic, and started to jump out. Kerstin shouldn't be so close to the unknown and possible danger. Bennett should've dropped her at the station before responding. "I'll send an officer over to take you to your hotel. *Do not* leave the car until he comes to get you. Understand?"

Kerstin nodded but grabbed Bennett's arm, and the situation outside her vehicle faded into the background. The pleading expression in Kerstin's eyes held Bennett. The warmth of Kerstin's hand penetrated her rough, polyester shirtsleeve and swirled through her. For an instant, she forgot where she was and why. A shout from outside reminded her that George needed her. The officers counted on her. She reached for and missed the door handle, unwilling to fully disengage. "I should go." For a second, Bennett thought Kerstin might ask her to stay.

"Please…be careful, Ben."

"Always."

Bennett jogged to Jazz's position, still uneasy that Kerstin was nearby. "What do we know?"

"A neighbor called in. George was ranting about life not being worth living anymore. She said he'd been out of sorts for several days and looked confused this morning when she checked on him. He told her his affairs were in order and for her not to come back."

"What did the primary officer see?"

"Nothing. George wouldn't let him inside."

"I want to talk to him face-to-face."

Jazz shook her head. "You know the protocol for a barricaded suspect."

"I don't care about protocol. This is George, one of our father's best friends. If you're okay letting him blow his brains out, I'll back off."

"Of course I'm not, but as the watch commander I can't let you go in either."

"Sorry, Jazz. If we wait for the special-ops guys, I'll miss my chance. I'm giving you a direct order. Stand down, Lieutenant." She headed toward the house but turned back. "Have someone take Kerstin back to the Proximity Hotel. She's in my car."

"But, Ben—"

"I'll be fine."

"Are you even wearing your vest?"

"Won't need it. Keep everybody out until I'm clear." She walked across the street, through the overgrown lawn to the rickety steps, motioning the officers back as she advanced.

The curtains of the residence were drawn shut, and the morning paper rested against the shredded screen door. No prickly neck-hair danger signals, always a good sign. She inched beside the door frame and listened. Whiskey, George's collie, was barking at the back of the house. She took a deep breath and gave the door a triple tap she'd learned from George.

"Go away."

"George, it's Bennett Carlyle."

"Ben?"

"Yeah. I'm alone. Let's talk."

"Nothing to say. Best if you don't see this, Ben. Think too much of you for that."

A lump formed in Bennett's throat as she imagined what had driven this once-proud cop to such a dire conclusion. "Please, George. I've lost my dad. I can't lose his friends too."

"Leave, Ben. I'm nothing to you."

She pounded on the door, desperate to get through to him. "But you are. Let me in, George. Just for a minute."

The house was quiet again, and Bennett waited. Jazz called her on the radio, but she turned down the volume, focusing on George. The black HNT van pulled up, but she didn't acknowledge the negotiator waving at her from the window. She was putting Jazz in a predicament because the hostage negotiations team should now assume responsibility for talking with the subject. She started to turn away, resigned to the inevitable, but then the door opened slightly.

"Just you."

She slid inside the darkened house and waited for her eyes to adjust. George stood in front of her in flannel pajamas, a scraggly beard, smelling like he hadn't bathed in days. His skin was pale and wrinkled. He'd aged badly since the last time she'd seen him. Old newspapers and empty water bottles littered the floor, and remnants of take-out containers with stale food dotted the horizontal surfaces. "What's going on, George?"

"Didn't they tell you, kid? I'm ready to check out. Have everybody leave and come back tomorrow. It'll all be over then."

She reached for his arm, but he pulled away. "Let me help, George." She hadn't seen him in months, and guilt hit her hard.

"Why do you care now?"

"I've always cared, but like everybody else, I get wound up in my own stuff and neglect what's important. That's no excuse. You matter to me, George."

"Why, because I worked with Bryce years ago?"

"You and Pete were his closest friends. You're part of our family, and you help keep him alive through your stories. Please don't take that from me. You're all I've got left. Besides, with this new job, who's going to keep me in line if you're gone?"

"Yeah. Saw those railroad tracks on your collar, hotshot."

"Just more headaches. Can we sit for a minute?"

"How long you figure we got before they storm the place?"

"As long as we need."

George crumpled onto a recliner and buried his face in his hands. "I don't know what's going on, Ben. I feel like I'm going nuts or something. I'm hungry and thirsty all the time, but nothing satisfies. My hands and feet tingle. I've passed out once, and you know I don't drink."

"Have you seen the doctor for a checkup lately?"

"That's another thing. My insurance lapsed, and I don't know how to fix it."

"We can make that right with a couple of phone calls. You think you've got problems? An old high school girlfriend of mine turned up out of the blue. Can't fix that with a call."

George laughed and shook his head. "I hear you. The widow next door brings me the worst God-awful casseroles."

"She's hot for you. We need each other to work out our woman troubles."

"Good point. I always liked you, Ben. Your dad and I used to laugh about your girlfriend shenanigans on boring night shifts. Kept us awake trying to help you figure out your girl problems. He was proud of you. You know that?"

"Sometimes." Why wasn't she as sure as everybody else seemed to be? Why did she question if she'd done enough or proved herself yet? She returned her attention to George. In this situation, only saving her friend would be enough.

"The question now is how do I get out of this mess I've gotten myself into?"

She placed her hand lightly on his shoulder. "Leave it to me. Get dressed while I cancel the circus outside. We'll figure the rest out as we go."

George rose and held out his hand. "Thanks, Ben. Guess Bryce sent you to me today, and I'm sure glad he did."

"We're all family, blue bloods through and through."

He disappeared into the bathroom, and Bennett radioed Jazz that everything was under control and to start clearing the units. She also texted Jazz so there would be no confusion about her intentions. *No charges will be filed.* While she waited, she grabbed the trash can from under the kitchen sink and bagged some of the debris throughout the house. While she worked, she looked for weapons and found none, not even George's service pistol. This whole incident seemed a cry for help, and she was glad she'd answered it.

George emerged from the bathroom a changed man—shaved, smelling of soap and aftershave, wearing clothes slightly wrinkled but clean. His bloodshot eyes filled with tears as he scanned the room. "You didn't have to pick up my mess. Place needs a deep clean."

"I know someone. I'll send her over while we're out, if that's okay with you."

He nodded.

"I hate to ask, George, but do you have any guns in the house?"

"Hell, no. I didn't even take my free service weapon the day I retired. Read too many obituaries of washed-out cops eating their guns."

Bennett brushed her hand through her hair. "Then how were you planning to—"

"Pills, but I couldn't find any. Sad excuse for a suicide attempt."

"You needed help and, like all hardheaded cops, didn't know how to ask."

He grasped Bennett's hand and started toward the door. "Maybe, but you don't have to babysit me anymore. I've got this."

"I know you do, but I'll have Jazz take you to the city's benefits specialist and get your insurance sorted, then to see your doctor. Agreed?" Bennett held the doorknob waiting for his response.

"You mean I'm not going to jail or the psych ward for all this hullabaloo?"

"That's not how we treat family, George."

He swiped at a tear and tried to speak but tipped his head instead.

"You ready?"

George nodded and straightened as they walked onto the porch. Several officers were still securing the scene, standing by their patrol cars. As Bennett and George passed on their way to Jazz's vehicle, each officer saluted.

"These guys really like you," George whispered.

"They're not saluting me." Bennett winked as a flash of movement to the left captured her attention. George's gray-haired, fairly attractive neighbor ran toward them. "Incoming."

"I can't talk to you right now, Marion, but would you look after Whiskey until I get back? I'll call you later."

The woman squeezed George's arm and nodded. "I'll wait."

"Like I said, woman trouble."

"Back at you," George said, nodding toward where she'd parked her car.

A couple of officers waved Kerstin back as she attempted to break through the police line. Bennett made eye contact and shook her head for her to stay put.

"Jazz, George needs a ride to city personnel and then to his doctor's office. Can you help him, please?"

"I'd love to." Jazz turned to George. "Good to see you again, old friend. Right this way. Have I got some stories for you."

George laughed, and the pair climbed into Jazz's vehicle like friends off for a casual drive.

Bennett called after them. "We'll set an extra place at Sunday brunch. Bring Marion if you want." Then she took a deep breath and turned toward Kerstin. "Why are you still here?"

"What?" Kerstin's face was flushed and her eyes round with either excitement or fear.

Bennett motioned for an officer headed back to his vehicle. "Would you transport Ms. Anthony to the Proximity Hotel?"

"But I want to go with you." Kerstin's voice was almost shrill and trembled slightly.

"I'm busy." Not really true, but Kerstin didn't need to witness the effects of her adrenaline high. She'd faced the unknown and won. Nothing could touch her, but if she didn't find a way to blow off some energy, she'd be edgy and anxious. Kerstin shouldn't be around then, because Bennett wouldn't hold back the words she'd suppressed for years.

"I'll wait." Kerstin crossed her arms over her chest.

The officer motioned Kerstin toward his car. "This way, ma'am."

"I need you to leave." She wasn't sure how she'd channel this surge, but she had to get away from Kerstin. As the officer gently cupped Kerstin's elbow and led her away, Bennett remembered the police academy was in session, and the instructors were always searching for volunteers to play suspects in takedown scenarios. She steered toward the Church Street facility, grateful for a chance to role-play and release her energy in a productive way.

The incident with George reminded Bennett of her grandfather's secret to a successful career and family life—keep your personal and professional lives separate. Today they'd overlapped, but the concept was sound. Cops needed friends and lovers outside the job for their own sanity. Her dad had told her on many occasions that when a cop retires, the force forgets him.

What about Kerstin? Did she fall in the professional or personal category? The answer should be obvious, but keeping Kerstin at arm's length wouldn't be easy, especially while riding an adrenaline high easily extinguished with sex. Yet Kerstin wasn't a wham-bam kind of girl. Was she? Bennett had no idea what Kerstin was like now, and that annoyed her.

Chapter Five

Kerstin was still groggy as she dressed at six the next morning. She'd drifted between sleeplessness and vivid images of Bennett entering a black door marked Danger. In her dream, Kerstin had foolishly charged the police lines to stop Bennett and failed. Her heart hammered again with the anxiety she'd experienced watching the scene unfold. She'd feared for Bennett, been protective of her, and rationalized she would've been concerned for anyone walking into harm's way. Maybe the charged situation had magnified her insecurity and safety issues.

Bennett as a police officer didn't jive with the cocky rebel from high school. Perhaps she'd simply cloaked her reckless side behind a respectable façade. Her adolescent pranks had entertained and occasionally annoyed, but her latest performance could've ended quite differently. She was probably still an adrenaline junkie but now took more dangerous and potentially life-altering chances. When the incident ended, Bennett could hardly stand still, and her body radiated some kind of feral energy. She had always been hyped before and after big volleyball games. Had she chosen her career for a similar type of excitement and challenge?

Kerstin still stung from Bennett's hasty dismissal yesterday. What had prompted the borderline rude behavior? She didn't have answers to any of her questions and probably shouldn't inquire. Her relationship with Bennett was strictly professional. Yesterday had been an anomaly. She wouldn't cross the lines into Bennett's risky world again.

At ten o'clock, she waited outside Bennett's closed office door for their meeting. She checked her watch and then her cell. No message about a time or location change. After a few minutes, she paced the narrow hallway from the entrance back to the office. Maybe Bennett had gotten another emergency call and something had happened. She stopped abruptly. Why had she automatically assumed the negative? As she reached for her phone again, the door at the end of the hall opened, and Bennett strolled in waving a white paper bag in one hand.

"Sorry I'm late, but this will definitely make up for it."

"Where have you been? I was worr—thinking I had the time wrong." Admitting she was actually worried about Bennett was a leap she wasn't ready to make.

Bennett unlocked the door and waved her inside. "Again, I'm sorry. I picked up a couple of breakfast sandwiches from Ma Rolls. You're going to thank me."

"I'm really not hungry." Her stomach was still in knots from too little sleep, too much speculation about Bennett's job, and the woman beside her looking and smelling like she was ready for anything. She placed her tote on the floor and sat down in front of the desk.

"You're in for a treat." Bennett dragged a straight-backed chair between the two leather ones and placed the paper bag on the seat.

"Like I said, I'm really not—"

"Humor me, please, as a peace offering." She dug into the bag and pulled out two wrapped sandwiches. "Bacon or sausage?"

It couldn't hurt to accept Bennett's olive branch, might even relieve some of the tension. "Bacon, please."

Bennett handed her the heavenly-smelling bundle and then darted toward the door. "Forgot the coffee. Be right back. And you look fantastic, by the way. Nice suit."

Kerstin straightened the jacket of her blue wool Jones of New York suit. She'd debated casual clothes, jeans and a sweater, but opted for the suit. Attire, timelines, and rules facilitated an orderly workplace, clarified professional boundaries, and reminded Kerstin of the place she'd established for herself in the world.

In Bennett's absence, Kerstin noted the additions that had been made to the office since her last visit. A picture of Bennett's father and grandfather, both in uniform, graced the desk, along with a badge on either side encased in Lucite. A family photo occupied a place of prominence on the file cabinet, and a couple of motivational prints added color to the walls. She scanned for other personal touches revealing Bennett's interests or other connections, but found nothing.

"I'm not much of a decorator." Bennett placed two mugs of coffee on the chair and dug cream and sweetener packets from her shirt pocket. "Wasn't sure how you take yours."

"Baby coffee, lots of cream and sugar, probably an affront to the real coffee drinkers of the world, like cops."

"Yeah, that's wrong, but to each her own. Let's eat." Bennett unwrapped her sandwich and took a big bite. She chewed with gusto, practically inhaling her food. "This is heaven." She licked her lips, and Kerstin swallowed hard and reached for her coffee.

"So, what's Ma Rolls?"

Bennett wiped her mouth with the back of her hand, and Kerstin handed her a napkin from the bag. "My mother and grandmother started a food-truck business several years ago, initially out of boredom. The few sandwiches they served officers at breakfast grew into a larger variety and stops at several locations three days a week."

"Umm." Kerstin pointed to her breakfast and jerked a thumb up. "And how does your dad feel about all the time your mom spends away from home?"

The grin on Bennett's face vanished. She placed her sandwich on the corner of the desk and reached for her coffee, struggling to swallow a few small sips. Kerstin wondered for a moment if she was going to answer the question. "He's gone—killed in the line of duty the year after I graduated."

The missing twinkle in Bennett's eyes suddenly made sense. She and her father had been inseparable. Young tomboy Bennett Carlyle worshipped her dad. "I'm so sorry, Ben."

"Thanks." She sat quietly for several minutes while the pain on her face slowly faded. "What about your folks?"

Kerstin winced, searching for an answer to honor Bennett's sincerity while revealing little on this slippery slope of sharing personal details. "Divorced."

"Sorry."

"Yeah." Bennett stared, urging more information from her, but Kerstin was desperate to shift the conversation back to Bennett. "I had no idea about your father's—"

"Well, you were gone too."

Bennett's tone was flat, hurt laced with anger. Kerstin started to defend herself, to explain the things Bennett had no way of knowing, but it would serve no useful purpose. What was done was done.

Bennett cleared her throat. "I'm sorry. That's not fair."

Kerstin hesitantly reached out to Bennett, uncertain if she should touch her, afraid of what she'd feel, but she had to know what drove Bennett to pursue such a dangerous profession in light of her family's tragic history. She inched her hand closer, then withdrew and let it fall back onto her lap.

"Ask your question, Kerstin." Bennett's voice softened again, her eyes urging trust.

"I don't mean to sound insensitive, because I have nothing but respect for your family and law enforcement. Why join the profession that claimed your grandfather and father? In school, you were headed in a different direction."

"Yeah, mostly downhill."

"Not exactly what I meant."

Bennett reached across her desk and picked up the picture of the two Carlyle men. "I already told you how I caught the bug as a kid. When Dad died, I was lost for a while. Everything I'd done seemed insignificant and disrespectful to his memory. He didn't live to see me change from a party girl bouncing from job to job to pay for clubs and liquor."

Kerstin remembered that person, popular and eager for the next thrill. "So your job is about proving something?"

Bennett carefully replaced the picture but continued looking at it. "I joined an honorable profession, and we prove ourselves every day. I'm a woman in a historically male field, so my burden is greater, expectations higher. I spent nineteen years dodging responsibility because I didn't feel quite up to par. So, yeah, I have tons to prove. Don't you?"

Regret and pain laced Bennett's tone. She scanned the room but couldn't look at Kerstin. She'd hit a nerve. "I assumed—"

"Don't assume anything about me based on the past. You'll probably be wrong, and we've already established you don't want me to clarify any misconceptions."

Kerstin couldn't let it go. Something urged her to dig deeper to understand Bennett. "You're in charge of officers and assignments, but *you* went into that house yesterday not knowing if the man was armed. You could've ordered someone else in."

"I don't ask my officers to do something I wouldn't do myself." Bennett's shoulders relaxed as if the comment released part of her burden. "It's my job."

"You're required to distribute assignments and assure the work gets done, not necessarily do it yourself. It's called delegation." Her battling emotions had tricked Kerstin into a discussion they shouldn't be having, and the pain on Bennett's face made her regret it even more. "I'm sorry, Bennett. I guess the excitement yesterday affected me more than I thought. I have no right to question your life. I couldn't be a police officer, facing the unknown, risking my life for strangers, never sure if I'd go home again. Policing takes courage, and I don't even stand up to my arrogant boss."

"Really?"

"Let's not go there." She couldn't stop probing into Bennett's life while cautiously guarding her own. "Is the man okay? I heard he's a friend of yours."

"George McIntyre. He has type-two diabetes and didn't know. He'll be fine if he listens to the doctors." The corners of Bennett's mouth curved into a smile, revealing those damn sexy dimples. "So, you were worried about me yesterday?"

"Let's get back to the project." Bennett's crooked smile and the invitation in her eyes ignited something in Kerstin. Should she give in to Bennett's charisma and enjoy a more congenial working relationship, maybe even a few nights of pleasure? Then what? No. She'd satisfy her sexual needs back in New York, where she'd be safe from entanglements. She pulled the architectural plans out of her tote and pointed to the small conference table in the corner. "Shall we?" She'd almost given in and touched Bennett when she exposed her vulnerability. Damn it, she couldn't afford such emotional lapses. It was time to get this meeting back on solid ground and concentrate on facts instead of fickle feelings.

"Does that mean you're actually willing to work together now?"

"I need this project to complete my portfolio."

"And I need it for my position. So it's all about our jobs." Before Kerstin could respond, Bennett asked, "Does this mean we can clear the air about our past as well?"

"No."

"You've asked some pretty personal questions. Turnabout is fair play."

"Not at all." But Bennett was right. Kerstin had pried into her life but quickly slammed the door the minute Bennett ventured across her boundaries. This wasn't high school where open, trusting Bennett and curious, optimistic Kerstin matched each other tit for tat. Talking about the past opened doors she needed to remain closed. "Let's get to work." She'd been right about Bennett needing to prove something, and not only to the police department. Would she be wrong to admit her motivation? Revealing the truth would expose her to emotions, temptations, and eventually failures she couldn't afford.

Bennett joined her at the table. "Okay, work it is. Hope I don't let either of us down."

"You'll catch up quickly." Kerstin rolled the plans flat and handed Bennett a folder. "Here's the original brief, the department's statement of needs." Bennett paused before accepting the papers, possibly afraid of what she might find or maybe what she didn't know. "And thanks for breakfast. Definitely an amazing sandwich." Kerstin was anxious to be back in control, not swirling around in Bennett's dangerous and emotionally charged world. She breathed a sigh of relief, ran her hands over the textured floor plans, and settled into her rhythm.

Bennett opened the file and stared at the first page, pretending to concentrate while taking a few seconds to calm her emotions. Kerstin's questions threw her off kilter. Jazz was usually the only person who read her so easily. Kerstin had possessed the knack in high school, but Bennett practiced shielding her feelings after joining the police department. Working with Kerstin and remaining all business might be difficult because she'd glimpsed the warmth and concern beneath her cool, professional exterior. She even offered Bennett a napkin, just like in the old days when she'd ruined T-shirts by wiping her mouth down the sleeve. Something was still there between them, but how to get Kerstin to see it?

She redirected her attention to the file, which read like an administrative course on doublespeak. "You've got to be kidding."

"What's wrong?"

"Have you read this?"

"I concentrated on the architectural plans, assuming Gilbert and Warren had addressed the details. Is there a problem?"

"Listen to this. 'It's imperative to balance secure internal space and publicly accessible space for the mission of the department. The building must be designed to make visitors feel welcome, while ensuring officer and departmental safety.' Have you ever heard such a load of total crap?"

"We advise our clients to use broad strokes in the initial statement of needs, which allows the architects more flexibility on the planning end."

Bennett raked her hand through her hair, trying not to lash out. Kerstin wasn't at fault because Arthur Warren had no idea what officers needed in a substation. "So where did the specifics you have on this plan come from? You do have specifics at this point."

"Of course." Kerstin didn't look as certain as she sounded. Her azure eyes scanned the drawing as if searching for something concrete. "There." She pointed to a street view of the plan.

Bennett leaned closer, inhaling Kerstin's light citrus perfume. Their shoulders brushed and reminded Bennett of lazy afternoons sprawled across a single bed, barely touching, while they pored over their senior project. The memory stoked warmth and comfort in her chest and an unfamiliar burn lower. She settled into the natural-feeling closeness until Kerstin pulled away. "What are you pointing to at the front of the building?"

"The main entrance."

"But that's all glass."

"Yes."

"We've found our first change. A glass front invites trouble, and besides, the main public entrance is on the parking-lot side, not off this street. A single metal door with restricted access would work better and save a lot of money. This area," she pointed to the space inside the current glassy front, "should be a small canteen with snack machines for the officers."

"A canteen?" Kerstin flipped through the other pages of the floor plans and back to the front. "I don't see a canteen, but here's a cafeteria at the back for—"

"Seriously? A cafeteria? We haven't discussed a cafeteria in any of our proposed substations. We don't have money to up fit a full kitchen, for staff or food."

"If these first two things are so wrong, what else might need changing?" Kerstin shook her head, and confusion, plus something deeper, crossed her face.

Bennett started toward her but stopped. This was work. Kerstin was work. For the first time since she'd returned, Kerstin looked rattled and uncertain, and Bennett desperately wanted to reassure her.

"This can't be right. Maybe I picked up the wrong set of plans." She checked the date in the corner of each page. "Current." Her full lips pressed together in a tight line as she studied the file she'd shown Bennett. "We have to make corrections quickly. Every day the contractors aren't on site, we're losing money and falling behind on the timeline."

"The chief really wants this station open for National Night Out in August."

"Normally that would give us plenty of time, but…"

"B-but?" Bennett's throat was suddenly so dry she had to force the single word out. Delays translated not only into loss of money and time but to failure, her failure. "We have a meeting with the full project committee soon. Maybe we should let them weigh in before we move forward."

"No!" Kerstin's high-pitched objection was almost a shout. "I mean, let's investigate on our own first. We shouldn't sound a false alarm if we have only the two issues. Right?"

Bennett really wanted a second opinion but blamed her apprehension on inexperience with an assignment of this type and magnitude. She'd follow her gut and trust Kerstin's expertise for the time being. They both deserved this chance. "What do you suggest?"

"I'll check the initial paperwork on the project and make sure I haven't missed anything. Then we'll visit the site and see how far along the builders are on the renovations in the two areas we've identified. How about a walk-through the first of next week?"

"Next week? Why not right now?" Bennett didn't want to explain to the chief why the builders weren't working every day on his pet project.

Kerstin stood and gathered the plans together. "I understand you're anxious to move this along, and so am I, but the original files are in New York, which is where I'll be for a few days. I'll get back to you as soon as possible. Here's my cell number." She handed Bennett a business card and started toward the door.

"Kerstin, it's the first glitch in a long and involved process. We've got this."

"You're right, of course." But the fire of excitement had dimmed in Kerstin's eyes, replaced by a darker shade of doubt.

As the door closed behind her, Bennett hoped she'd sounded more enthusiastic than she felt. If the tension between them and the problems they'd found were any indication of things to come, she and Kerstin were in for a rough ride.

Chapter Six

Bennett hadn't heard from Kerstin in four days, and the anxiety of waiting drained her worse than manual labor. In the meantime, the substation site stood vacant, all work at a standstill. She'd almost called Kerstin several times for an update but didn't want to ratchet her stress level with unnecessary pressure. The silver lining today was family brunch, and George McIntyre joined them for the first time in months.

"Ryan, say grace so we can eat," G-ma said.

"Grace?" Ryan shuffled like any eleven-year-old put on the spot, probably wondering like everybody else why certain Sunday brunches deserved a blessing and others didn't.

"Yes, please."

Ryan glanced up at his mother, got a nod, and bowed his head. "Rub-a-dub-dub, thanks for the grub. Yeah, God." He giggled and reached for his milk.

"Good enough." G-ma raised her mimosa in a toast. "I love having our table full of friends and family. Welcome back, George." She'd lost too many people in her life, and George had almost been added to the list.

"Thank you, Norma. I wouldn't be here if your girls hadn't helped me out the other day."

Mama gave Bennett one of her what-the-hell-is-he-talking-about expressions. She needed to head off more questions before the situation became uncomfortable for George. "Jazz and I helped with some insurance issues. No big deal. Let's eat." She winked at George and passed him the platter of bacon.

"So, how's the substation coming along?" Jazz asked, smoothing the distinctive shock of white hair along her ear. Not the best topic at the moment, but she was helping divert attention from George's situation.

"I haven't seen much activity the past few days on our runs over that way," Mama said. "Is something wrong?"

"Not really. Kerstin is checking the original plans to ensure we're on the same page before we continue. Our predecessors may have been a little lax with details."

"Kerstin?" Dylan turned sideways in her chair and stared at Bennett. "Kerstin Anthony, as in your old high school heartthrob?"

Simon almost sprayed his mimosa across the table. "Do people still use that word?"

"A better question is since when do we grill each other about personal matters in front of company?" Stephanie asked, wiping a dab of ketchup from Riley's chin.

"As long as I've been joining this family for Sunday brunches." Vanessa Brandon, Simon's lesbro at the firehouse, offered her two cents.

Simon punched her on the arm. "That's because you're not a guest, Van. You're family."

Between chews George added, "I'd forgotten how entertaining your family meals are."

"Et tu, Brute?" Bennett gave him a pointed stare, but he shrugged and smiled, a very welcome sight.

Dylan waved her napkin in the air. "Point of freaking order. Back to the original question, please. Are you talking about *that* Kerstin Anthony? For real?"

Everyone at the table kept eating, but their eyes were on Bennett. "Yes, and before any of you wander down some matchmaking trail, we're working together. That's all."

Dylan shook her head. "You moped around for months over her, and all we get when she reappears after seventeen years is 'we're working together'?"

"All there is to say." Bennett cast her mother a pleading glance. She didn't want to revisit that time in her heart and mind, and definitely not in front of family and friends.

"I remember Kerstin," Mama said. "Invite her over for a meal sometime to welcome her home."

Not exactly the help Bennett hoped for. "She's not home, Mama.

She's the architect on this job. When the contract ends, she'll go back to wherever she lives now."

Dylan scooted her chair closer. "So, she's an architect. That's pretty cool, right?"

"She was always the smartest one in the class," Jazz added. "Makes sense." She passed Bennett a basket of fresh bread. "Does anybody care about my first few days as a new district lieutenant?"

Bennett shot Jazz a grateful smile for taking the heat off her. She grabbed a slab of bread, smeared it with warm butter, and took a bite. She glanced sideways, and Dylan was giving her one of her psych-rotation-doctor stares, but she ignored it.

After brunch, G-ma announced, "Everybody to the front porch if you want coffee or tea. Gayle, Bennett, and I will bring it out."

Jazz gave Bennett an apologetic shrug as she passed. "See you on the flip side, if you make it."

Being sandwiched between G-ma and Mama in the kitchen meant a chat about things she didn't want to discuss but couldn't escape. Bennett took drink orders and followed the matriarchs into the kitchen. "Two chamomile teas, the rest coffee."

G-ma pushed the coffeepot button, and Mama started the electric kettle. Then they both turned to Bennett, and G-ma said, "So, has Kerstin changed?"

Bennett couldn't weasel out of answering their questions. It was either now or later. Might as well get it over with. "She's still gorgeous, smart, and as driven as ever."

"But?" Mama asked, her hand resting lightly on Bennett's forearm.

"She seems more cautious, maybe even suspicious, and definitely less optimistic than I remember. And she's standoffish, almost cold, at least with me."

Mama placed cups on a serving tray, Bennett filled them with coffee and hot water, and G-ma dropped in the tea bags. "You two were close in school, despite the money differences between our families. I thought you'd end up together. You didn't talk about what happened." The unasked question lingered, a dense cloud hanging between them. "You were brokenhearted for a very long time."

"I don't know what happened, Mama. I brought up the past a couple of times, but she shut me down. I'd really like to have the conversation someday." How much she wanted to surprised her.

G-ma brushed her hand down Bennett's back. "Sounds like she's been hurt too. Give her time to get to know you again."

"I'm not sure she wants to. Nothing can happen anyway. It's complicated."

"Isn't it always where the heart is concerned?" G-ma said. "We'll see."

"Hey, where's my coffee?" Simon called from the front of the house.

"Hold your horses, Paul Simon Carlyle," Mama answered. She offered Bennett the loaded tray but held on when she tried to take it. "You have your family, and we love you."

❖

"Valerie? Valerie, where are you?" Elizabeth called from her bedroom, her voice rising with each syllable.

Kerstin jumped out of bed and ran down the hall. "Mother, I'm here. Are you okay?"

Elizabeth flailed in the covers, her hair wild, and her gaze scanning the room.

"I'm here." Kerstin placed her hand lightly on her mother's arm to reassure her.

"Oh…I'm…Kerstin?"

"Val is away for the weekend." Her mother's dazed expression reminded Kerstin her recovery was ongoing. "We're holding down the fort. Ready to get up?"

"Maybe I am." She looked around as if trying to get her bearings in her bedroom of seventeen years.

"Would you like to shower first or have breakfast?" Her mother's preferences changed from day to day now, unlike her steadfast routines of the past.

"I'll shower, dear, then make breakfast." Elizabeth edged the covers back with her left arm, trying to appear as normal as possible, her limited range of motion slightly improved. "Start the coffee, dear. I'll be in shortly."

"Don't you need help?"

"I've showered myself for more years than you've been alive. I'll manage."

Kerstin kissed her mother's cheek and returned to her old bedroom, feeling almost as helpless as she had in her younger years. But the past three days with Elizabeth had been much better than she'd hoped. They'd gotten along with minimal problems, and her mother seemed more grateful for her help. Maybe giving Val an occasional break was good for everyone.

She dressed quickly, grabbed the architectural drawings she'd brought home from the office, and headed to the kitchen. After pouring herself a cup of coffee, she studied the documents again, hoping for a different result. She'd been surprised by the lack of details on the original statement of needs and on the plan itself. How had Gilbert gotten by with such incomplete work? Had Leonard even reviewed the design? Maybe she should call Bennett and have her start from scratch with a comprehensive brief. If she had that, an assessment during the walk-through would be easier.

She pulled her cell from her jeans pocket and stopped mid-dial. Was it really necessary to talk to Bennett right now? For the past four days, she'd avoided thinking about their last encounter. Bennett's attentiveness as Kerstin had explained the plans, her brown eyes wide, reminded Kerstin of the eager teenager engrossed in their senior project. When their shoulders had touched, Kerstin's body heated, evoking an urge to run. She glanced at the phone in her hand, shivered, and dialed again. This was work, and it was important.

"Hello?" Bennett's throaty voice turned sexy and sent another shiver through her. "Hello? Is anyone there?"

"Ben—Bennett, it's Kerstin."

"Hi. Is everything okay? You sound stressed."

Why was she so damned nice and considerate? Kerstin heard voices in the background and immediately regretted the call. Maybe Bennett was with a woman, a date, or, more specifically, a lover? She still imagined Bennett as the free-spirited, noncommittal girl of their youth. She placed her hand over her pitching stomach. "I'm sorry. You're busy."

"Sunday brunch with the family. They're like a sports team on steroids. I'll go into another room." A door closed, and Kerstin heard a loud exhale before Bennett came back on the line. "Okay, what news?"

"Nothing good. I probably shouldn't tell you this, but my coworker didn't include enough details in the initial phase of the project."

"In other words, you don't have specs from the department."

"Some, but certainly not enough. I'm so sorry, Bennett."

"How did that happen? Aren't you people sticklers for detail?"

"Yes, and I take full responsibility for the oversight. My job *is* the details, but I gave Gil the benefit of the doubt, unfortunately." She chastised herself for revealing her distrust of her coworker and for not being more thorough in her examination of the plans initially. "Will you start a list of necessities for the station? We can compare it to the plans when I get back. Maybe Gilbert was working off a list in his head. According to his notes, he and Captain Warren were in daily contact."

"I'll work on the list this afternoon. And thank you, Kerstin. You probably hate taking over a project from someone who isn't as organized and efficient as you, but don't worry. We'll make the station a showpiece."

Bennett's kindness and sincerity again put Kerstin completely at ease. How could Bennett know exactly how Kerstin felt? She'd anticipated that working with Gil's drawings would be a nightmare, but she'd dropped the ball on the details.

"Kerstin!" Elizabeth's voice echoed down the hallway as she headed toward the kitchen.

"Who was that?"

"Sorry, Bennett. I have to go. I'll return to Greensboro tomorrow, and we'll set up another meeting."

"Kerstin, where are you, dear?"

"Good-bye, Bennett." She ended the call and hurried toward her mother. "Is something wrong?"

"I heard voices. I thought we were alone. Did I hear you say *Bennett*?"

Kerstin didn't want to discuss Bennett with her mother again, but the only way around the conversation was a lie. Their relationship had suffered enough. "Yes."

Elizabeth put her good hand on her hip and leaned against the counter. "Not Bennett Carlyle from North Carolina?"

"Yes."

"Can you say anything except yes?"

"Yes." She grasped for a way to soften the blow of her news. In the past, her mother always preferred the truth. "My new project is in Greensboro, and I'm working with Bennett."

Elizabeth's face paled. "I see."

"When she walked into the conference room, I was definitely shocked."

"I'll talk to Leonard and have someone else take over."

"Please don't, Mother. I appreciate the offer, but I'll handle my career."

"Even this situation? Have you forgotten what happened to us in that town?" Her mother's face twisted in anguish, the pain still so cruel. If only Elizabeth could've chosen which memories the stroke erased.

She moved to her mother's side and placed her arm gently around her waist. "Of course I haven't forgotten, but you can't blame Bennett Carlyle. She's not the reason Dad left."

"But the whole distasteful mess between the two of you expedited things."

The whole distasteful mess was the kernel around which Kerstin had constructed her walls, the foundation of her determination to succeed, and the pain she vowed to never feel again, but she wasn't the reason her parents' marriage had failed. "You obviously disapprove, but I will see the project through, and not because of Bennett." Was she being totally honest?

Elizabeth hugged her, and Kerstin relaxed into her mother's arms. "I only want the best for you, my dear, not bouncing from person to person with no hope of a stable future."

"And I love you for caring, Mother." But she'd definitely tested her lesbian wings in college while also appeasing her mother by dating every eligible bachelor she shoved in Kerstin's path, until she finally admitted her lesbianism. If she'd learned anything from her dating experiences, from Bennett, and her parents' divorce, it was that love wasn't worth the trouble. The only thing worth fighting for was her safety and place in the world, and she excelled at self-preservation.

CHAPTER SEVEN

On Monday morning, Bennett stood on the front stoop of Fairview Station and watched Kerstin gather her belongings from the yellow cab, her shapely butt sheathed in tight skinny jeans. She hoisted her heavy bag onto squared shoulders, her vivid-blue cashmere V-neck sweater shifting to reveal more cleavage. Bennett caught a full breath and admired the classy casual look she remembered from years past. Her heartbeat trebled as Kerstin walked toward her, her posture rigid, head down. Bennett wanted her to look up, to acknowledge her, to smile, to be happy to see her, but as Kerstin got closer, Bennett noticed dark circles under her eyes and tension around her mouth.

"Good morning," Bennett said. "We do have such things as rental cars in our small town, if you're interested." She tried for a bit of humor.

"I'm not here often enough to justify the expense to the firm. Cabs are fine." Her dour expression didn't alter.

"Are you all right?"

"Of course."

"Did everything go okay in New York this weekend?"

Kerstin stopped on the bottom step and looked up, her tired blue eyes telling much more about her mood than anything she was about to say. "I found the original plans, as I told you, and we have a lot of work to reconcile the police department's needs with the design. We should get started." Her boundaries clearly drawn again, she proceeded around the building.

Bennett wanted to ask about the woman she'd heard in the background when Kerstin called, the one who called her dear. What was their connection—family, friend, or lover? But Kerstin wasn't about to reveal anything personal. Resigned to keep things professional, Bennett said, "Let's start with the public entrance." She unlocked the heavy glass door and held it open. "After you." The space they entered was large and open as far as Bennett could see, no dividing walls or separation.

Kerstin unrolled her drawings and looked back and forth between the physical space and the design, while Bennett remained silent, determined to let Kerstin engage.

"Okay, this is good."

"What's good?"

Kerstin pointed to the drawing. "No unnecessary walls to tear down. Great start."

Bennett suppressed the urge to point out the obvious incompetence of Kerstin's coworker and Arthur Warren, and Kerstin's naïveté about safety needs in a police substation. Instead, she produced the small scrap of paper containing her scribbled notes. Getting upset wouldn't help Kerstin's already sour mood or their working relationship. "But we definitely have issues to address in the space."

"Such as?"

The blue of Kerstin's eyes deepened and became pinpoints directed at her as she turned her attention from the plans. Bennett's skin heated and she licked her lips. "I…this area should serve multiple purposes, which will definitely require walls."

"Explain." Kerstin maintained eye contact, one hundred percent total focus.

"Here," she motioned in front of them, "is the public entrance, conference slash training slash meeting room, and a couple of unsecured interview rooms off to the right. But over here," she waved left, "should be the records and reception area. We'll need a completely enclosed counter with enough space behind it for desks, computers, and file cabinets for our receptionists and crime-analysis folks."

"Oh, I—"

"And a secure door should separate the entire front area from the officers' space in the back."

Kerstin's gaze softened, and a smile threatened the corners of her mouth. "You said you didn't know anything about architecture." Her tone was almost teasing, and the mood between them became slightly more relaxed.

"I don't, but I've walked through the building several times recently and imagined how it could be configured to accommodate my officers."

Kerstin moved to the hallway. "Could we place the security door farther down?"

Bennett followed, excited by Kerstin's apparent acceptance of her suggestions and willingness to negotiate. "I guess. Why?"

She motioned to the left. "If the public has access to the front of the building, these restrooms will have to be accessible."

"Good point." Bennett nodded toward what would become the records and reception area. "That means we'll have to add a secure door to that area as well. We can't have MOPs going to the restroom and wandering in on our staff."

"MOPs?"

"Police speak for members of the public, but not to their faces, of course."

Kerstin smiled for the first time today. Her smile always made everything in Bennett's world seem right, but everything wasn't right—not anymore. The sadness she'd sensed in Kerstin earlier still clung to her, weighing her down. Bennett wanted to know what was wrong but hesitated to break the work rhythm they'd established. Kerstin had become focused and visibly energized as they discussed the project in detail. Architecture was obviously her passion. "Shall we continue?"

"Yes, please." Kerstin preceded her down the hall past the restrooms.

Bennett dropped her gaze to Kerstin's ass, captured in tight denim and swaying hypnotically. She'd filled out beautifully since high school, and Bennett imagined how those full hips would feel in her hands and wrapped around her—Kerstin stopped suddenly, and Bennett almost plowed into her.

"And right here," Kerstin formed a box in the air with her hands, "is the perfect spot for the secure door. Would you prefer a keypad entry or card swipe?" She turned toward Bennett, and they were almost toe to toe. "Focus, Carlyle."

"Totally focused."

"Not on my ass."

Bennett fought the warmth sweeping up her neck. "How did you—?"

"Some things don't change."

The heat charging through her shifted from arousal to embarrassment. She wanted Kerstin to take her seriously, to forget the immature kid she'd been, but she was behaving exactly like a horny teenager. "But you look absolutely edible in those jeans."

"Bennett, please."

"Not what I meant to say, totally unprofessional, but it's still true."

"You're still not good at hiding your feelings. One of the things I liked about you."

"And you always kept me guessing, Kerstin Anthony." Bennett inhaled the citrusy fragrance of Kerstin's perfume and a mixture of coffee and mint on her breath. Which flavor would dominate if she sucked Kerstin's tongue into her mouth? She licked her lips and swayed forward but stopped seconds before Kerstin stepped back.

"Let's keep going," Kerstin said.

Her voice sounded low and raspy, and her pupils dilated. Their closeness had affected her as well, but she didn't want to acknowledge that fact. "Yes, let's."

"Hey, Cap." A couple of officers headed toward them in the hallway.

Kerstin lightly touched Bennett's forearm but quickly released, chastising herself for the gesture. "They shouldn't be in here during construction, liability issues." And Bennett's proximity was a control issue.

"I'll take care of it." Bennett smiled at Kerstin before turning toward the officers. "Hey, guys. What's up?"

One of them answered, "We wanted to check out our new digs."

Bennett guided the two officers back toward the front of the building, chatting and laughing like old friends instead of subordinates. She moved farther away, and Kerstin breathed easier as the air around her cooled. Bennett had been staring, openly admiring her, and their heat pulled them closer and mingled as if they belonged together. Kerstin should've been annoyed, immediately stopped the flirtation, but she enjoyed the attention. The admission unsettled her, but her attraction to Bennett was simply chemistry. What warm-blooded lesbian with a pulse wouldn't be flattered? But Bennett's concern about her sour mood was perceptive, something Kerstin hadn't expected.

Her preoccupation with Bennett was a problem for the project and her career. When she added attraction to their tentative truce, the mixture created a recipe for disaster. She conceded her discomfort wasn't entirely about the past. Forgetting certain things didn't erase the memory of what she'd left behind or prevent them from resurfacing. One thing was certain: she needed to discourage future one-on-one, potentially flirty sessions with Bennett.

She unrolled the plans and scanned the rest of the details. She had some idea about the officers' needs in the public area of the substation now and could bring the contractors and builders back. She'd get Bennett's priority list and conduct another walk-through on her own to nail down other modifications to the design. Maybe she could still keep the project on track and meet the deadline.

"Ready to continue?"

Kerstin jerked. She'd been so focused she hadn't heard Bennett walk up behind her. "Not necessary. I have enough to start."

"Don't you even want to see my list?" Bennett offered a small scrap of paper with writing on both sides.

"That's your brief?" She tried not to smile but failed. "Looks like a mangled grocery list." Bennett's laugh filled the narrow hallway, and Kerstin fought an urge to poke the dimples on either side of her mouth and kiss her until she begged for air.

"Rush job, but I'll make it pretty for you."

"A typewritten page I can add to the draft would suffice." She pressed her back to the wall and inched past Bennett on her way to the exit. "Why don't I schedule a meeting with the full committee day after tomorrow to fill them in?"

"Don't you think we should go over the rest of this first, finish the walk-through?"

"We'll be fine." She hoped she was right as she hurried through the door and toward the parking lot, where she abruptly stopped. She didn't have a car.

"Need a ride? The thing about taxis, you actually have to call them before they show up."

"Very funny. I have the company on speed dial, and they're usually very prompt." She hit the button and placed her request, silently hoping Bennett would keep her distance. She hung up, and Bennett stood shifting from foot to foot, her hands stuffed in her pockets. "What's on your mind, Carlyle?"

"I'm supposed to ask if you'd like to come over for brunch on Sunday, with the family."

"You're *supposed* to?"

"I mean I want you to come, but G-ma and Mama told me to ask, and I'm not brave enough to disobey either of them."

She didn't answer immediately, enjoying the slight blush on Bennett's cheeks.

"Would you? Come?"

Kerstin's insides quivered as she read another meaning into the innocent question. "I…I'm sorry. I'll be back in New York this weekend."

The expectant expression vanished from Bennett's face, replaced by a heavy sigh. "Will you go back every weekend?"

Kerstin nodded.

"Because of the woman I heard in the background when you called?"

The question surprised her. Bennett had heard her mother call out but didn't know their connection. Was she searching for personal information or being kind? "Yes."

"I see." Her answer was almost inaudible, and Kerstin started to clarify, but the cab's arrival interrupted her. "I'll text you about the next meeting. Can we use your conference room?"

"Of course," Bennett replied without looking up again.

As the taxi pulled away, Kerstin regretted leaving Bennett with such a wrong assumption, but it was probably best. If she thought Kerstin was unavailable, both their jobs would be much easier. And right now, Kerstin could use a bit of easy in her life.

Chapter Eight

Police. Open up," Jazz called from the front of the cottage. A loud banging on the door followed the announcement.

"Go away." Bennett shoved her head under a pillow and pulled the covers over the top.

"No can do. If you're not alone, say so now because I'm coming in."

"Jazz, if you like me even a little, go away."

"I love you, sis. That's why I'm here." The door opened, and heavy footsteps sounded through the small space to Bennett's bedroom door. "Are you decent?"

"I'm afraid so." She tugged on a threadbare T-shirt and shorts, her version of pajamas, and sat up as Jazz plopped down on the side of the bed. "To what do I owe the displeasure of your company so early?"

"Early? It's seven in the morning. I've been on duty for over an hour. Come ride with me for a while, see the troops in action, and survey your queendom. You've holed up in your office for the past two days, pretending to work. Why are you still in bed?"

"Contemplating moving somewhere my family doesn't have such easy access. What if I'd had someone in here?"

Jazz arched an eyebrow. "Really? When *was* the last time a woman stayed overnight? For that matter, the last time you spent the night with a woman after you sexed her up?"

"Seriously? What does that even mean? And we're not talking about my sex life at seven in the morning. What *are* we talking about, by the way? Why are you here?"

"You haven't been to the house for a meal since Sunday. Dylan, your mini-me, hasn't even seen you. So, you know what had to happen."

When the family worried about Bennett, Jazz got reconnaissance duty. If Dylan went AWOL, Bennett checked things out. Since her meeting with Kerstin on Monday, she hadn't been in the mood to mingle with anyone, family or otherwise. "I'm fine. Besides, Sunday was only three days ago."

"You or Simon don't show up for meals? Something is definitely wrong."

"Stop it, Jazz." Her voice sounded harsher than she intended.

Her sister winced, her brown eyes suddenly guarded. Her first foster parents had been critical and impatient, and Bennett was occasionally reminded of how much Jazz had overcome and surprised by how a word or tone could still disturb her.

"I'm sorry." Bennett didn't want to talk about Kerstin again, but the effect of her tone on Jazz made her soften. "I didn't mean to take it out on you. Forgive me?" She couldn't bear to be the person who made her sister uncomfortable for any reason.

Jazz nodded, but the uneasiness between them lingered.

Bennett scooted closer and hugged her lightly. "I'm really sorry. Sometimes I can be a real shit. Do you have time for coffee?"

"I always have time for coffee." She punched Bennett on the arm and headed for the small kitchenette. Everything was right again.

Bennett made coffee, and Jazz perched on a barstool, her radio interrupting the silence with calls for service. "Sounds like a busy morning. Anything significant overnight?"

"Not really. A robbery, assaults, and several drunk-driving arrests. The usual." She plugged her earpiece into the radio to silence the chatter and glanced at Bennett as she poured the coffee and handed her a cup across the bar. "Should I wait until you finish your first dose before I ask what's going on?"

Bennett hopped up on the counter and cradled her mug in her hands. "I'm not sure about the situation with Kerstin." Jazz waited. "We had a meeting on Monday to walk through the substation, and I assumed we'd spend most of the day working through plan changes, but she cut it short with no explanation. Haven't heard from her since."

"Uh-huh."

Once she'd said the words aloud, her reason for being upset sounded lame. She added some urgency to the situation. "We have a big meeting soon, and a lot of stuff is still unresolved. We're wasting time and money every day the builders aren't on site."

"What's really bothering you?" Jazz paused, no doubt giving Bennett time to come to the truth on her own. She didn't respond, so Jazz continued. "Sounds like you had expectations of spending time with Kerstin, and they didn't work out." Jazz gave her a skeptical look.

Bennett took several sips of coffee, hiding her face and guilty expression in her mug until she could answer honestly. "She phoned from New York on Sunday, and I heard a woman's voice in the background calling her *dear*. Might have something to do with my foul mood. She wouldn't talk about her. And she goes back to this woman every weekend."

"I see."

"That's all I get?"

"You don't need me to tell you what to do, Ben. You know what's right."

The problem was she wanted a second chance with Kerstin after all these years. Right or wrong? She needed to focus and prove her worth on this project and to Kerstin as well. Wrong or right? She was torn between loyalty to her profession and desire for a woman she harbored unresolved feelings for. "What if the right thing isn't what I want?"

"You'll have to negotiate with yourself, with her, and with your career until you can both live with the outcome. Mixing business and pleasure isn't easy. Add a painful past, and things get really tricky. Think carefully before you go there."

"Yeah. Really."

Jazz cocked her head to one side, and a serious look crossed her face as she stood, finished her coffee, and gave her a two-fingered salute. "Duty calls, but I've got a few minutes, if you want to get dressed."

"Maybe I'll catch you later. I'm not in the mood to rush."

"You know where I'll be."

"What? No last words of wisdom?"

Jazz paused at the door. "I keep repeating myself. Be patient, follow Kerstin's lead, and let her make the first move. Can you?"

Bennett started to answer yes immediately but hesitated. She'd been in limbo most of her life waiting for the right woman, and her patience was running out. "Honestly, sis, I don't know."

❖

Kerstin crinkled another sheet of tracing paper into a ball and shot it toward the tiny overflowing hotel wastebasket with her other failed efforts of the morning. She was exhausted, her shoulders a mass of bunched, tense nerves and muscle. She hadn't engaged in her go-to stress buster since the project started, and her body objected strongly. Her quick runs back to New York weren't long enough to visit her regular haunts, and with her mother in residence, she couldn't employ a service for a much-needed house call. Maybe she'd establish at least one source she could utilize while trapped in small-town USA, but where would she look for a casual partner guaranteed not to get attached or broadcast her personal business? She shook the ridiculous idea from her mind and returned to the plans spread out in front of her.

She'd easily blended Bennett's suggestions for the public space into the original floor plans, but anticipating other changes frustrated her. What did cops need or want in a precinct house? Damn, she hated feeling inept. A hammering headache kept her up half the night, and a slightly upset stomach welcomed her this morning. Her whole system seemed out of sync. The only thing that affected her this much was losing control of a situation, and she was definitely out of her comfort zone with Bennett Carlyle intruding into her professional life.

If they'd completed the walk-through, she might've finished the revisions before the full committee meeting this afternoon. Maybe Bennett would view her early modifications as an act of good faith and back her up with the group. One of her mother's old sayings came to mind: "If you trust a person to do what they've always done, you'll never be disappointed." The maxim didn't bode well for Bennett or their working future, but she didn't have a choice. Time was not on her side, and the question needled her repeatedly.

She rose from the confining desk, stretched her back, and walked to the large windows overlooking a partially wooded creek bed. Cooler overnight temperatures had created ground fog hovering above the surface of a stream that curved and eventually disappeared from view.

The condensation ebbed and flowed on a slight breeze, giving the area an otherworldly aura. One of the reasons she'd booked into the Proximity was the hotel's designation as the nation's first to receive honors from the U.S. Green Building Council. Supporting the environment and sustainable housing were ideals she planned to adopt in her firm.

Taking a deep, steady breath, she allowed the vision of sky and earth to soothe the real quandary roiling inside—what to do about Bennett. She was torn over her attraction for Bennett, the woman, her respect for Bennett, the dedicated police captain, and her memories of a reckless teenager. Any time they got too close, Kerstin bolted like a scared animal, abandoning work and self-respect. The possibility of a relationship had vanished years ago. Yet her fanciful adolescent dreams remained entwined with hopes for the future. If she teased apart one small tangle, the rest might unravel and bury her.

The alarm on Kerstin's phone sounded, a reminder she had only two hours before the first meeting with the full building committee, and she was no closer to a completed plan she could sell to everyone. She rolled the drawings, placed them in her tote, and headed toward the shower. Maybe her trust in Bennett Carlyle wasn't misplaced this time.

❖

Kerstin paused outside the conference room and steeled herself for the first glimpse of Bennett since her indecorous exit on Monday. She opened the door slowly, squared her shoulders, and plowed ahead. Her preparation failed. Bennett wore her black, tailored uniform complete with gun and handcuffs that elicited vivid fantasies. She shook her head and willed her pulse to slow. Bennett was engaged in light, friendly conversation with the other committee members at a small table covered with food. She usually held center court with her charming personality, and food couldn't hurt in an obligatory meeting. Their eyes met, and Bennett smiled. Kerstin's stomach took another acrobatic dive.

Bennett waved her over. "Come meet everybody and try these. Ma Rolls sent some snacks, meat treats wrapped in filo, whatever."

"Pass on the food." She waited as Bennett introduced her to the three men. The public-works and city-planner guys focused on filling paper plates and barely looked up, but the third eyed her as she walked over.

"And this is Chip Armstrong, rep from the manager's office."

What self-respecting adult male allowed people to call him Chip? And he looked like her stereotypical image of a Chip—tall, blond hair, blue eyes, expensive trousers and shoes, fancied himself a ladies' man in spite of the wedding band on his finger, and oozed a cocky attitude that probably turned more women off than on.

Chip stepped forward, offered his hand, and held hers way too long after the mandatory shake. "It's a pleasure indeed, Mrs. Anthony, or is it Miss?" His eyes traveled the length of her body and back up to her breasts.

"Ms. Anthony." She started to ask if he stared at other women's breasts in his wife's presence. The comment wouldn't help their working relationship. "Nice to meet you all. Shall we get started?" Everybody looked toward Bennett. Damn. Kerstin had overstepped because Bennett served as the committee chair. "When you're ready, of course."

Bennett gave her a quick smile, passed the plate of food around again, successfully redirecting everybody's attention, and nodded to her. "Carry on, Ms. Anthony."

Kerstin could've kissed her for the save. She left her drawings in the bag beside her seat, hoping no one would ask to see them until she'd completed the revisions. "On behalf of Parrish Designs, I'm honored to be part of Greensboro Police Department's first substation project. I look forward to working with each of you as we make this the absolute best facility possible." Political niceties out of the way, she dove into the meat of the issue. "As you're aware, loss of the original architect and police manager stopped work on the project while Captain Carlyle and I reassessed the plans."

"Is there something wrong with the original drawings?" the city planner asked.

Kerstin shifted, uncomfortable telling a group of city employees and the man who held the purse strings for the project that her predecessor was, in her opinion, a professional embarrassment. "There's nothing necessarily wrong, but we need to flesh out some details."

Public-works guy, his mouth half full, asked, "Is that polite-speak for a screw-up?"

Kerstin considered throwing Gilbert Early under the bus. He hadn't done anything to help her career, exactly the opposite, but being vindictive was counterproductive. "We have different architectural ideas and styles. Captain Carlyle and I have done a partial walk-through and discovered a few issues we'll need to address."

"Can work resume immediately?" Chip asked. "The manager's office is anxious for the facility to be finished on time and certainly on budget."

"I think we can start back next week with a few minor revisions while we make further assessments on larger items." She'd studied every option critically before reaching a workable solution that allowed preliminary work coupled with continuing evaluation.

"Wait. What?" Bennett's eyes widened.

Kerstin's heart pounded erratically. "Bennett—"

"I'm not comfortable resuming work. We haven't completed an evaluation of the current plan or a walk-through of the building. Construction should be held up until we're finished."

Her brown eyes were dark and their gold flecks sparked. The strained tone of her voice suggested considerable control, but Kerstin sensed underlying anger. "We talked about the public lobby space—"

"Yes."

"And security between the lobby and police spaces, so—"

"And that was as far as we got."

The three men's heads pivoted back and forth with each exchange, and Chip leaned forward in his chair as if hoping for a catfight.

"If you'd let me finish a sentence, I'd—"

"Stop." Bennett held up her hand and touched the listening device protruding from her left ear. "I'm sorry, but I have to go."

"What?" Kerstin stood and waved toward the others. "We're in the middle of a meeting."

"Reschedule." Bennett headed for the door.

"Guess we'll have to get used to the captain rushing out," Chip said.

Kerstin's worst fear unfolded—thrown under the bus by her supposed partner on the most important project of her career. She'd trusted Bennett, but finding out in public she'd made a mistake was the ultimate betrayal. She grabbed her tote and charged after Bennett. "You might have to, but I don't."

Chapter Nine

"Wait." Kerstin raced down the hall to catch Bennett, but she wasn't slowing.

"I don't have time."

Kerstin came alongside her before she reached the exterior door. "You threw me to the wolves, and I don't even get an explanation?"

"I really *cannot* talk right now."

Bennett met her gaze for an instant before pushing through the door, and Kerstin saw sadness and something akin to anguish etched in the lines of her face. But she wouldn't be put off, emergency or not. She followed Bennett to her vehicle and climbed in. "We *are* going to talk about what happened, now or later."

"You shouldn't be here."

"Then I guess you'll have to take the time to put me out because I'm not leaving."

Without looking at her, Bennett said, "Then you better hold on." She spun out of the parking lot, steering with one hand and dialing her phone with the other.

Kerstin pulled her seat belt tighter and grabbed the dashboard, feeling queasy at the abrupt change in direction.

"Jazz, what do we know?"

Kerstin couldn't hear the other side of the conversation, but from Bennett's expression, something was terribly wrong.

Bennett pressed her lips tightly together while she listened and barreled through intersections. "I see. How badly is he hurt? Any fatalities?" She flinched at the response. "I'm sure you've already done so, but make sure an officer stays with the family once they arrive. I'll see you at the hospital."

"What's going on, Bennett? Why are we going to the hospital?" The last place she wanted to be was in a medical facility of any kind. She'd spent too many days and nights in those places after her mother's stroke. Kerstin shook her head to clear some of the horrible images. Her sweaty palms slid off the dashboard, and her shoulder rammed into the door.

"Hold on, please." Bennett shot her a concerned look. "Officer injured. High-speed chase. One fatality, innocent bystander." She slowed at an intersection and stared at her a second longer. "You okay? You're really pale."

"I don't like hospitals."

"You don't have to come in. Probably best if you don't." Bennett slid the car to a stop near the emergency bays. "Taxis come and go regularly outside the main entrance."

Bennett sprinted away before Kerstin could reply, and she suddenly felt petty for chasing her to discuss something that now seemed insignificant. Someone was dead, and someone Bennett cared about was injured. Choking down her discomfort, she opened the car door and slowly followed Bennett's path inside. She was easy to spot in the crowded waiting room surrounded by a group of uniformed officers, talking in hushed voices. Kerstin edged closer.

"Is everybody okay?" Bennett looked to each officer and waited for his or her response. "Were any of you involved in the actual chase?" A young female and an older male nodded, while the others shook their heads. "Okay. Don't talk about it with anyone else or each other until after the Internal Affairs interview. Understood?" They nodded again. "Have we gotten an update on our officer yet?" The group fell silent.

An attractive redheaded nurse approached and touched Bennett's forearm, smoothing her hand back and forth like a woman familiar with the terrain. Her smile was warm, her tone full of concern, exactly what a good nurse should be, but Kerstin found her physical familiarity improper under the circumstances.

"Ben, I have a small conference room, if you'd like to move your officers somewhere more private to wait," the nurse said.

"That would be great, Jen." She motioned to the officers, and they followed the nurse, Bennett bringing up the rear.

When the last officer took a seat in the small space, Jen said, "I'll have coffee brought in and let the ER doc know where to find you."

"Thanks."

Bennett held Jen's hand a bit longer than necessary before letting go and turning back to the officers. Kerstin's fleeting thought that *she* should be supporting Bennett quickly vanished. They couldn't even get through one encounter without clashing, and the unpleasant outcome at the meeting didn't bode well for their future. She stood outside the doorway, unsure if she should interfere with the gathering. Her eyes met Bennett's for a second before motion at the end of the hall distracted her. A man in a white coat fast-walked toward her, and she signaled to Bennett.

She stepped out into the hall. "How's my officer?" she asked, still several yards away.

Kerstin cringed at the anguish on her face and in her dark eyes. She remembered Bennett's comment about not asking her officers to do something she wouldn't and wondered if Bennett would take the injured officer's place if possible.

"He's sustained serious injuries, none appear to be life-threatening at this time, but we'll know more after the X-rays and other tests. Has his family been notified?"

"His family?" Kerstin's question was almost a gasp. "You said the injuries weren't life-threatening."

"He's still unconscious. I'll need permission for further treatment beyond stabilization," the doctor explained and looked back at Bennett. "You understand."

"Of course. My lieutenant is contacting the family." The doctor turned to leave, and Bennett added, "Please keep me informed." She glanced at Kerstin and didn't seem to register who she was for a moment but finally said, "You really should go. I have to call the chief, visit the accident scene, and I'll be here until I know my officer is out of danger. Are you sure you're okay?"

Kerstin nodded.

"Well, you don't look it."

"So you've said. I just don't like hospitals."

"So *you've* said, but not why." Kerstin avoided her stare, and Bennett looked back toward the waiting officers. "I should brief them. Excuse me."

"I'll wait for you…if that's all right."

"You're welcome to wait with us."

"I don't want to intrude." She purposely eased her hand closer to Bennett's until they touched and then held it momentarily. The connection reminded her of a simpler time when she believed in dreams and the possibility of their fruition. She withdrew so quickly it seemed almost comical. "Go. Your guys need you. We'll catch up later." She didn't wait for a reply before rushing toward the exit, the walls blending into an institutional-beige haze. Why had she touched Bennett when they were both so emotionally vulnerable? Hospitals and emotions, never a good mix.

Since her mother's stroke, hospitals reminded her of desperation and pain. Now she could add another feeling to the jumbled mixture. She needed to breathe deeply, to push down the unwanted memories and cravings. Once outside, she ran to Bennett's car and leaned against the side, pulling for breath.

"Are you okay, ma'am?" asked a paramedic exiting an ambulance.

"Needed some air."

"Hospitals can have that effect." The young man walked away, glancing back until the emergency room doors closed behind him.

Kerstin kicked off her shoes and climbed onto the hood of the car, burying her face in her hands to stop the memories—her mother lying helpless, blue eyes begging to understand what was happening; Kerstin walking the halls every day and curled in a small recliner at night waiting for the results of endless tests; the smells of blood, vomit, and the deodorized scent of cleaning chemicals.

Her experience today wasn't as personal, but certainly disturbing. She'd been helpless and unable to reach her mother during those first hours in the hospital because of her condition. And today she couldn't truly connect with Bennett or help her at all because of their distance.

Her nerves jangled, a slow unraveling of control. Neither of those situations had been within her power to alter. She let the truth sink in. Slowly her frustration and discomfort from the meeting evaporated in a desire to help, but she had no idea where to start. Bennett's officers were as stoic as she'd tried to be. She slid off the car and slipped her feet back into her shoes. At least she wouldn't complicate things any further. She'd talk to Bennett about work another time. Giving her bag that rested on the floorboard a final glance, she walked toward the front of the hospital, texting Bennett on the way: *Got a taxi. Bag in your car. See you tomorrow. Good luck.*

Several hours later, Bennett glanced down at Kerstin's text and tapped in a response.

Sorry I couldn't talk. My office at ten?

Okay.

She dialed Mama's number and stepped into the hall. "Are you terribly busy?"

"I heard about the accident. G-ma and I are whipping up some wraps to bring to the hospital. What else can I do?"

Bennett slumped against the door frame, relief and gratitude making her weak. "How do you always know exactly what I need?"

"I'm a mother, and I've had lots of experience with cops. How are you, honey?"

"Trying to keep the guys' spirits up until we hear, and you know cops and food. I love you, Mama. See you shortly." She enjoyed the feeling of being truly known and loved for a few seconds before returning to the tension in the waiting room. The two original assist officers and their supervisor still waited to hear more about their squad mate, after she'd sent the others home or back to their shifts. "I've ordered something decent to eat, not canteen food."

"Thanks, Cap," the sergeant answered.

The officers nodded and continued to pace a pattern around the table and each other. She understood the need to vent nervous energy. She considered a stroll through the parking lot herself but decided on a few laps around the hospital. "I'll be back in a few, Sergeant. Call me if you hear anything."

The sergeant nodded, and Bennett walked down the hall toward the canteen, the farthest distance from their location, taking long, deliberate strides to stretch her muscles. The movement released some of her anxiety but couldn't relieve the weight of the situation. A police chase resulting in the death of an innocent bystander was a worst-case scenario. Her officer would likely second-guess his decision, relive the incident over and over, and perhaps reconsider his career choice. The grieving family could never be consoled or compensated for their loss.

And she couldn't do anything to help either of them. After three laps around the floor, she slowed her pace. She was on her final pass when she saw a familiar figure slouched forward on a table in the snack area, her head resting on her hands.

"Emory?"

Emory Blake turned her head to the side, wiped her face and eyes with a napkin, and raked her fingers through tendrils of auburn hair that had escaped her usually tight French braid. She finally faced Bennett. "Hello, Ben. How are you?"

"Okay." Just like Emory to be more concerned about others. She was a social worker with the hospital, and the job fit her nurturing personality perfectly. "May I join you?" When Emory nodded, Bennett pulled a chair closer and placed her hand on Emory's forearm. "What's wrong?"

Emory sniffled and shook her head. "The usual. Child abuse, pretty bad case. How can people hurt children?"

Bennett's insides clenched into a hard knot. "No idea. It defies decency and common sense. Want to talk about it?"

"Not really. Just needed a good cry. I'll be okay now."

"Will you? Will any of us who see these things on a regular basis? I sometimes wonder what it does to our souls, and if we'll continue to believe in love and kindness."

"Bennett Carlyle, you're starting to sound like an old philosopher."

"Nah. Just a realist or maybe a skeptic."

"How's your officer?" Emory asked, slipping into professional mode.

"So far so good. How did you know about the accident?"

"Hospital grapevine. How are you holding up?"

Bennett, focused on feelings other than her own, wasn't sure she had an honest answer, and Emory was the kind of woman who expected the truth. Bennett's shoulders ached and a headache pounded at the base of her skull. "I'm devastated for the family who lost a loved one in the accident, worried about my officer's condition, and I'm contemplating the details that could turn a routine internal-affairs investigation into a nightmare. Under the circumstances, I guess I'm okay. A lot to think about."

Emory leaned forward, now the nurturer, and briefly cupped Bennett's hand. "And none of it is your fault. You understand, right?"

The statement caught her off guard, and she simply nodded.

"Do you really?"

The intensity of Emory's green-eyed stare made Bennett wonder how close she and Mama had become through the years working together on hospital social events and fund-raisers. "Intellectually, yes, but sometimes it's hard to separate professional responsibility from personal accountability."

"It is indeed, but for our own sanity, we have to master the art. Just like with my cases."

"How did you become so smart?"

Emory shrugged and offered a quick smile. "Maybe it's the decade and a half of experience I have on you. How's your family? Simon and Stephanie? Dylan?"

"Good. Simon and Stephanie live on the same street in Fisher Park, but you probably already know that. G-ma and Mama want all their children close, even when we fly the nest. Dylan still lives at home for the time being, a financially challenged ER doctor."

"I see her occasionally passing in the halls. She's quite impressive." Emory broke eye contact and brushed a wisp of hair from her face. "And…Jasmine?"

"Jazz is great. Made lieutenant a few days ago and is settling in like a pro. You haven't seen Jazz in years, have you? I mean since we graduated? She went away to college for a few years."

Emory shook her head. "Strange too. You'd think our paths would cross at some point, professionally, I mean. I see you and Dylan, so…" A light blush colored her cheeks.

"Maybe we should make a proper introduction some time, off the job."

"Oh, I'm not—"

"Captain?" One of Bennett's officers stood at the canteen entrance. "A nice lady dropped off the food, if you're hungry."

"Thanks. I'll be right there." The officer walked away, and Bennett turned back to Emory. She wanted to continue their conversation, but Emory grabbed her bag and headed toward the door. "Want to join us for something to eat?"

"No thanks. I need to get home. Early day tomorrow."

Bennett smiled. "Hope I didn't make you uncomfortable."

"Not at all." Emory gave Bennett a hug and discreetly whispered in her ear, "And don't worry about the substation cither. You'll work it out."

"What?"

"Delays and old friends complicating life. It'll work itself out. You'll see."

"How do you know about—"

"Hospital gossip. Nothing is sacred on the grapevine. Good night, Bennett." Emory gave her arm a final squeeze before leaving.

On her way back to join the officers, Bennett thought about Emory's comment regarding the substation. Definitely not good that people were talking about her personal challenges with Kerstin, even worse that the project was a subject of rumors and speculation. She hoped the chief wouldn't hear any of it.

Chapter Ten

Jazz's soft voice cut through Bennett's sleepy haze "Ben? Ben?" She raised her head from the table, and Jazz stood over her with two cups of coffee. "Have you been here all night?"

Bennett looked around, getting her bearings, momentarily unsure of where here was. Uncomfortable hospital waiting room. "More or less. Went to the scene for a quick look-see."

"Sleep much?"

"Must've dozed off. I wanted to know about the surgery. What's the time?"

"Almost ten." Jazz placed the coffee on the table and joined her.

"Great commander I am, right?" She took a long sip and prayed for a swift jolt of caffeine to clear her head.

"As a matter of fact, you are. I stopped by the nurses' station on my way in. Jen said the procedure to repair the compound fracture of the officer's femur went well. He'll be out of commission from four to six months, but he will recover."

Bennett let out a long sigh and relaxed slightly. "That's great. I'll let the guys know when I get to the station."

"I briefed the morning sergeant and asked him to notify oncoming shifts."

"You're one hell of a 2IC, Jazz Perry."

"Of course. You wouldn't let any jackleg be your second-in-command. We make a good team, which brings me to the next item of business. You need to rest, Ben, and I'm not channeling G-ma and Mama. You've been up all night and look like hell. I checked by the station, and you don't have anything urgent on your calendar, unless you didn't tell me."

"Did you say it's almost ten o'clock?" Bennett pushed back from the table and stood too quickly. Her vision blurred and the room spun. She grabbed the arm of the chair for support. "Crap. I've got a meeting with Kerstin."

"Hold on." Jazz guided her back toward her seat, but she pulled away.

"I'm serious, Jazz. We had a disagreement during our last meeting and didn't have a chance to talk before the accident. I can't blow her off."

"I don't think it's a good idea for you to do anything important until you've rested."

Bennett finished her coffee and started toward the door. "I appreciate your concern, sis, but this really can't wait. Thanks for the coffee…and for being the voice of reason even if I don't follow your advice."

"I figured you'd barrel through, so I've got you a clean uniform in my car." She tossed a key to Bennett. "Leave it under the mat. I have a spare."

"Aren't you coming?"

Jazz stared at the floor, a sheepish look on her face. "I'll be along."

"Interesting nurse on your radar, sis?"

"Go, nosey."

"On the subject, I saw somebody last night I'd like to introduce you to, or I should say reintroduce you to," Bennett said.

"No thanks. I don't need your help getting a date. Ever again."

Bennett raised her hands and backed away. "Have it your way, but I expect details."

Jazz laughed. "Not likely."

Ten minutes later, Bennett dropped Kerstin's tote in her office chair on the way to the shower. She peeled her wrinkled uniform and undergarments off, dropped them on the floor, and stepped under the cold water. She gritted her teeth as the icy spray brought her fully awake, her first clear thought of Kerstin. She'd been really upset after their meeting yesterday, but Bennett couldn't quite pin down the reason. They'd resolve things this morning.

After an invigorating scrub and a rinse with hot water, Bennett toweled off and reached for her uniform. She unbuttoned the shirt, and a small plastic bag hung from the hanger. Jazz remembered everything. Bennett pulled on her boy-cut briefs and sports bra, feeling almost human again. As she reached for her trousers, the door burst open and Kerstin glared at her. The stare was as potent as her tender touch last night at the hospital. Bennett's knees trembled.

"Oh…the officer out front said you were…I didn't realize you'd be…" She scanned Bennett's body slowly, her gaze a lingering caress. "I'll wait for you out—"

"No need." Bennett forced her voice to remain calm in spite of her quivering insides. "I can dress while you talk. Might as well get this over with."

"In…inappropriate," Kerstin said.

"Kerst, you've seen me practically naked before."

"Seventeen years ago…in gym class. You were nothing…like… this." She waved toward Bennett. "I'll wait in your office." Before Bennett could respond, Kerstin was gone.

Arousal dampened the inside of Bennett's thighs, and she shivered. Heat tingled her skin and left her sticky. Kerstin's words were clearly meant to distance, but she couldn't hide the longing in her eyes. The desire was mutual, but what could she do? Jazz told her to be patient, let Kerstin take the lead. What if Kerstin continued to deny her feelings?

Bennett finished dressing and walked toward her office, pausing outside the door to put on her game face. She hated pretense, but she'd have to ease into a conversation about feelings. Adjusting her utility belt, she stalled and prayed for divine intervention. She stepped into her office, and Kerstin was rummaging through her bag, effectively avoiding eye contact.

"Sorry to keep you waiting."

"Thanks for bringing my bag. How is your officer?"

"He'll be fine. Thanks for asking."

"When did you leave the hospital?"

"About ten minutes before you found me in the locker room." They were both stalling.

"Are you sure you want to do this now? You must be tired."

Kerstin's words warmed her because she wanted Kerstin to be concerned about her. "I'm good, but thanks for asking."

"Who was the nurse you were talking to? Jen something? You seemed very friendly."

Kerstin's tone held a hint of irritation, and Bennett caught a glimmer of something fiery in her eyes before she looked away. Bennett almost laughed, deciding to play it out. "A friend."

"A *good* friend, I'd say, by the way she clung to you."

"We went out a few times. She's a good nurse and a—"

"Stop." Kerstin raised her hand. "Sorry. I don't really have the right to ask about your personal or dating life."

"True, but you have my permission to ask anything you want." She was jealous, and Bennett took great pleasure in the knowledge, which affirmed the next thing she needed to say.

"Bennett, I—"

"Kerstin, can—" They spoke at the same time. "You first."

"No, you, please."

Bennett motioned for her to sit and then pulled another chair closer. She tried to gauge Kerstin's mood by the set of her jaw or the shade of her blue eyes, but nothing provided a clue. "We need to talk about the past, our feelings. They're getting in the way of...of everything."

Kerstin stared at her hands clasped tightly in her lap and shook her head like she was trying to shake something loose. "We have a more important issue to discuss. Trust."

"Probably the foundation of our problems. I feel you're sending mixed signals. Your words are totally business, but your eyes say something else. In the locker room, you threw serious heat my way, and you seem jealous of Jen. I'm more than a little confused. I want to trust you, and I want you to trust me, but we have to be honest."

Kerstin's eyes softened momentarily before a blink shuttered any emotion. "I'm talking about yesterday, Ben, about how you blindsided me with the committee."

Bennett jerked her head back. "Blindsided you?"

Kerstin skirted around Bennett's personal observations without even a grunt, much less a comment. Irritation rolled off her in waves as she said, "We reached an understanding about working together, but you basically called me incompetent in front of the others. Your remark about needing more changes before the builders came back cast the design and my assessment into question. And quite honestly, your comments seemed personal."

Bennett closed her mouth finally, struggling for an appropriate response. How had the topic changed from feelings to being accused of professional and personal attacks?

"I should've known you'd do it again." Kerstin grabbed her chest and turned away as if embarrassed by her words.

"Do what again, Kerstin? I *know* you're not talking about the past because it's apparently off-limits."

Kerstin's back was still to her. "I shouldn't have…I don't like being used or deceived."

"I'm sorry you feel I did either, now or in the past. It certainly wasn't my intent, and if I made you look incompetent, I sincerely apologize." She let her words sink in, and after several seconds of silence, Kerstin faced her again.

When she spoke, her voice was calmer, her words more measured. "So what point were you trying to make with the committee?"

"Only that we had other issues to address, and another walk-through would be a good idea before the workmen returned. Better planning now might prevent another work stoppage later. I was excited about sharing my needs list with you." She reached for Kerstin's hand but reconsidered and pulled back. "I was only thinking of the best possible outcome for both of us, professionally, but the accident happened before I could clarify. I'm really sorry I upset you."

Kerstin hung her head. "I'm afraid the committee left with an unfavorable impression."

"Then we rectify their impressions at our next meeting."

Kerstin regarded her cautiously and eventually nodded. "What do you suggest?" The spark returned to her eyes as she spread the substation plans across the conference table, any personal discussion effectively bypassed again.

What choice did Bennett have but to go along? She placed two sheets of typed notes on one side of the drawings. "We sit down and really evaluate the possible changes. My list is pretty comprehensive, and with your knowledge of architecture, we come up with an idea of what can and can't be changed and also how much of a cost difference we're facing."

Kerstin took Bennett's list and glanced back and forth to her plans. "This is interesting. We need a block of uninterrupted time. What works for you?"

"Not right now, I'm afraid, too many details about the accident still need my attention. And I'd like to visit the family of the man who was killed."

"Consoling family members is part of your job?"

"It's the right thing. Why don't you come by the family place around six? G-ma and Mama have ladies' night at the police club, Dylan and Jazz are working evenings, and if Mama's not cooking, Simon and Stephanie fend for themselves. We have an eight-foot table, perfect for your humongous drawings." She pointed to the sheets of paper hanging over the small conference desk like a tablecloth.

"Are you sure you can concentrate after your all-night vigil at the hospital?" Kerstin's brow wrinkled, as she appeared to consider the pros and cons of the offer.

"Totally."

"Okay." She didn't sound convinced.

Kerstin made a few changes on the drawings, fully immersed in her work, until a subtle throat clearing cued her that Bennett had asked a question. "I'm sorry?"

"I said, do you need a ride back to Proximity?"

"Took your advice and rented a car. Made sense."

"Okay. I'll see you later."

"Can I hang out here for a bit?"

Bennett picked up her briefcase and started toward the door. "Sure, as long as you want. Jazz might pop in and out, but she's mostly in the field. Let her know if you need anything."

Bennett stood beside her for several seconds, their closeness distracting. The smells of soap and shampoo wafted from her freshly showered body, and Kerstin leaned in for another whiff before backing away. "Thanks, but I shouldn't be much longer."

"I look forward to this evening."

Bennett's tone sounded hopeful, and Kerstin clarified the boundaries once again. "You understand we're having a work meeting."

"Of course, but a girl has to eat. I'll order in. Don't worry." Without waiting for a response, Bennett closed the door behind her.

Once Bennett's scent cleared from the room, Kerstin breathed more easily. Bennett had been patient and sensitive in her explanation of her intentions with the committee. Maybe Kerstin had overreacted to everything, especially Nurse Jen. What was *that* about? She certainly wasn't jealous. And why did she accept Bennett's invitation to her house? She was tempting fate.

The huge Carlyle home would be empty except for the two of them, giving Bennett home-court advantage, physically, psychologically, and emotionally. Tonight was truly all about business, so why was she worried? Because Bennett's magnetic personality won people over, and Kerstin had succumbed more than once to her charm. Was she strong enough to resist now? Did she even want to?

She glanced at the program brief Bennett had prepared, which showed considerable thought and research. Did she still judge Bennett by her high school reputation as a cavalier, reckless teenager not to be taken seriously? Kerstin couldn't imagine being judged by her immature, cowardly past. Maybe she'd give Bennett a break. If they talked about the past, perhaps they could resolve their trust issues, which apparently emerged unbidden.

Kerstin spent the remainder of the day studying plans and walking through the substation site before dashing to the hotel to change clothes. She rifled through every outfit she'd packed before finally settling on jeans and a V-neck sweater, hoping for casual without sexy. As she approached the large Southern-style residence, her pulse soared, and she wanted to run. Her jeans were too tight and the sweater too low-cut and form-fitting. Why had she agreed to a private get-together with the only person who could totally shatter her control with a single smile or glance? She paused on the sidewalk, reconsidering, before the front door opened, and Bennett waved her in.

"Having second thoughts?" Bennett stood aside as she entered.

"Of course not." But she couldn't meet Bennett's brown eyes. Instead, she took in the Carlyles' warm, traditional decor, which had remained the same as long as she could remember.

"G-ma and Mama are nothing if not consistent," Bennett said as if reading her mind.

"Not necessarily a bad thing." She'd always gotten a sense of warmth and acceptance in their home. "It's nice, comforting."

Bennett led the way down the hall to the kitchen at the back of the house. "Guess you don't need a tour. The pizza is here, half meat-lovers, half ham and pineapple. Hope you still like the combo." She finally turned to Kerstin, and her eyes painted a slow trail down her body. "Wow. You look…hot. Sorry. Am I allowed to comment on your level of hotness?"

"Business, remember?"

"Okay, but as G-ma would say, the truth is welcome in heaven."

Their eyes met, and heat oozed through Kerstin so slowly it was painful. She wanted to blame her sudden spike in temperature on the woodstove glowing in the corner but couldn't deny the truth. Maybe they should have *the talk* tonight. She would present the facts calmly enough to convince Bennett the past really was past.

"Pizza now before it gets cold?"

Kerstin nodded and reached for a slice of ham and pineapple. She folded it and bit into the salty-sweet combination. "Mmm, I'd forgotten how good pizza tastes if done properly. We have so many places in New York I have trouble choosing. Where did you get this?"

"Sticks and Stones on Walker Avenue, the best in town."

They ate in silence, Kerstin slowly savoring every bite of the delicious slices. Bennett tore off chunks and chomped with the same gusto she performed most tasks with. Bennett retrieved another drink from the fridge, and Kerstin stole a glance at the low-slung jeans hugging her hips and the stretchy T-shirt outlining her breasts. She ignored her guilt for saying one thing and thinking the opposite, but in an odd way she felt entitled to enjoy herself…and yes, with Bennett. The familiarity of the place and the woman somehow seemed right.

"Shall we get started?" Bennett cleared the empty pizza box from the table and moved her drink to the side.

Kerstin took a long pull from her Coke to cool her insides and focused on business. She rolled the drawings across the long table and placed Bennett's list between them. "I'm impressed with your specs. You were very detailed, exactly what we should've had in the beginning."

"Thanks." Bennett smiled and edged nearer. "But I was hoping we'd talk about us first."

Kerstin swallowed hard. The closer Bennett got, the more difficulty she had thinking, and if she did, her thoughts proved totally unproductive. "Oh. We should get business out of the way. You know, in case things go badly on the *us* front, at least we'll get some work done."

"More stalling, Kerst?"

The tension in Kerstin's stomach said yes, but she didn't have the courage to admit it. "Makes sense to work first."

Bennett moved to a leather chair in the corner and relaxed, stretching her legs out toward the woodstove. "Okay, let me know if you need me to clarify anything on my list."

Kerstin finally gathered a full breath and turned her attention to the drawings. She'd reviewed most of Bennett's list this afternoon before leaving her office but still had a few more modifications. "This shouldn't take long, and then we can talk."

Kerstin homed in on the minutiae of her plan, flagged the specifics Bennett listed with red ink, and left space for costs. She stopped on something she didn't understand. "What did you mean here?" She pointed to an item on the list.

"Hold on…a…second…" Bennett leaned forward in her chair, got halfway up, and slumped back, obviously exhausted.

"Never mind. I'll figure it out or ask you again tomorrow."

"Thank…s…" Bennett's voice faded.

Soon Kerstin was consumed by the work again, forgetting where she was or even the time. After she'd reviewed and marked all the items, she rolled her shoulders to release the tension and stretched her back. She glanced at her watch, surprised three hours had passed. She turned, momentarily startled by her surroundings, until she saw Bennett.

She was asleep in the old leather chair beside the woodstove, her long legs stretched out, hands splayed across her abdomen, and her head tilted to the right as if she'd been watching Kerstin when she drifted off. The glow from the stove cast a soft sheen on Bennett's face, highlighting wisps of brunette hair across her forehead and dark lashes resting against her cheeks. At rest, her features settled into a contented smile, lips slightly parted, dimples barely visible. She was so gorgeously innocent in the moment that Kerstin felt protective and something tender and deeper. She admired how hard Bennett worked and that she gave one hundred percent to the people who depended on her.

She debated going to her, cupping her face, and kissing her until she'd purged all her suppressed feelings. She rehearsed again the words she should've said seventeen years ago, questioned waking Bennett to deliver them, but wasn't sure she could be that vulnerable. In the end, she chose reason over emotion. What Bennett really needed was sleep, not a misguided attempt to correct past wrongs.

Kerstin scribbled a note and placed it on the table.

> *Thanks for the pizza, the huge work area, and the peace and quiet.* ☺ *See you in the morning at the site, 10:00 sharp.*

She knelt beside Bennett and whispered, "I'm sorry, my darling. Life wasn't fair to either of us." She lightly kissed Bennett's lips, savoring the lingering salty flavor of pizza. One tiny taste of Bennett's lips, and Kerstin desperately wanted more, but she forced herself to stop and crept out of the house.

Chapter Eleven

Bennett paced in the parking lot of the future Fairview Station next morning, working the kinks out of her back and legs from sleeping all night in a chair. She ached everywhere but felt mostly embarrassed she'd fallen asleep on Kerstin before their talk. To complicate matters, she'd dreamed Kerstin had kissed her and had woken up aroused. She paced faster, images of Kerstin hunched over Mama's dining-room table and kissing her playing on a mental loop.

"Careful or we'll have to replace the asphalt."

Bennett looked up seconds before bumping into Kerstin. "What?"

"You're pacing a rut in the parking lot. Something wrong?"

"I'm so sorry about last night. I haven't fallen asleep with a beautiful woman in the room ever. I'm mortified and—"

"You were exhausted, and I couldn't bear to wake you. We'll talk, soon."

"Promise?" She was uncomfortable about blurting without filtering but couldn't stop. She really wanted Kerstin to set another date. "When?"

"Soon. Would you please get the box from the backseat of my car?"

Bennett didn't move, surprised at Kerstin's question, not at all responsive to her inquiry. It was evident no further explanation was forthcoming, so she pulled her hands out of her pockets and shuffled over to Kerstin's vehicle. She'd hoped her honesty would spark the conversation they didn't have last night, but Kerstin was business as usual. She retrieved the item as Kerstin unlocked the side door of the substation and waited for her. "What's this?"

Kerstin slid a large cardboard box into the center of the room and rested the smaller one on top. “A 3D model of Fairview Station.”

“Like Legos?”

“Sort of, but a more sophisticated version with all the internal bits. If I recall, you’re a more kinesthetic learner, a doer, so a model might help translate the drawings into reality.”

Bennett flashed back to the two of them kneeling beside Kerstin’s bed developing a drainage system for the soccer field on a sheet of drafting paper. Bennett’s practical applications and Kerstin’s design won them both excellent grades on their senior project. The only part Bennett really enjoyed was working with Kerstin and getting to know her better, a lot better. Kerstin remembering something personal and positive about her, and going to the extra effort of providing the useful aid, filled Bennett with a type of joy she didn’t totally understand. She grinned and nodded, basking in the attention.

She walked around the model, glancing between Kerstin’s drawings and the replica. She looked in through a window. “I wish I could see the inside better.”

Kerstin edged her aside and gently removed the roof. “Your wish is my command.” She cleared her throat, and her cheeks turned a light shade of pink.

“Don’t I wish? Sorry. You left yourself wide open.”

“Can you focus, please? I marked all the changes you want inside with red ink. My next step is to calculate costs. You might have to compromise on some things.”

“Like what?”

“I’m not sure until I run the estimates, and then we can talk again.”

Bennett studied the model, which made a lot more sense than the pen-and-paper version. The room dimensions and solid walls were clearly distinguishable from doors and windows. She easily saw what needed to be moved or added. “Thank you for this. It really does help.” She looked up, and Kerstin was staring at her mouth. “Please don’t look at me like that. Last night I dreamed you kissed me, and the expression on your face isn’t calming my libido.”

Kerstin’s blue eyes darkened and she licked her lips. “Sorry.”

“I did only dream you kissed me, right?” Kerstin started to say something, but Bennett's phone interrupted her. She pulled it off her belt and groused at the caller. "Yeah. Carlyle."

"Ben, it's Pete Ashton. Bad time?"

Bennett straightened. "No sir, Chief. How can I help?"

"I'm at Fairview Station and everything's locked. Where are you?"

"Come to the parking-lot side." She hung up and turned to Kerstin. "He didn't sound happy. You don't have to stay. I'll brief you later."

"Whatever the problem, we'll face it together." Kerstin touched Bennett's arm like a physical connection was a natural thing and made eye contact, holding it until the space between them started to close. "Understand?"

The flush of arousal assaulted Bennett's senses and threw her heart rate into a climb. The only thing she understood at the moment was how much she wanted to hold and kiss Kerstin until everything else disappeared, but now was definitely not the time or the place. "Perfectly. I'll be right back."

She sprinted to the entrance and unlocked the door. "What brings you to the field, Boss?"

"Police business, of course." Chief Ashton nodded to Kerstin. "Ms. Anthony." Then he scanned the open space and shook his head. "I got a call from Chip Armstrong."

"And?" Bennett waited for the secondhand report from the manager's lackey.

"He said the builders hadn't worked for a while, and from the looks of this place, I'd say he's right. He also said you and Ms. Anthony were having, how did he put it, 'fundamental differences.' What's happening, Ben?"

Kerstin stepped forward. "Chief, I can exp—"

"Ms. Anthony, no disrespect, but you don't answer to me. I need to hear from my captain."

Bennett was embarrassed by the chief's assumption and elated that Kerstin took up for her, but this was her boss, her fight, and her reputation. "We reevaluated the architectural plans and made some necessary changes."

"Why?" Bennett met Ashton's unwavering stare. "What aren't you telling me, Ben?"

"Things had gone a bit off the rails."

"How so?"

"Chief, if I may?" Kerstin tried again.

"Very well, Ms. Anthony, since my captain seems reluctant to speak candidly."

"What Bennett doesn't want to say is her predecessor did a horrible job on the initial brief, which left out several necessary specifications completely. And my predecessor wasn't very thorough either. So we've been cleaning up their sloppy work. I can't allow workmen to return to the site until they have a completed set of drawings and accurate material and cost estimates."

Bennett stared at Kerstin as she spoke, pride rising in her chest. Kerstin was confident and professional and wasn't about to let the chief of police bully either of them.

"Makes sense," Chief Ashton said. "I'm sure I don't have to say this again, but I will to impress upon both of you the importance of this project. The manager's office has reason to be concerned. If these changes put us over budget or over our deadline, the whole project could be scrapped. You both understand?"

"Yes, sir," Bennett answered.

"I do, Chief." Kerstin waved toward the 3D model. "Want to look at the floor plan?"

"No time today." He nodded toward the door for Bennett to accompany him. "I'll see you later, Ms. Anthony, and thank you for your candor." They got outside, and the chief said, "So why didn't you want to tell me about Arthur Warren?"

"Didn't see the point. He's gone. The project needed attention, and I didn't think you wanted excuses."

"I wanted what I've come to expect from you, the unvarnished truth."

"Yes, sir." Bennett looked down, suddenly unable to meet her boss's eyes. She'd disappointed one of the few remaining people who'd mattered to her father.

"I admire your loyalty, but Warren doesn't deserve it. Now get to work and keep this project on schedule." He gave her a slap on the back before getting into his car.

Kerstin walked up beside her. "Well, that could've been worse."

"Yeah, and could've been better."

"Did I do something wrong? Shouldn't I have told him about

Warren?" Kerstin's blue eyes held the shadowy sadness Bennett had seen before when one of her parents criticized her.

"You didn't do anything wrong. I should've told him about Warren." She wrapped her arm around Kerstin's shoulder, surprised she didn't pull away, and led her across the parking lot toward the street. "You were fierce."

"I know, right? No idea where the courage came from, but he went after you, and I…"

"If your boss could've seen you, he'd probably think twice about messing with you."

Kerstin seemed to consider her comment before noticing they were heading away from the substation. "Where are we going?"

"Lunch. I skipped breakfast."

"Well slow down, speedy. I can't keep up."

The small food-truck window opened, and G-ma and Mama waved as they approached. "Get over here, you two."

"*Kerstin Anthony?* Is that really you?" Mama hurried out the back of the trailer and enveloped Kerstin in a hug. "It's been ages." She held Kerstin at arm's length and spun her in a circle. "You still look the same."

"Filled out in some places. Right, Ben?" G-ma added from inside the trailer.

"G-ma, please." Bennett gave Kerstin an apologetic shrug.

"Hi, Mrs. Carlyle," Kerstin said, blushing at her comment. "Good to see you both again."

Mama passed the sandwiches and drinks to the lunch crowd as G-ma handed them to her and collected money. "Welcome back, Kerstin."

"I'm not really back, Gayle."

Bennett leaned closer and whispered. "Lighten up. Southern hospitality."

"Come over for dinner," G-ma said as Gayle rejoined her in the trailer. "Ben says you go back to New York every weekend, so Sunday night? Seven o'clock? We're changing brunch to dinner for the occasion."

"We are?" Bennett and Mama said in unison. The sacred Sunday brunch time hadn't changed since Simon announced his proposal to Stephanie, twelve years ago.

"Won't take no for an answer," G-ma said, giving an authoritative nod.

"Well, I really should—"

"If you don't say yes, she'll keep pestering you," Mama said.

Bennett nudged Kerstin. "Please?"

"Okay. I'd love to come for Sunday dinner."

"Good. It's settled." Mama tossed two sandwiches to Bennett, followed by a couple of canned drinks. "Enjoy."

As they walked back across the street, Bennett pointed to a large, freshly mowed grassy area with a couple of picnic tables behind the substation. "Mind if we eat outside? Be a shame to waste such a beautiful day."

"I'd love to." Kerstin settled on one side of the bench and turned her face to the sun. "I don't take time to enjoy this in New York. And if I have time, the skyscrapers seem to gobble all the warmth, or grumpy people complain so loudly I can't enjoy myself." She sniffed the air. "What's that fabulous smell, sort of ripe apricots and black tea, very dainty and demure?"

Bennett took a whiff around her. "Beneath the fresh-cut grass, smells like tea olive, the evergreen-looking bushes to your right with the tiny white blossoms. Hard to believe something so small produces such an aroma, isn't it?"

"I love the fragrance." Her tone sounded forlorn, almost wistful.

"Why do you stay in New York?"

Kerstin glanced at her as if considering whether to answer. "I have responsibilities I can't walk away from."

"The woman I heard on the phone?"

"Yes."

The word landed with solid finality, and Bennett debated asking for clarification. Here in the outdoors with nowhere to run, Kerstin would either refuse to be honest with her or they'd finally have a real conversation. "Is she your partner, your lov—er." The word hung in Bennett's throat, an affront to every unfulfilled desire she held for Kerstin.

"What?"

"She called you *dear*."

"Elizabeth. My mother."

The tension that held Bennett's breath finally released. "Your mother?"

"You thought…no…there isn't anyone…special."

The admission seemed to injure Kerstin with each word, a disclosure of some perceived failure or perhaps a difficult conscious choice. Bennett didn't even try to suppress the smile consuming her face. "I can't say I'm sorry, but if you're unhappy, why can't you leave?"

Kerstin glanced at her unwrapped sandwich before pushing it aside. "Mother had a stroke. She needs me…well, she needs constant care at the moment."

Bennett moved around the table, wrapping an arm around her waist. "I'm so sorry, Kerst. I didn't know." Kerstin relaxed against her. "Guess there's a lot I don't know." She waited, gauging Kerstin's willingness to reveal more. "Do you manage the situation all alone?"

"My aunt Valerie is with her when I'm away. She's really been a godsend. I can't imagine how I would've survived without her. She lives with us and, I have to admit, has a much better rapport with Mother than I do."

"I'm glad you have someone to help out. Her condition certainly explains your aversion to hospitals. I imagine the process has been long and difficult for all of you."

Kerstin again turned her face to the sun and closed her eyes as if soaking up the warmth like a balm. She either didn't notice or didn't mind that Bennett still held her close.

A few minutes later Bennett asked, "What happened to us, Kerst?"

Kerstin's body stiffened before she backed away, an incredulous look on her face. "Why are you so obsessed with the past? It obviously didn't slow you down."

The comment was as harsh as it was unexpected. "What?"

Kerstin looked at the ground and shook her head. "That comment was unnecessary and insensitive. I apologize. Let's move on."

Bennett had been on the receiving end of Kerstin's deflection many times when she was upset or uncomfortable, but her words still stung. "And I suppose you're still a virgin?" Neither she nor Kerstin were cruel or vindictive people, and Bennett immediately regretted the snarky comment. "Now I'm the one who's sorry."

"We're both attractive women and have probably had numerous partners."

Bennett winced at Kerstin's confirmation of her sexual growth. Had she wanted Kerstin's life frozen until…until what? How ridiculously seventeen of her. "I'm way out of line. I'll leave you in peace." She rose from the table and walked away.

"Don't go." Kerstin's voice was so low Bennett almost didn't hear her. Kerstin blew out a deep breath and sagged against the table. "I'm the one avoiding the truth and trying to change history. Sit. Let's talk."

Bennett slowly returned to Kerstin's side, afraid any sudden movement would break the spell and throw her back into avoidance. Bennett sat quietly, anticipating the long-awaited explanation.

"You kissed me," Kerstin finally whispered.

Bennett leaned in so Kerstin had to make eye contact. "And you kissed back."

"I—"

"Please don't tell me you didn't or, worse, you've forgotten."

Kerstin shook her head. "I could never forget. I feel the intensity of that kiss in my dreams, snuggle up to its warmth on cold New York nights, and masturbate to the sensations it still summons. But that was a…" She swallowed hard, as if unable to believe she'd said those things out loud. "Long time ago."

"Kerst, I—"

"That kiss, our *only* kiss, changed my life. And you acted like it didn't matter. You actually said, 'This is nothing. We're just experimenting.' What did you expect me to do?"

Kerstin's total recall landed like a physical blow, and Bennett recoiled. "What?" The blue of Kerstin's eyes darkened and misted, tears on the verge of spilling over.

"Those were your exact words. You were terrified."

"Of course I was terrified, Kerst. Your father walked in on us, without knocking, which he did quite a lot when your bedroom door was closed."

"He was a bit intrusive."

"Overbearing was more like it. And when he saw us kissing, he was enraged. I was protecting you in a very bad situation." She paused, her chest tightening as old feelings surfaced. She struggled for the strength to explain what she hadn't gotten the opportunity to clarify all those years ago. "Denying was the only thing I could think to do at the time. I didn't want him to be angry at you or forbid us from seeing each other, which obviously didn't work." She reached for Kerstin's arm, but she jerked away.

"Instead, he divorced my mother, and she and I moved to New York."

The statement carried no emotion, a simple set of facts. How long had Kerstin managed and concealed the wounding memories? "And you blame me for everything?"

Kerstin's eyes softened slightly, but old pain still tugged at their corners. "Of course not. The whole situation was the excuse he needed to leave an unhappy marriage. My mother hated North Carolina and wanted to move back to New York to be with her family and friends. The argument was a constant battle, which he finally won that day."

"So why are you so upset with me?"

"You belittled our feelings, denied them. Denied *me*. I wanted you to care enough to fight for me, but you folded like a cheap chair and walked away." Kerstin's features hardened again, and her hands fisted in her lap. All the pain she'd buried was broadcast across her face.

"I didn't…well, I said the words, but you had to know I didn't mean them." Kerstin's expression didn't change. "You stopped showing up at school the last two weeks, and I called your house, every day. I didn't hear back, so I assumed you didn't care—"

"Seriously? I was shattered. And I didn't get any messages."

"I had no idea. You always kept your feelings close to the chest. I wanted so badly to explain, but you were gone." Bennett couldn't bear the distance any longer. She edged closer to Kerstin, pressing her leg along the length of Kerstin's thigh. "I poured my heart out in your yearbook. Remember? Please say you believe me."

"I doubted everything you'd ever said to me. And then my life changed so fast after the kiss. The divorce decision. My mother and I moving in the middle of the night so the neighbors wouldn't gossip. Receiving my diploma in the mail instead of graduating with my class." She looked toward the sky and slowly shook her head. "I can't believe my father didn't tell me about your calls." She paused before adding, "Yes, I can. He was absolutely livid."

"I'm so sorry, Kerst. I should've tried harder, but I was devastated too." The *what ifs* and *maybes* Bennett had pondered through the years vanished, and with them, the knot of grief and uncertainty she'd carried.

Kerstin stroked Bennett's cheek and skimmed her lip with her thumb. "All this time I believed you didn't care or, worse, you betrayed me. Oh, Ben, I—"

"Bennett, I've been texting you." Jazz jogged across the parking lot toward them but stopped short. "I'm sorry, but we have to go. Serious assault in Irving Park."

Kerstin's hand dropped and a single tear slid down her cheek.

Bennett released a heavy, frustrated sigh. Irving Park spelled old money, prestige, political influence, and immediate police response when infrequent crimes occurred. She desperately wanted to remain at the small park bench on the secluded patch of grass in the company of the woman she'd loved since childhood, but the urgency in Jazz's voice reminded her of other responsibilities. She squeezed Kerstin's hand where it rested in her lap. "I'm so sorry, Kerst. I have to go. Please don't change your mind about dinner Sunday night."

Kerstin nodded.

"And maybe we can talk more afterward?"

"I'd like that."

Bennett rushed after Jazz, glancing back several times, her heart tugging her in one direction, her sense of duty in another.

Chapter Twelve

On Sunday morning while Kerstin searched the closet in her old bedroom for something comfortable to wear, a tattered dress box on the top shelf caught her eye. She'd left the box along with most of her other teenage memorabilia when she moved into her own condo. Her prom dress, homecoming trinkets, and baubles from friends strained the corners of the frail cardboard. She carefully lowered it and, supporting the bottom with both hands, placed it gently on the bed. The items inside belonged to another time, to a more naive person. Why she hadn't tossed this collection of junk she wasn't sure. She debated leaving it undisturbed, but Bennett said she'd poured her heart out in Kerstin's yearbook. She didn't remember. Maybe this once the past was worth revisiting.

She checked that her mother and Val were still sleeping before she raised the box lid slowly. She peeped under the corner, foolishly afraid of ghosts or memories capable of changing the person she'd become. Reaching for the first rectangular item on top, she stopped, recognizing the yearbook. The cover imitated an old-fashioned wooden door with wrought-iron hinges and handle. In the center, a white window insert contained the gray whirligig emblem of Grimsley High School. The book looked harmless, and her desire to open it had become palpable. What did she hope to find? What did she pray wasn't there?

She flipped past the front pages where the teachers wrote their best wishes and stared at the final sheet glued to the cover. In the hurried style indicative of everything she did in those days, Bennett's scrawled message occupied the entire page. She raked her hand over the writing as if divining feeling from the words. They tempted her to read and remember. She resisted but ultimately failed.

Dearest Kerst,

What can I say to the person who stole my heart the minute I met her? You probably think I'm too bold, and I am, but I'm also honest. That's me. I feel I've known you forever. You own me. Totally. Now and always. And I don't say those words lightly. Please don't forget me or the time we spent together. I never will.

You'll probably end up at Princeton or Yale next year, and I'll be ducking classes at some community college. You're destined for greatness. Don't let anyone kill your dreams and never doubt your potential. I don't.

If you want, I'll come to you wherever you end up. All you have to do is ask, and I'll find a way.

In bold block print, she'd added a quote Kerstin didn't recognize.

"All I refuse, and thee I choose."

Love, Ben

She slammed the book and brushed away tears falling on the cover. Ben's words seemed genuine, but her actions proved otherwise. How had she forgotten, and why had she dredged up these feelings again? They only confused and tormented her about something that never was or ever could be. Opening her heart would be much more complicated than reading a few lines of old text, no matter how sincere. She placed the lid on the box and shoved it in the back of the closet out of sight. The little voice in her head taunted her. *I told you not to open it. Serves you right.* She crawled back in bed, pulled the covers over her head, and slept until Valerie tapped on her door announcing lunch was ready.

"Earth to Kerstin." Valerie stopped stacking the lunch dishes in the dishwasher and perched her hands on her hips.

"Huh?" She was daydreaming about her conversation with Bennett, again, and had missed her aunt's question entirely.

"Exactly. I asked what's been bothering you all weekend. I'm starting to wonder who has the short-term memory loss."

"Not funny. I'm fine, but I have a lot on my mind."

"Work or something else? I haven't seen you so distracted by a job. Do I dare hope you've found something more personal to occupy your time?"

Her face flushed, and she attempted to distract Valerie. "This coffee sure is hot. Did you add some kind of spice?"

"Nice try. What's up? Quickly, before your mother wakes from her nap."

Kerstin topped off her cup and headed toward the wingback chairs facing the park view. "Do you remember a girl named Bennett Carlyle from Greensboro?"

"You were in high school together, right?"

Kerstin nodded.

"And if I recall, you two had a big crush on each other." Valerie paused and stroked her chin for several seconds as if searching for buried details. "OMG. Was *she* the girl your dad caught you kissing in your bedroom? The girl he forbade you to see again? The reason you and Elizabeth ended up in New York?"

"Nothing wrong with your memory." Kerstin sighed, took another sip of coffee, and finally continued. "I'm working with her on my latest project."

"I bet Elizabeth isn't happy. Wait. Does she even know?"

"Sort of. She walked in while I was on the phone with Bennett, and of course she remembered all that history. Whether she recalls our conversation the other day is another matter. For seventeen years, I believed Bennett totally betrayed me when my dad found us together. Apparently, she'd tried to get in touch, but Dad blocked her."

"Sounds like you two had quite a chat."

Kerstin nodded. "And I was emotionally off the charts, pissed one minute and fighting back tears the next. I'm not normally an ambivalent person. Now I'm not sure what I believe or what to do. I haven't trusted her because of the past, and my distrust causes complications on the job."

Valerie relaxed in her chair and studied Kerstin. "Maybe you should, especially since your dad was the reason the two of you lost contact."

"Dad was an easy scapegoat at the time, and in retrospect I guess he's the person I really don't trust emotionally. But still, I have to accept some of the blame. I didn't want to be gay on top of everything else—a teenager, the divorce, my parents using me as a pawn, and moving away from my friends. Besides, I watched you struggle with your sexuality. Your family wasn't too happy in the beginning. I couldn't bear to go through the same thing, alone with Mother. I ran away from my feelings, and I guess I'm still running."

"Some things don't change."

"What do you mean?" Kerstin wasn't sure she really wanted to know.

"I shouldn't."

"You don't usually hold back, and you might actually help."

Valerie leaned close and lowered her voice. "I'm not judging, simply an observation. You can't use clubs and sex services to escape your feelings forever. Hookups lose their luster eventually."

Kerstin's face burned, and she stared out the window to avoid looking at Valerie. "How do you know about my private activities?"

"It's a small community, and I know people who work with a couple of the elite companies you frequent. The owner of the Cubbyhole is an old friend too. She mentioned that you seemed to be struggling."

She was still processing the fact that her aunt knew she occasionally utilized escort services for sex. "Struggling, huh?"

"Not acquiring partners but sustaining connections. I think she called you a serial troller."

"You haven't said anything to Mother?"

"Of course not. My point is, do you think strangers can satisfy you long-term?" Kerstin didn't immediately respond, and Valerie added, "If you've identified a pattern of running from relationships with serious potential, maybe it's time to reevaluate."

Kerstin stared into her coffee cup and shook her head. "Can you blame me? Dad didn't fight for his family. I haven't dated anyone who wanted a relationship enough to work for it."

"Did you ever consider they might've if you'd been willing?"

Kerstin mentally ticked through her series of short-term relationships and the reason each had ended. She didn't answer Valerie's question. The smug look on her face said she already knew she was right. "I'm not sure what's holding me back with Bennett."

"Are you still attracted to her, still care about her?"

"I certainly got quite a surprise when she walked back into my life. What those feelings mean, if anything, I have no idea."

"But you want to find out?"

Kerstin recalled the emotions surrounding her last conversation with Bennett and searched for the truth before answering. "Yes, I believe I do, but I might be too late. Neither of our lives has been on hold. Women flock after her like they did in high school, and I'd probably have to wait in line. So not my style."

"But she excites you after all these years. That's worth something."

"No matter what happens between us while we're working together, a liaison of any kind can't change my life. I have plans, a business to establish, and my mother to consider."

"Your mother to consider about what?" Elizabeth stepped into view from the hallway. "What have I missed? And why are you discussing me behind my back?"

Valerie moved to her sister's side, always the devoted caregiver. "Don't you know we always talk about you behind your back? You're the driving force of our lives."

Kerstin considered the truth in Valerie's words as she vacated her mother's favorite chair. "Would you like something to drink?"

"No, thank you, dear. Why is your suitcase by the elevator?" Already her mother had forgotten the discussion she'd interrupted. Sometimes her memory challenge had unanticipated benefits.

"I'm returning to Greensboro tonight. I have a meeting." Only a little white lie, but it bothered her to mislead her mother. "I wanted to say good-bye. I hate to leave without seeing you."

"You're always working," Elizabeth said as Kerstin leaned down to kiss her cheek.

"And you're getting more independent every day. Soon you won't need me or Val."

Elizabeth waved her off. "And when the day comes, I'll leave you both in the city and head to Florida, permanently. All my friends are there already."

Kerstin had started toward the elevator but turned back. "Do you really want to join your friends, Mother?"

"Of course. I don't want to live in the cold indefinitely, with you two hovering all the time. Where's the fun?"

The possibility of her mother living an independent life again hadn't occurred to Kerstin, much less that she'd want to be anywhere but New York. "Whatever makes you happy."

Valerie walked Kerstin to the elevator and out of Elizabeth's earshot. "Your mother knows exactly what she wants. Take a page from her book. Don't push your emotions aside forever, Kerstin. Figure out how you feel about Bennett. We'll work out the rest as we go. You deserve love and happiness, and I need to know you'll be okay before we part company."

"Back at you, Auntie," Kerstin said, giving her a long hug before stepping onto the elevator. "I haven't forgotten about your vacationship with the flight attendant. Every time I bring it up, you change the subject. Is she special, or have you already broken her heart?"

"Stop meddling or you'll miss your plane. We'll discuss her later."

"Pot. Kettle. Promise?"

"Maybe."

"I'll keep in touch by text. Let me know if you need anything. And thanks, Val."

On the two-hour flight, Kerstin considered Valerie's advice about sorting her feelings for Bennett. She admitted that being in Greensboro again tasted of freedom—no caretaking responsibilities, doing the work she loved without her intrusive boss—and was consumed by guilt. Bennett's presence added one more thing to the guilt pile—wanting more—a life with someone she loved. Maybe Valerie was right. Her mother's improvement prompted Kerstin to at least consider her life beyond work and caretaking.

She retrieved her rental car from the airport parking garage and headed to the Carlyle home for dinner, more optimistic than she'd been in months. Was she making a mistake mingling business with potential pleasure? Maybe her libido needed a little exercise, something she hadn't tried in Greensboro. Her body tingled at the possibility, but her mind returned to Bennett. Their last conversation had ended in mixed feelings and no resolution. They owed it to themselves to resolve the past, for the sake of both their futures.

Her body still hummed with sexual energy as she parked in front of the sprawling house and a gorgeous, slightly younger version of Bennett sprang down the steps toward her.

"Hi, Kerstin. I'm so glad you're here. Everyone is running around like they're preparing for royalty. Mama wouldn't let Ben greet you, so G-ma put her to work in the kitchen. Not pretty." The young woman took a breath, and Kerstin took the opening.

"Dylan?"

"What was your first clue?"

"You look so much like—"

"Ben? I get that a lot. She calls me her mini-me. You look almost the same, prettier though, which shouldn't even be possible."

"Thanks. You were barely a teenager the last time I saw you."

Dylan laughed. "Yeah, with braces, no boobs, and a serious crush on the girl next door."

"The first two have definitely changed."

"I still have girl crushes but no time to act on them."

"Now you're a doctor. Congratulations. Well done," Kerstin said.

"Yep. I'm all kinds of awesome. Now if my family would give me some props." Dylan gave her a self-deprecating smile, looped her arm through Kerstin's, and guided her up the steps. "Thought I'd come out and offer moral support before you go into the lions' den. If you need something stronger, I have drugs."

"A handful of Valium wouldn't go awry."

"I feel the same at every Sunday brunch, but I won't let them grill you too hard. If they ask something you don't want to answer, say pass."

They'd stalled on the front porch, and Kerstin drew in several deep breaths. "And that'll actually work?"

"Probably not." Dylan tugged her forward and opened the door. "Better get inside before Bennett comes looking. She's been pacing Mama's floor for the past hour."

"Why?"

"Oh, come on, Kerstin." Dylan gave her an incredulous stare she didn't want to decipher. "Let's face your case of nerves head-on." She waved her inside.

Bennett appeared in front of them in the hallway. "Nerves? Why? Nothing's changed since you were here last."

A wide smile lit up Bennett's face, but her eyes were shadowed, a contrast of hope and anxiety that caught Kerstin off guard. She hadn't considered that Bennett might be worried about this evening too.

"Don't be so literal, Ben," Dylan said. "The place hasn't changed, but everyone inside certainly has. Facing people you haven't seen in seventeen years is nerve-wracking."

Bennett nodded toward Dylan. "My sister, the doctor. Too smart for her own good sometimes." Her voice almost quivered, and pride lit her eyes as she looked at Dylan.

Dylan stepped aside. "Okay, so I'll see you guys at the table. Hurry. You know how grumpy Simon gets if his food is late." Dylan bounded off after a quick wink at her older sister.

Bennett slid her arm around Kerstin's waist. Dylan's touch had offered comfort, but Bennett's carried heat and sexual energy. Kerstin flinched from the possessive gesture, her first instinct to pull away, but Bennett tucked her closer to her side and escorted her to a living area off the entry, and her resistance dissolved.

"I'm so glad you came. I was afraid you'd change your mind." Bennett's whiskey-colored eyes turned dark as she focused on Kerstin's lips. "After dinner, come back to my place? We can finish our conversation. From Friday." Bennett stood so close Kerstin felt the quick breaths from her erratic words, smelled the musky fragrance of her perfume, and saw a glimmer of hope in the gold flecks of her irises.

"Your place?"

"The cottage out back."

Kerstin leaned closer, succumbing to the urge to kiss Bennett, to claim her, finally, but a voice from the back of the house stopped her.

"Dinner's on the table."

Bennett lightly kissed her forehead and lingered until Kerstin was on the verge of begging for more. "Can we? Talk after dinner?"

"Yes." The word was barely a whisper, her lungs full of Bennett's scent, her body trembling for her.

"Are you okay? You're shivering."

"I'm…you…fine. I'm fine."

Bennett rested her hand in the small of Kerstin's back and guided her toward the kitchen. The comforting gesture grounded her in the moment, to this familiar place, and to the woman at her side. It also created heat much lower. They reached the dining area, and the Carlyle family stood around the table, ready to welcome her back. Kerstin remembered being here frequently and feeling she belonged.

"Kerstin!" G-ma and Mama embraced her from either side, burying her in a warm hug.

Simon shook her hand, but Kerstin pulled him in for a quick embrace. "Hey, you."

He nodded to the woman at his side. "This is my wife, Stephanie, and those two gorgeous creatures," he said pointing to the table, "are our twins, Riley and Ryan."

"A pleasure, Stephanie. Hi, guys." She hugged Stephanie and waved to the twins, who barely looked up from their phones.

"Into the basket with those bloody things," G-ma said.

"You know better, guys," Stephanie said and gave them a stern grimace.

"And I'm sure you remember Jasmine," Mama said, smiling proudly at her daughter.

"I do indeed. Good to see you again, Jazz." She took the seat Dylan patted beside her, which placed her next to Bennett as well.

Kerstin inhaled the delicious food offerings, and her stomach growled. She was suddenly starving. A roast with what appeared to be caramel-crusted topping occupied pride of place on the table. Roasted red potatoes, carrots, and onions flanked the meat on a huge serving platter. Steamed broccoli, creamed spinach, and fresh-baked bread finished the offerings with a splash of color. A pecan pie, banana pudding, and red velvet cake topped the nearby sideboard. Her mouth watered.

"Well, we don't usually drink, but this calls for a celebration." G-ma motioned to the center of the table, where two bottles of champagne rested in copper chillers. "Bennett, would you do the honors?"

Bennett grabbed the bottleneck with her long fingers and unwrapped the foil. She popped the cork, and as it flew across the room, bubbly spilled over her hand. Bennett made eye contact and slowly licked the champagne off before pouring everyone a glass. Kerstin almost came undone.

"To our guest of honor," Simon said, raising his coupe.

Bennett passed another glass to Kerstin, and their fingers slid together, a lingering touch, subtle yet more arousing than any caress with a casual lover. She licked her lips and tugged the coupe toward her, desperate for something to soothe her parched insides. Dylan elbowed her, and when she looked up, everyone held a flute aloft.

"To a friend who's returned to us after a long absence," Mama said. "Welcome back, Kerstin. Please visit often. You'll always have a place at our table."

"Thank—you." The words choked past emotions hung in her throat. Even before they left Greensboro, her parents' relationship had been contentious, making meals tense at best, confrontational at worst. She'd sometimes served as a peacekeeper, sometimes a pawn in their decline toward divorce. Watching the Carlyle family exchange tidbits of their day and encourage each other, she hoped for this feeling of family and love, one day.

Dylan passed the breadbasket and leaned closer, whispering. "Are you okay?"

"Thinking—not a habit I recommend."

"Got you covered." Then she spoke louder. "Kerstin, do you know how the Carlyle kids got their names?"

"Oh, no." Simon groaned from the other end of the table.

"Really, sis?" Bennett waved her fork at Dylan. "I'm sure she knows."

Some of the tension between Kerstin's shoulders dissolved as she enjoyed the easy banter between siblings. "No, I don't."

Jazz laughed and pointed to Dylan and Kerstin. "You two are trouble."

"Well…" Dylan breathed a dramatic sigh before turning to Mama. "You should probably do the honors since I wasn't around for the actual naming."

Mama leaned back in her chair and gazed up at the ceiling as if searching for a memory—or the strength to go on. "My beloved husband, Bryce, and I adored sixties music. We were fanatics about the era and attended every concert we could afford."

G-ma cupped Gayle's hand briefly. "Bryce worked every day after school and weekends saving money for those blasted concerts. He'd sneak out at night after Garrett and I went to sleep, meet up with Gayle, and sneak back in before daybreak."

"Some of the best times of our lives were spent playing groupie. Our eldest," she pointed toward her son, "was named after Paul Simon, one of our favorites. When our next child came along, we'd already decided to name him or her after Tony Bennett, an amazing jazz crooner. Our little Jasmine came already tagged with an outstanding name, so we didn't mess with perfection." She gave Jazz an adoring smile. "And our baby had to be christened for the incomparable Bob Dylan because of his songs about social unrest of the time. This one," she patted Dylan's arm, "would take a different path." She looked around the table, placed her hands over her chest, and added, "I'm so proud of you all. You're my heart."

Tears clung to the corners of Bennett's eyes, and adoration radiated from her face. Kerstin ached to be the recipient of such a loving expression. Bennett was no longer the irresponsible girl from high school. She was the woman who sacrificed her own safety for her father's friend, spent hours at the bedside of an injured officer, and exhibited tremendous patience with Kerstin's whiplash emotions. This Bennett Carlyle was vulnerable and sexy as hell, and Kerstin wanted to know more about her, regardless of where her exploration led.

She reached under the table and squeezed Bennett's hand where it rested on her thigh. Suddenly she craved everything they'd missed as teenagers—the first tentative press of Bennett's naked body against hers; the pads of Bennett's fingers tracing a path across her breasts; the scent of her mingled sweat and sex; the silkiness of Bennett's arousal on her fingers, in her mouth; her ragged breathing before she came; and her unbridled moan of pleasure as she climaxed. Kerstin released Bennett's hand, unable to endure the intensity of their body heat and her erotic thoughts.

"Kerst?" Bennett placed her arm on her chair, leaned in, and whispered, "All right?"

Everyone was staring at her. She cleared her throat. "Naming your children after your favorites is a lovely way to remember them, your courtship, and your husband." The mood around the table was weighted, full of family memories and her desire. "And can any of your children sing?"

"Of course they can, but seldom on key." G-ma laughed as she took a big gulp of champagne. "But we love them exactly the way they are."

"It's a good thing too," Bennett said. "By the way, I saw Emory Blake at the hospital the other night. She looked great and asked about the family."

"She's a wonderful woman," G-ma said. "She, Gayle, and I have worked on several volunteer projects through the years. I hoped she'd end up in the family." She continued eating while everyone quieted. When she looked up, Bennett drilled her with a pointed stare. "Oh, sorry, dear. Don't mind me. I ramble."

The comment and Bennett's sheepish expression produced the same queasy feeling Kerstin had when Nurse Jen fondled Bennett at the hospital. She swallowed another sip of champagne to settle her stomach and steered the conversation in a safer direction. "And what event is up next, at the hospital?"

Mama shook her head. "Not sure yet, maybe the annual fund-raiser."

G-ma pushed her champagne glass away. "And this is why we don't drink much. It makes us forgetful."

Silence stretched until Simon cleared his throat. "Bennett tells us you're an architect, Kerstin."

"I guess you could say I followed in my father's footsteps. As a child, I imagined we'd go into business together, specialize in sustainable housing, but…" But her father never warmed to the idea or to her beyond a fierce protectiveness of her virtue.

"Life happened," Dylan said. "Like it always does."

She smiled at Dylan appreciatively. "Exactly."

"She kicks serious butt as an architect." Bennett eased her arm around the back of Kerstin's chair again. "You should see the design she has for the substation. Our place is going to be outstanding."

"So how is working together?" Jazz asked, purposely avoiding Bennett's glare.

"Nothing like high school," Bennett offered.

Kerstin gave her a quick smile. "Well, I wouldn't totally agree. Some things seem very familiar."

Bennett faced her, an amused grin on her face. "Such as?"

"I'm doing all the work." Kerstin laughed. "Sound about right?"

"Hey. I'm doing my part."

"Sleeping in a chair while I pore over the design."

"I'd had a long night," Bennett said.

"And trying to decipher your horrible handwriting. You should've been a doctor too."

"It was a rush job."

"And there's the never-ending discussions about form versus function." Kerstin enjoyed the back-and-forth until Bennett shifted uneasily and the light in her eyes dimmed almost imperceptibly.

"Wait a minute. It's not my fault some jackleg messed up the police-department specs before I came along."

"And my predecessor wasn't exactly thorough. Can't blame his incompetence on Bennett." Kerstin couldn't bear the pained look on Bennett's face any longer and put her out of her misery. "I was only kidding."

At the end of the table, Simon broke out in a full belly laugh. "That was fun to watch."

But Bennett's discomfort remained, evident in the crease across her forehead and her unwillingness to look at Kerstin. The poignant comment about doing her best in a new assignment returned, and Kerstin leaned closer. "I'm really sorry. I shouldn't have said that." Then to the group, she added, "Actually, Bennett has practically rewritten the entire police department brief, and we're about to put together a killer update to the plans."

Bennett finally smiled and said, "And Kerstin made this model to help me understand how it will really look."

"A model?" Riley's head snapped up from her pie. "Can I see?"

"Me too," Ryan chimed in. "Me too."

Stephanie waited for an indication from Kerstin or Bennett that the request wasn't entirely out of the question before commenting. When Kerstin nodded, she said, "You'd have to be very careful, because Kerstin and Aunt Bennett need the model for work. You can't throw pieces of it at each other like you do Legos. Can you behave?"

The kids answered in unison. "Yes!"

"Guess it's a date. What do you think, Captain Carlyle?"

"Definitely."

"Thank you," Simon said as the kids debated which one should examine the model first.

After the main course, Mama served pecan pie, banana pudding, and red velvet cake along with coffee or milk. Kerstin forced down a tiny bit of each so she wouldn't hurt G-ma or Mama's feelings…and because she just couldn't decide between the three choices. She took a final sip of coffee and pushed away the table. "I can't possibly eat another bite."

Bennett rose and placed her hand on Kerstin's shoulder. "Would you like another cup of coffee or some water while I help with the dishes?"

"Nonsense," Mama said. "I believe it's Dylan and Simon's turn to clean up."

Dylan started to say something, but Simon interrupted. "You're exactly right, Mama. Come on, Doc. You can tell me about your latest challenging ER case." He herded Dylan toward the sink and winked at Bennett.

"Dinner was delicious, as usual, Mrs. Carlyle," Kerstin said. "Thank you all for welcoming me into your home again. It was like old times, really nice."

"Glad you liked it, dear. Come back often. We always have plenty of food."

Bennett again placed her hand in the small of Kerstin's back and guided her toward the back door. "Let's make our getaway while the getting's good." They walked toward the garden. "I'm so glad you came. You fit right in."

Kerstin didn't admit it, but for the first time in months, she'd actually let her guard down and allowed her emotions to rise. What had surfaced was another spark, which heightened her sense of belonging, and that feeling further amplified her arousal. She refused to think about her mother, the job, or the past. She focused on the feeling of being alive.

They walked a bit farther before Bennett spoke. "It's a full moon. Would you like to sit by the koi pond for a bit?"

Kerstin glanced at Bennett standing beside her, and the image stopped her. Moonlight shimmered across the planes of her face and cast sexy shadows. Her eyes glistened in the dim glow and seemed to beckon to Kerstin. Enchanted by a combination of feelings and the champagne, she said exactly what was on her mind. "No, not really." She grabbed Bennett's hand and pulled her toward the cottage at the rear of the garden.

CHAPTER THIRTEEN

Bennett allowed Kerstin to drag her into the cottage. Very soon, Kerstin would come to her senses and run the other way. She always did if they got too close. But for the moment, Bennett savored the desire seeping from Kerstin's pores and the craving it released in her.

She closed the door behind them, and Kerstin stepped into her body space and stared at her, begging her to understand and accept. The usual crystal blue of her irises turned stormy, but she didn't speak.

Bennett swallowed hard at the hunger in Kerstin's eyes. "Is there something you'd like to talk about or—"

"Absolutely not." With no preamble, Kerstin pushed her against the closed door and kissed her.

An urgent kiss so demanding Bennett struggled for breath. Kerstin's hands fisted her hair and held her close while heat swelled and surged between them. Bennett's legs trembled and she clung to Kerstin's hips. She wanted this so desperately. She dreamed about sex with Kerstin, but her dreams were better choreographed and way more intimate. "Kerst—"

"Shush." She scanned the small living space before resting her hooded eyes on Bennett again. "Bedroom?"

Bennett nodded toward the back of the cottage. "But shouldn't we—"

"We've been dancing around this since I came back. Let's get it out of our systems and move on." She grabbed Bennett's waistband and pulled her to the bedside.

"Like this?"

"Please stop talking, or I'll change my mind." She reached for Bennett's shirt buttons but stopped. "Do you want me to change my mind?"

"Of course not, but—"

"Then *please* be quiet and let me have you, my way." She ripped the front of Bennett's shirt open, stripped it off, peeled her sports bra over her head, and stood back. "Oh, my. You're more…everything… than I imagined."

Bennett gasped, a combination of cool air on her steamy skin and Kerstin's open appreciation. Bennett had fantasized about having sex with Kerstin, but she was the assertive one, gradually seducing Kerstin and slowly tormenting her until she begged to be taken. Bennett stepped forward with her arms open, an invitation for intimacy, but Kerstin backed away.

"Take off your jeans, slowly," Kerstin said. When Bennett hesitated, she added, "Do you want me to say please?"

Bennett's hands shook as she loosened her belt, unzipped her jeans, and folded them away from her body. She didn't get nervous with women. Ever. But Kerstin wasn't just any woman.

Kerstin laughed and pointed at her jeans. "Lucky you. Really?"

Bennett paused, uncertain. Maybe Kerstin noticed her discomfort, or maybe she didn't look as good in her jeans as she imagined, but she glanced down and laughed as well. "The Lucky jeans motto."

"Guess we'll have to see how lucky I am, won't we?" She knelt and skinned Bennett's clothes off, tossing them and her shoes into a pile on the floor.

Kerstin Anthony on her knees in front of her—a fantasy come true. Bennett's mouth dried while the inside of her thighs dampened. She shifted to close her legs.

"Don't, please." Kerstin slid a finger between Bennett's thighs, and Bennett's knees buckled. "Oh. My. Ben, you're soaked. Lie down."

"What about your jeans and—"

"I want you. Now. Just like this." She placed her hand in the center of Bennett's chest, shoved her onto the bed, and crawled on top, straddling her pelvis. "If you expected the shy, confused girl from high school, she's long gone."

"I—"

Kerstin placed a finger over her lips. "Again with the talking." She shifted lower and settled a thigh against Bennett's center. Her mouth found one of Bennett's breasts, a hand the other. "So firm. So hot."

Bennett tucked a hand inside the shoulder of Kerstin's sweater, caressed her supple skin, and moaned at Kerstin's responsiveness. She tilted Kerstin's head for a kiss, searching for an intimate connection, but she resisted.

"Need this." She feasted on Bennett's breasts while riding her thigh, her pace harder and faster with each stroke.

The rough fabric of Kerstin's jeans scrubbed her tender flesh, creating more heat and moisture. She bucked against the pressure, desperate to come but more desperate for intimacy. She wanted to kiss Kerstin and feel her need reciprocated, wanted the gentle exploration of first sex. She wanted to make love, not fuck. As she started to object, Kerstin pinched her nipples between her thumbs and forefingers, held on, and slid down her body.

"Kerst, please…"

The only response was a groan as Kerstin buried her head between Bennett's thighs. Her tongue tormented Bennett's clit. Her left hand teased a breast while her fingers slid slowly into her. Heat boiled inside Bennett and her muscles contracted. The sensations overpowered her as Kerstin feasted, and the initial surge of orgasm rose too quickly. Bennett urged Kerstin up her body for a kiss to prolong their contact and to slow her steady climb toward climax.

Kerstin raised her head and gazed into Bennett's eyes. "Please… let me…"

She would give Kerstin anything—in the past, now, and forever. And with those pleading words, Bennett surrendered, shattered by the orgasm ripping through her. She barely heard Kerstin cry out and go still on top of her.

Hours could've passed before she moved again, her body a mass of satisfied flesh, and when she did, Kerstin moved with her.

"Turn over."

"What? Come here, please. I want to kiss you." Bennett again attempted to bring her in for a hug, but Kerstin straddled her and rolled her onto her stomach.

"Relax. You're going to like this."

"Kerstin, I need—"

"I'll give you exactly what you need, very soon." Kerstin eased onto Bennett's back and kissed along the tops of her shoulders and down her spine while she cupped the sides of Bennett's breasts. "You feel so awesome. I can't get enough of you."

Definitely not the shy Kerstin Anthony she recalled from high school, the nervous kid barely confident enough to kiss Bennett, once. Had she desired the earlier version, expected her as Kerstin suggested? Present-day Kerstin orchestrated every move as if she'd planned the entire scene. Bennett enjoyed Kerstin's eager assertiveness, but Bennett could've been any other woman. Kerstin wasn't really seeing her.

"Kerstin, I need…" Kerstin slid a hand under her and words disappeared. In seconds, Bennett writhed against the sheets begging for relief. She rode Kerstin's expert fingers until the second orgasm hit and she collapsed. Kerstin withdrew and stroked Bennett's ass until she moaned her release in Bennett's ear.

"That was amazing. You're so responsive." Kerstin nudged Bennett onto her side and spooned her from behind. "Thank you, Ben, for letting me take charge. I'm guessing that's not your preferred style, but I was desperate." Bennett tried to roll over, to embrace Kerstin, but she resisted again. "Just let me hold you for a while. Enjoy the moment."

Bennett stretched back into Kerstin's arms. She felt sexually satisfied but emotionally torn about their lack of intimacy. If she wanted more, she needed to ask. She took a deep breath, but Kerstin's steady breathing stopped her. "Kerst?" No answer.

She crumpled under the weight of sadness and disappointment. She could write off their lack of affection as awkward first-timers' sex. But what if Kerstin preferred fast, frantic, and detached liaisons? Bennett's distress deepened. Kerstin cared about her. Bennett refused to believe anything else. They could talk tomorrow, deconstruct the entire evening, like women do, and move forward. She finally relaxed in Kerstin's arms, hoping at last they'd come full circle.

❖

Kerstin steadied her breathing and pretended to sleep. Bennett wanted to talk, but Kerstin couldn't find one honest thing to say that wouldn't expose her as a fraud. She'd treated Bennett like a meaningless hookup, like some men treated women, and her stomach roiled. She wouldn't cuddle and play make-believe like a couple of teenagers, and she couldn't admit this was only about sex. Was she afraid Ben would want more or that she would? Her choices were land mines, deceptive and damaging, and the results would haunt her going forward.

Bennett's hold eventually loosened, and Kerstin slowly eased out of her grasp. She stood beside the bed, mesmerized by Bennett's naked beauty and the innocence etched across her face, wishing she could offer more, knowing she couldn't. And then she crept into the night.

She unlocked her car and slid behind the wheel as Jazz pulled in front of her and parked her unmarked police cruiser on the street. Headlights lit up the inside of Kerstin's vehicle, like a suspect in a lineup, complete with mussed hair, bruised lips, and Bennett's scent all over her. She almost waved from sheer nerves, but maybe Jazz hadn't seen her. She didn't want to draw even more attention to her awkward situation.

Mercifully, Jazz killed the lights, gathered her equipment from the backseat, and walked toward the house. One day Kerstin might laugh about this, possibly even thank Jazz for her discretion, but tonight she couldn't get away fast enough. The Carlyles' front door closed behind Jazz, and Kerstin sped off without even turning on her headlights.

Why was she embarrassed? Why did she feel guilty? She and Bennett had sort of cleared up their misunderstandings about the past. They were attracted to each other. So, what was the problem? She'd snuck out of bed and crept away before Bennett woke up. Why hadn't she stayed to talk as she'd promised? She just wasn't sure she could be that intimate or vulnerable.

"If you've identified a pattern of running from relationships with serious potential, maybe it's time to reevaluate." Her aunt's observation flashed through her mind, but she dismissed it. She wasn't running. She'd simply decided to return to the hotel for a decent night's sleep and left Bennett to do the same.

She dove into bed, clothes and all, praying for dreamless slumber, but sleep refused her. She imagined the press of Bennett's body against hers, Bennett's wetness on her fingers, and the taste of her. Bennett's essence lingered on her clothing and her hands. She inhaled deeply and desire flared. She groaned and rubbed the heel of her palm between her legs. Her body ached for Bennett again.

She'd allowed herself and Bennett only one kiss, a hard, possessive signal that she was in charge. She took Bennett like every other woman she'd had sex with, refusing intimacy as old habits and muscle memory kicked in. She should've picked up a stranger in a bar, called a service, *anything* except bed the one person who could destroy her career and derail her life.

Flinging the covers off, she sat up in bed. The whole point of having sex with Bennett was to purge the desire from her system, but her plan backfired. She wanted her even more. And now she'd shown her cowardly side by sneaking away without even a thank-you or goodbye. Maybe an anonymous, controlled tryst was all she could handle with anyone. Maybe she wasn't capable of true intimacy.

When she saw Bennett at work today, she'd either continue her detached act or she wouldn't. Revert to type or be honest about her feelings for once. She'd make her decision when the time came. No need to struggle unnecessarily.

Chapter Fourteen

Bennett stretched, and the muscles below her waist and in her back ached in protest. She smiled, and excitement swirled when she remembered why. She breathed in Kerstin's scent, still clinging to the sheets, and her body readied for another round. They had finally given in to their attraction, proving they had feelings for each other. So why the hint of melancholy? She reached across the bed, but the covers were cold. Her feelings of intimacy and closeness faded as she remembered the truth. She'd given Kerstin everything she wanted, exactly the way she wanted it. Didn't she deserve at least the courtesy of a good-bye?

She rolled onto her stomach, and the bed sheets grazed her tender pelvis, arousing desire again. She'd surrendered to Kerstin in every way possible—something she hadn't done with another woman, but it wasn't enough to keep Kerstin by her side. Bennett fisted the sheets and groaned into the mattress. Was it a mistake to have sex with Kerstin? If not, why did she feel like a trick or a one-night stand?

Bennett slid out of bed and slowly moved to the shower. The steamy water cut through her sleep fog. What did she expect from a woman she hadn't seen in seventeen years and never slept with before—an immediate declaration of love; a long recap of the night, a replay; maybe a cup of coffee and a friendly chat before work? Did she really want a chance to reconnect and start fresh? She didn't have such hopes with other women.

Realization hit like a fist to the gut, and Bennett grabbed the side of the shower. She *had* expected more with Kerstin—more tenderness, more intimacy, more time—and was upset with herself. Kerstin's quick exit indicated she had no such sentimental hopes. Reality check. She'd had sex with a woman with no promise of a repeat. If they hooked up again, she'd be more emotionally prepared. Problem solved. But she didn't feel any better after her resolution. Maybe seeing Kerstin soon would help. She'd probably behave as if nothing happened between them, which made Bennett feel strangely validated but simultaneously quite empty because last night had meant so little to her.

Bennett pulled into the lot of the Parks and Recreation building and started toward the entrance, but activity from the substation across the street caught her eye—a lot of activity. Vehicles dotted the parking lot, men in construction hats filtered in and out of the side door, and Kerstin was talking to a man beside a big truck.

Her gut clenched at the first glimpse of Kerstin. She wore jeans, a black sweatshirt with a red-and-white Cornell logo on the front, a yellow hard hat, and work boots, and she looked delicious. At this distance she appeared as young, adventurous, and available as she'd been in high school. As Bennett grew closer, the girl morphed into a woman, and the challenges of time and circumstances became more visible in the set of her shoulders and the tiny worry lines around her eyes and across her forehead.

So many things ran through Bennett's mind—images of their night together, words she should've said, and confusion about how to behave the morning after. She pulled the shell casing from her front shirt pocket and rolled it between her fingers as she crossed the street. *Dad and Grandpa, if you can hear me, I need strength today.*

She stopped behind Kerstin, who was hunched over the building plans spread across the tailgate of a truck, pointing to something on the drawing. She listened while Kerstin explained to the man beside her the changes to the public entrance the two of them had discussed. Bennett smiled, proud of her contribution, and then Kerstin turned to her, and her smile widened.

"Oh, good morning." Her eyes scanned Bennett and came to rest on her lips before licking her own. Kerstin still wanted her. "I was filling Henry, our contractor, in on the changes we made. Do you have anything else to add?"

Bennett shook her head, her voice temporarily abandoning her.

"Okay then." She spoke to Henry. "Make sure the guys know what we're doing, and I'll get more specs to you by end of play."

Henry walked away, and Kerstin faced her again. "Did you sleep well after I left?"

Bennett shook her head again, unable to believe Kerstin was actually referring to last night so openly. She'd totally misjudged Kerstin's reaction today, certain she'd just pretend it never happened.

"I had a great time. Sorry about the pace. I needed a quickie, and to be honest, I'm not good with intimacy. And I'm sorry for skulking out like a burglar, but we both needed to rest and regroup before work started back today. Hope you won't hold it against me." She rolled the plans, cupped Bennett's elbow, and gently guided her toward the picnic table at the rear of the building. "Maybe we can do it again sometime? I'll try to be more compliant."

Unsure what to say, Bennett could only nod. Never before had a woman snuck out of her bed, been cordial the next day, thanked her for a good time, and alluded to a repeat like it meant no more than having coffee together.

As they walked, Kerstin leaned in and whispered, "Did I fuck you mute?"

Her grin was pure mischief, but damn, the words hurt just enough. If Kerstin wanted to play it cool, Bennett would oblige. If Kerstin thought they were on the same page, Bennett had a better chance of spending more time with her. She could do casual. Maybe. "Not mute…and yes, I'd like a repeat of last night…sometime." Kerstin startled, her blue eyes wide. Bennett had surprised her. "So, what are *we* doing today?"

After a few seconds, Kerstin recouped and spread the plans across the picnic table. "Let's make some cost assessments and keep the guys working on the changes. Sound good?" Her brows knitted together as she studied Bennett's face.

"Sounds perfect. Let's get to it." Kerstin didn't immediately shift into work mode, so Bennett asked, "Something wrong?"

"What have you done with the real Bennett Carlyle?"

"Sorry?"

"Where's the relentless woman who wants to talk about everything? We had sex, and you don't want to talk?" Her tone held a hint of disbelief.

Bennett considered her response, not wanting to downplay the significance of their night or overplay the casual angle. If Kerstin wanted a relationship, she'd have to open up, and Bennett was willing to allow her time to adapt. "You're a woman of action. Now I understand. I can adapt. We had sex. It was good. We might do it again."

Kerstin nodded and smiled, but the smile didn't brighten her eyes as usual. "Okay." She pointed to the drawings. "Tell me what other changes we need."

Bennett slid onto the bench seat and pulled the folded list from her back pocket, marking off the items as she went. "Well, we already have the canteen slash cafeteria issue sorted, the glass windows on the front, and everything in the public area. I assume the workmen started there this morning?" She looked across at Kerstin, and she was staring at her mouth again instead of the plans. "Kerst?"

"Yes…the public entrance. Sorry."

"Shall I start at the front of the building with the other items, go down my list, or give them to you in priority order?"

"Read them to me, and I'll mark each area on the drawing."

"Bullet-resistant glass on the lineup area, and before you object, I know it's expensive, but based on the number of assaults on officers recently, I think we can justify it. Regular glass would be too much of a temptation, sort of like shooting fish in a barrel."

Kerstin placed an X on the plans and circled it. "This will be a cost discussion."

"Fair enough. There's currently no regular door at the rear of the building. We need a locked entry off the loading dock for prisoners. Inside that area, we'll have to separate the large space into smaller interrogation rooms and add a bank of gun lockers to secure weapons."

"So far it doesn't sound too expensive." Kerstin brushed Bennett's arm as she reached for another pen, and they both stopped, silently acknowledging the heat rising between them. "Go—on." Her voice cracked.

Bennett swallowed hard against the desire to kiss Kerstin and redirected her attention to her list. "Right now, you have a huge area marked as a lineup room, but we can divide the space into lineup, reports, gun-cleaning, and evidence lockers. These won't need separate security because they're already in the police-only section of the building. A few walls here and there should do it, right?" This time she didn't look up but waited for Kerstin to respond.

"Probably. What about—"

"Hey, Kerstin," Henry called from the substation entrance. "There's fresh coffee if you two want some, and it's pretty good."

She waved to Henry and said, "I'll get us a cup," before sprinting toward the building.

Bennett released a long breath and her shoulders relaxed. Being around Kerstin, wanting to touch her again and pretending casualness she didn't really feel was hard work. She forced out a few more deep breaths, tensed her entire body, and relaxed again as Kerstin returned with their coffee.

She placed the cups on the table. "And look what else I found." She held a snack bag in each hand. "Cheetos or pork skins?"

"You're kidding, right?" Bennett grabbed for the skins. "Southern girl through and through. Cholesterol wins over orange carcinogen any day. Thanks."

Kerstin purposely brushed Bennett's hand as she passed her the snack and immediately wished she hadn't. Bennett was a magnet pulling her closer, and she desperately wanted to follow. She'd hoped work would occupy her mind today and their sexual romp would fade like with other women, but Bennett proved the exception. Damn it. Her mind said she'd made the wrong decision about sleeping with Bennett, but her body disagreed.

Bennett bumped her shoulder.

"What?"

"I said, are you ready to continue?"

"Yeah. Sure."

"Okay, the administrative complex can be significantly reduced. Jazz and I don't need all that real estate, and my sergeants can use more office space and access to the conference room."

Kerstin watched Bennett's lips as she talked, wishing she'd kissed them more last night, taken time to explore them, and experienced the magic they could undoubtedly release on her body. If only she'd been more focused on lovemaking and less on the mechanics of fucking, control, and release.

Bennett waved her bag of treats under Kerstin's nose. "You really should try these."

"No, thank you."

"Where's your adventurous spirit? We used to eat all kinds of weird things."

"*Used to* being the operative words." She offered Bennett her Cheetos, but she declined. "See?" She pulled a single Cheeto from the bag and tossed it across the table. It landed in an orange puff on Bennett's black uniform shirt, leaving a path as it tumbled to her lap. "Oops."

"Seriously?" Bennett swept at the messy streaks, but they only spread. "What, are we seventeen again?" The light brown of her eyes darkened as her long fingers brushed places Kerstin wanted to explore again and again.

Kerstin caught her gaze, held steady, and whispered, "I certainly hope not."

Bennett tossed a pork skin at her before taking her seat and pointing to her list again. "Let's get back to work. I'm almost finished here."

"Finished? So soon?"

"Thought you'd be pleased to finish the planning phase so you can get back to drawing and number-crunching."

"Of course." But she wasn't pleased at all.

"I'd like a secure door into the detectives' area. Most of them would like me to believe they carry their weapons at all times, but I'm willing to bet they don't. I was a detective once, and sitting at a desk all day with a gun poking in my side got really uncomfortable. So in case of a breach, I'd like an extra layer of security to allow them a bit more time to retrieve their weapons from a drawer." Bennett glanced at Kerstin as she refolded her list.

Bennett hadn't asked anything of Kerstin, but her eyes begged for answers buried so deeply Kerstin wasn't even sure she could excavate them anymore. "Okay."

Bennett seemed to have lost her focus as well. "Okay what?"

"It's a reasonable request."

"Right." They continued to stare at each other until Bennett finally rose. "Okay. I'll leave you and get back to my real job. We won't see as much of each other from this point, but I'll drop by to check on things occasionally and will attend the group meetings."

Their time was ending? How had she not seen this coming?

"If you need *anything* from me, don't hesitate," Bennett said as she walked away.

Her emphasis on the word anything turned Kerstin's insides to needy, pathetic mush. "O—kay." Bennett played the cool card better than Kerstin, and now she was the infatuated teenager she'd been all those years ago instead of a professional.

Chapter Fifteen

"Car 100, show me on the domestic call on Charter Place." Bennett wanted a read on the two newest rookies in the district, and the best way was to watch them in action. En route her mind drifted again to Kerstin. She couldn't stop thinking about her no matter how many hours she worked. They hadn't seen each other or spoken in two days. Bennett busied herself in the field answering calls with the troops almost twenty-four seven, but she was constantly distracted.

"Ten-four, 100."

She pulled up to the duplex, and the two rookies were already out of their vehicles. They used caution in their approach and posted on opposite sides of the door instead of the more dangerous position in front. She heard screaming from inside as soon as she exited her car but hung back, allowing the officers to handle the situation. She waited until they were inside before approaching to observe.

Bennett stood on the porch and watched through the screen door as the rookies separated the two arguing individuals, one male and one female, according to protocol. The female officer urged the female suspect to the opposite side of the small efficiency space, and the male officer did the same with his suspect, who sipped from a bottle of beer. Bennett listened as they calmed the two irate individuals, the female officer making more progress. Just as she decided the rookies could handle the situation without her, she noticed subtle movement of the male suspect's right hand, which rested by his side.

He slowly worked his fingers along the body of the beer bottle until he gripped the neck like a club. The rookie focused on the man's eyes, not the threat in his hands. She started to call out to alert him, but her warning would've been more distracting than helpful. As the suspect raised the bottle, the action seemed to shift into slow motion. Bennett opened the screen door.

"Officer, weapon."

The suspect flicked his wrist, smashed the beer bottle against the sink, and with the jagged neck, lunged at the officer. The rookie froze.

Bennett burst through the door, shoved the rookie aside with one arm, and grabbed the suspect with the other. She wrestled him to the floor, a mass of struggling arms and legs. Her vest shifted up, and she felt a sharp pain rip through her right side just above her belt. "You're… under…arrest."

"Fuck you, bitch."

"Stop resisting."

"Go to hell."

They rolled over on the floor again, and Bennett temporarily straddled the suspect. She shouted at the still-stunned officer. "Grab his other arm and help me cuff him!"

"You're bleeding, Captain." The rookie grabbed his radio and yelled, "Signal-0. Officer needs assistance! Send an ambulance!"

As she scrambled around on the floor with the suspect, Bennett glanced to her left, where the female officer scuffled with the other suspect, keeping her from joining the fray. Bennett called to the rookie again. "Officer, snap out of it and cuff this man!" Outside sirens sounded in the distance and some fairly close, all responding to the frantic officer's emergency call for assistance. She struggled to keep the broken beer bottle away from her neck and the suspect generally contained until they arrived.

The male rookie finally snapped out of his daze and pointed his Glock at the suspect. "St—op or I'll sho—ot." His voice shook, and his wide eyes looked abnormally large against his ashen face.

The suspect stopped as if suddenly realizing he couldn't win. "Don't shoot." He released his hold on Bennett and tossed the bottleneck to the floor.

"Turn over and put your hands behind you." Bennett grabbed her handcuffs, jammed her knee in the suspect's back to hold him still, and snapped the cuffs around his wrists. "Stay down." She turned toward the officer, who was still pointing his gun at the suspect, his hands visibly shaking. "Holster your weapon, Officer."

"What?"

"Holster your gun, now. Step outside and get some air." She pulled her walkie-talkie from her belt. "Dispatch, cancel all emergency response to this location."

"Advise on ambulance proceeding, Car 100."

"Cancel the ambulance." She turned to the female rookie. "What's your name, Officer?"

"Brooks, ma'am."

"Is your suspect under arrest, Brooks?"

"Yes, ma'am, assault on an officer. She's already cuffed."

"Secure her in a vehicle, have the other officer watch her, and come back inside."

A few seconds later, Brooks stood at Bennett's side. "You do realize you're bleeding, right, Captain?"

"So I've been told. He must've caught me between the side panel of my vest and my utility belt. Locate the bottle and take some pictures before the scene is disturbed. You're in charge of security until your supervisor arrives. The place will be crawling with officers shortly. Make sure every officer who comes through that door signs the crime-scene entry log with his name and badge number. Don't let anybody bully his way in. Understand, Brooks?"

"Yes, ma'am."

Officer Brooks located the bloody beer bottle under a chair a few feet from where Bennett had struggled with the suspect and snapped pictures on her phone. She started toward the door, and Bennett added, "You did good."

"Thank you, Captain."

The first person on the porch was Jazz, and she wasn't happy. "Let me in this damn door, Officer, or I'll go through you."

"I'm sorry, Lieutenant Perry, but I can't let you in without authorization. Captain Carlyle's orders."

"Authorization? I'm your lieutenant, and I'm authorizing you to let me in the house." Jazz's tone held the high pitch of stress.

"Then sign right here, ma'am." Brooks held out the log, and Jazz impatiently scribbled the necessary info on the page.

"Let her in now, Brooks."

Jazz crossed the threshold, made eye contact with Bennett, and immediately came to her side. "Are you all right? You're pale…and there's blood everywhere. Is it yours?"

Bennett nodded. "Hand this guy over to one of the officers for processing. He's charged with assault on a female, two counts of assault on an officer, and resisting arrest."

Jazz quickly escorted the suspect to the front door, handed him off, and returned to Bennett. "He cut you." She was staring at the floor where the bottle neck had come to rest, and her tone said what Bennett had been thinking since the sting in her side occurred.

"I didn't have time to draw my pistol. The suspect was about to lunge, and the officer was like a deer in the headlights. I pushed him aside."

"You put yourself between a suspect with a weapon and another officer?" Bennett didn't answer, but Jazz cupped her elbow and guided her toward the door. "Let's get you to the hospital before you bleed out."

"The injury isn't that bad."

"You might wish you'd bled out once G-ma and Mama hear about your heroics."

Bennett took a deep breath to combat a sudden bout of dizziness as she stepped out on the front porch. Officer Brooks eyed her and started to reach out, but Bennett squared her shoulders and said, "I'm counting on you to brief the crime-scene tech, file a report, and make sure the proper charges are filed."

"Yes, ma'am. I won't let you down."

"No. I don't believe you will."

Bennett walked toward Jazz's vehicle, and the male officer who was guarding the female suspect said, "Captain Carlyle, I'm sor—"

"Don't." Jazz held up her hand to keep him away. "I'll deal with you later." She settled Bennett in the passenger seat of her vehicle, grabbed a bandage from her first-aid kit, and handed it to her. "Press this against the wound, hard." Then she drove toward the hospital, blue lights and sirens activated, without saying another word, her features a solid mask of anguish and her left hand worrying a few strands of white hair into a knot.

They parked at the emergency room ambulance bay, and Bennett said, "Don't be too hard on the rookie."

"What? He almost got you killed."

"He's new, and in case you hadn't noticed, I'm fine."

"You're not fine. You're bleeding all over my car, and you're as pale as G-ma's starched table doilies. Let's get inside." She wrapped her arm around Bennett's waist as the automatic doors swished open into the ER. "Even rookies should be able to keep their wits in an emergency. If not, they don't need to be in police work. Fear gets people killed."

"Can we talk about this later?" White spots danced in front of her eyes, and she reached for something to steady herself, missed the check-in desk, and slumped to the floor.

When Bennett opened her eyes again, her family hovered on one side of her bed in the small curtained exam area, anxious expressions on their faces. Dylan and Jen stood on the other side. "Hi, everybody. What's going on?"

G-ma play slapped her leg. "What's going on? You almost scared the daylights out of us, that's what."

"I'm fine."

"She keeps saying that," Jazz said.

Mama stepped closer and placed her hand on Bennett's forehead. "I'm so happy to see your pretty brown eyes again. You had us worried."

"But I just got here, right?"

"Afraid not." Dylan checked her pupils and adjusted an IV drip. "You've been out for several hours, long enough for us to stitch you back together and for two coffee runs and a doughnut-retrieval operation across town. Simon needed an injection of breaded sugar."

"Of course he did." Bennett laughed, but a sharp pain in her side cut it short.

"Easy." Dylan pointed to her right side. "You're very lucky. You've got a jagged laceration to your side, which required deep stitches."

"Hurts like hell, so what's the lucky part?"

"The suspect wasn't using a longer piece of glass or a knife. He lacerated the skin and fatty tissue, nicked the external oblique muscle before glancing off your rib cage and fortunately missing your liver. Like I said, lucky."

"Does that mean I can go home now?"

Mama shook her head like a bobble toy on steroids. "I don't think so, young lady."

Dylan placed her hands on her hips in a stance so much like Mama that Bennett had to smile. "That's probably not a good idea. Why don't we admit you for observation overnight, as a precaution."

"No thanks. I want to go home to my bed. And I want to go back to work, soon."

"I'm afraid the work part isn't happening as soon as you'd like. The skin will heal relatively quickly, but the muscles, which you need for twisting and turning, will take longer. If I know you, you won't stay behind a desk."

"So, what about going home then?" Being confined, unable to be in the field or even at her desk, made Bennett anxious and jittery.

"Come on, Ben, be reasonable," Jazz said. "We're not about to let you check out and go home alone. If you leave, you'll stay at the house so we can keep an eye on you."

"Listen to your sister," G-ma said. "She's making a lot more sense than you are right now."

"Could be the pain meds." Bennett glanced at her little sister and begged.

Dylan's expression softened as her resistance dissolved. "The only way I'll discharge you tonight is if you have around-the-clock care for the next twenty-four hours, either at your place or at home. I don't care which. Can you promise?"

"Of course." Bennett started to get up, but the pain again stopped her abruptly. "A little help, guys?" She scanned the faces gathered around her bed, but no one moved. She looked at Jen, and she winked.

"If it's all right with the family," Jen said, "I'm getting off in thirty minutes and would be glad to look after the grumpy invalid."

The family exchanged a few glances before G-ma and Mama reluctantly nodded. "At least she'll be close by," Mama said.

"It's settled then. Thanks, Jen." Bennett could tell by the look on Mama's face she wasn't happy about the arrangement but didn't want to create a scene in the hospital. "I'll be fine, Mama. Jen is an excellent nurse. Isn't she, Dylan?"

"Absolutely." Dylan leaned close to Bennett's ear and whispered, "You owe me *so* big-time for this one. I'll collect very soon."

Chapter Sixteen

Four days in New York would normally be a good thing, but on the last day Kerstin paced, her shoulders tense and her emotions totally out of sorts. She'd come back early for her mother's birthday and snuck out the past two nights after she'd gone to bed for a little recreational activity. The city provided ample distractions, but even her sexual rendezvous hadn't tamed her unease. Every time she touched another woman, she remembered Bennett's smooth skin, how responsive she'd been, and how desperately she wanted to caress her again. Kerstin's nerves were on edge, and she ached for a connection she'd never known. To make matters worse, Valerie and her mother were sneaking around, whispering, and laughing behind Kerstin's back, which didn't help her disposition.

"Yo, Kerstin," Valerie said. "Hell—o."

"What? Yes. I'm here."

"Doesn't seem like you're here this weekend." Valerie put her fingers to her lips and inclined her head toward Elizabeth's room. "Let's go for a walk before she wakes up."

Kerstin nodded and grabbed a light coat on the way to the elevator. An unusually warm spell had brought some of the flowers out prematurely in the park, and they dotted the path around the perimeter, their fragrance a welcome respite from dead, decaying leaves. "So, what are you and Mother up to this weekend? You're skulking around, obviously up to no good."

"We have a surprise for you when she wakes up."

Kerstin stopped, and a jogger almost slammed into her. "You know I hate surprises."

"You'll like ours. Promise." She nudged Kerstin forward. "Keep walking before somebody runs you over."

"Give me a hint?"

"You first."

Kerstin's attention shifted to a tall, lean woman stretching in the park. Her hair had the same rich color and wavy texture as Bennett's. "Sorry?"

"My point exactly. What have you been thinking about for the past three days? Bennett Carlyle perhaps?"

At the mention of Bennett's name, Kerstin stopped again, and this time Valerie pulled her off the path in time to avoid a collision. "Talk to me, Kerstin."

"It's annoying that you read me so well." She stopped to admire a few sprigs of goldenrod, but Valerie nudged her. "If you must know, the substation project is a big mess, and I'm not sure I can salvage it. Gil totally screwed up the plans, and the changes are going to put us over budget. Whizzing back and forth between two places every week and living out of a suitcase while trying to have a life isn't as easy or as much fun as I remember. And Greensboro is nothing like New York."

"In a good or bad way?" Valerie pointed to an empty bench.

Kerstin's feelings poured out without preparation. "Both, I guess. There's the obvious difference in social activities, ethnic restaurants, and sheer body mass. The people seem friendlier and operate at a much slower pace. Greensboro lives up to its name with lots of trees, flowers, green spaces, and parks and would probably be a great place to start my firm, especially with the emphasis on sustainable housing and an easier market to break into as well."

Valerie eyed her hard. "So far I'm not hearing anything good about the city."

"New York has significantly more entertainment, especially of the intimate variety. I was so desperate I actually…"

"You what?"

"Never mind."

"You're about to dish something real juicy."

"I shouldn't."

Valerie raised her hands. "Have you and Bennett at least had a conversation?"

"Sort of, partially, not really. We…I mean, I…" Her face flushed.

Valerie's expression indicated she knew exactly why Kerstin was stammering. "You had sex with her."

"Keep your voice down, please."

"Seriously? In New York City? I'm sure people are having sex right now, in this park, in broad daylight. Tell me everything."

Kerstin put her elbows on her knees and buried her face in her hands, unable to meet her aunt's questioning stare. Seconds ticked by as she gathered courage. "I did my usual thing." Valerie didn't have an immediate comeback, so Kerstin looked up.

Valerie shrugged. "I have no idea what that means. Without getting too specific, because I'm not sure I want the details of my niece's sex life, what are you saying exactly?"

"Yes, we had sex and I basically treated her like an escort—wham, bam, but without the thank you, ma'am. I tiptoed out in the middle of the night. Not my proudest moment."

Valerie stared at her for a few seconds. "That's only problematic if she wants more. Does she? Is she the fling type or the white-picket-fences forever type?"

"I have no idea. She seemed fine the next day, very cool and casual."

"And since?"

"Haven't seen her again, not even at work."

"But you've talked on the phone?"

Kerstin shook her head. When she said everything aloud, she sounded like a scoundrel. If a woman treated her the way she'd treated Bennett, she wouldn't speak to her again. Maybe that was why she hadn't heard from Bennett. Kerstin was very clear that she only wanted a fling, but maybe she and Bennett hadn't actually had the conversation. Damn.

"I should've known better, especially with a coworker. Always a bad idea." She glanced at Valerie, her eyes soft and sympathetic. "I've really messed up, haven't I?"

"Not necessarily, but it all comes back to the same point—knowing what you want and telling her." Valerie urged her to her feet. "Let's head back. Elizabeth is probably awake, and you could use the surprise I promised."

The elevator pinged at her mother's penthouse, and Valerie dashed down the hall toward Elizabeth's bedroom. Kerstin heard mumbled conversation and shuffling around for half an hour before they emerged.

Valerie peeped around the corner of the hallway and motioned toward the kitchen. "Move over to the kitchen island."

"What are you two playing at?"

"Get over there, please."

"Listen to your aunt, Kerstin Anthony," her mother called from farther down the hall.

"All right, I'm going." She grabbed her cell phone and perched on a stool at the large granite island. "In position." A sliver of anxiety crept up her spine as she waited for the big surprise.

Valerie cleared her throat and thrust her arms apart. "I give you Mrs. Elizabeth Grayson Anthony, high priestess of the order of independent women." She bowed and brushed her hands forward as if presenting the Queen.

Elizabeth walked down the hallway without her walker or cane and barely a detectable limp. Dressed in form-fitting black slacks and jacket with a bright-red blouse, her blond hair twisted into a tidy braid, she was the image of stately perfection. Her eyes rested on Kerstin as she moved, pleased but expectant.

"Mother, you're walking, without assistance. You're absolutely fabulous."

"Yes, I am."

"When…I mean…how?"

"Stop babbling, dear. It's unattractive." Her mother grinned, pride evident on her face.

"How long have you two been planning this little event?"

Valerie smiled but allowed Elizabeth the spotlight. "Since the day this dreadful thing happened. I've worked poor Valerie rather hard and been quite demanding."

"It was totally worth the effort," Valerie said, coming to her side. "Isn't this the best?"

"I couldn't imagine anything better." Kerstin slid off her stool.

Elizabeth held up her hand. "Wait. I want to come to you. And I do have one other little surprise for the day, if you'll indulge me."

"Anything," Kerstin said. "Today you've earned whatever you want." Tears slid down her cheeks, tears of pride and admiration at her mother's accomplishment. She'd once feared Elizabeth might not walk unassisted again or regain functional use of her left arm, but she'd underestimated her mother.

"I've taken the liberty of making a reservation for brunch at Peacock Alley. We can celebrate my newfound independence and have a nice meal before you head out of town again."

"The ritzy place in the Waldorf Astoria?" Kerstin groaned internally. The last time they'd gone there, her mother had set her up with the son of a lawyer friend.

"Yes, and I promise it'll be only the three of us. My treat."

Valerie, always within a couple of feet of Elizabeth's side, winked at Kerstin. "Well, who can resist a free meal?"

"Absolutely. Give me fifteen minutes." She stopped on the way to her bedroom and gave her mother a huge hug. Elizabeth squeezed her with both arms, and Kerstin's tears fell freely.

Kerstin dressed for their outing and wondered what decisions her mother would make about her future now. Where would she want to live? Would Kerstin figure into those deliberations at all? Should she? The benevolent and loving part of her was elated with her mother's progress, but the selfish and controlling part that wanted everything to remain the same was terrified.

CHAPTER SEVENTEEN

Kerstin hit the equal key on her calculator and drew a red circle around the total of the column of figures on the page. She dropped her pen and faced the setting sun, enjoying its warmth and the gentle breeze through nearby oak trees. She loved working surrounded by nature at the picnic table behind the substation. If she had questions, she ran inside, and if the contractor had issues, he knew where to find her. The memory of her first real conversation with Bennett in this spot still lingered and brought her a sense of peace and cautious hope.

"Ma'am?" A uniformed officer stood offering her a sandwich and a Coke. "Mrs. Carlyle asked me to bring this over. Sorry I'm a bit late. I had an emergency call."

"*Mrs*. Carlyle?"

"The Ma Rolls lady."

"Yes. Thank you." She accepted the offering, pulled some money from her bag, and stood to offer it to him.

"On the house, she said." He turned to leave.

"Thank you for the delivery. By the way, have you seen Captain Carlyle today?"

The young man scuffed his shoe in the grass and didn't make eye contact. "No, ma'am."

"Do you know if she's in her office? I checked a few hours ago, but the door was locked."

"Don't imagine she'll be around for a while."

The statement sent a chill through Kerstin. "What do you mean?"

"A rookie got her injured last week, put her in the hospital. She'll be out for—"

Kerstin's knees weakened and she started sinking.

The officer rushed to her side, clasped her hands, and helped her sit. "Here, easy."

"How…what…okay?" She couldn't find the right words, and the ones that came weren't enough to get the answers she needed. *"Tell me."*

The confused officer released her hands and stepped back as if preparing to give a report. "She responded with two new officers on a domestic. A male suspect attacked one of the rookies with a broken bottle, and Captain Carlyle intervened. The man cut her pretty bad. She's something else. Nothing like our former captain." He puffed his chest out, clearly proud of his new commanding officer. "Are you sure you're okay, ma'am?"

"Fine. Thank you." As he walked away, Kerstin folded her arms, the light breeze suddenly too chilly across her sweaty skin. She had to find Bennett, to see for herself if she was okay.

Ma Rolls. Norma and Gayle would have all the facts. She shoved the papers into her bag and sprinted toward the street where their food truck was usually parked. Empty. She ran toward her car and was unlocking the door when Henry called from the work site.

"Ms. Anthony, I need to see you before you leave."

"You'll have to wait."

"It won't take but a minute."

She slammed her car door and mumbled as she walked toward him, "It better not."

Henry's minute turned into two hours as she struggled to clarify one key point on her drawings. She was distracted, unable to focus and properly explain the changes she'd made—very unlike the controlled professional she professed to be. By the time she headed to Bennett's place, it was almost eight o'clock at night.

Cars lined the street in front of the Carlyle home, so Kerstin parked around the corner, entered the garden through a white wooden gate, and followed a solar-lighted path toward Bennett's door. As she approached, laughter drifted through the night air, a good sign. Halfway up the path, the front door opened, and a woman with short black hair exited, her young face glowing in a genuine smile. Maybe she should've called before showing up. Her last exchange with Bennett was tense and prickly. The woman nodded as she passed with the agile swagger afforded the very young or deeply enamored. Kerstin's steps faltered.

Was coming here a mistake? She had to check on Bennett for her own peace of mind. What if she wasn't alone? Kerstin argued with herself as she approached the cottage and stared at the door for several seconds before finally knocking. No answer. She pushed the door and it opened easily.

As soon as she entered, she wished she hadn't. Bennett, naked from the waist up, lay on her back across the sofa, and redheaded nurse Jen sat on the edge leaning over her. Jen's hands worked slowly on Bennett's naked torso as Bennett watched her movements with hooded eyes. They were totally engrossed. She shouldn't be here. The scene in front of her would never fade from her memory.

The women's intimate exchange made Kerstin queasy. She wanted to announce her presence but choked out only a squeaking sound. Bennett finally noticed her, and Kerstin mouthed *I'm sorry* and ran.

"Kerst, wait." Bennett called after her, but she didn't stop.

She was almost to her car before she heard footsteps behind her. Expecting to see Bennett, she turned, not sure what to say.

Instead nurse Jen stood with her arms crossed over her low-cut blouse and plentiful breasts. "Really?"

"What?"

"You don't call or come by for almost a week, and now you're throwing shade?"

"I need to know how she's doing. Anything else is your own business." Up close and under the glow of a streetlight, nurse Jen was even more attractive than Kerstin remembered. Her red, shoulder-length hair curtained a chiseled face and bright-green eyes that flashed angry stares at Kerstin as they faced off. Jen's comment finally registered. "You don't know me, so don't judge my behavior. And I'm definitely not shady."

"Have you seen Bennett since she was injured?"

"Well, no, I—"

"Maybe you were at the hospital, and I missed you?"

"I didn't—"

"Have you even called?"

"No, but—"

"That's all I need to know about you. If you sleep with a woman, it's polite to keep in touch, unless she was a one-night stand. Was she?"

The air rushed from Kerstin's lungs. "She *told* you?"

"Ben wouldn't. I guessed. Suppose I was right. The look on your face when you saw my hands on her body—"

"Stop." Kerstin turned away so Jen wouldn't see how deeply her words affected her. Why was she standing in the street talking to a stranger about a woman she, what? Hadn't quite forgotten after a decade and a half? Had sex with and couldn't wait to again? Cared about? Loved? Certainly not love. Was it? The thought unsettled her nearly as much as watching Jen touch Bennett's naked chest.

"I probably shouldn't put you out of your misery, but I'm a nice person and sworn by the Florence Nightingale Pledge to do no harm. I was changing Ben's bandage."

Jen's statement took a second to register while Kerstin played the scenario through her mind again with the new information. "But she looked…her eyes…"

"She's on pain meds. A guy wielding a broken bottle neck ripped through her skin, some muscle tissue, and nicked her ribs."

Kerstin flinched at the vivid description, trying not to visualize the damage to Bennett's body. "I see."

"Do you really? While she was hospitalized and heavily sedated, she called your name. She might not be special to you, but I'm pretty sure you are to her. Don't hurt her."

Jen's assumption fanned Kerstin's irritation into a rage. She bit back an angry retort, stepped closer, and spoke through clenched teeth. "You don't know how I feel, and unless Bennett confided in you, you don't know how she feels either."

"I've known her a long time, and we've been intim—"

"Again, stop with the details."

"The point is, I know her, probably better than you do. I've lived in this town all my life, went to school with Bennett, nursed her through breakups, and yes, even slept with her."

Kerstin cringed at the mental image of Bennett having sex with this pretty, intelligent woman. "Since you've known her so long, you must also know she has her choice of female companions, so I doubt I'm special." Her anger made the words taste bitter, but the truth didn't always leave a pleasing taste.

Jen laughed like she'd told a sidesplitting joke. "Granted, she has quite a rich dating pool, but she seldom dips into it. Don't get me wrong, she's not celibate, but she doesn't indiscriminately bed every available woman. After you left the first time, she was gutted."

Bennett grieved for her? She hadn't pictured Bennett as anything but her usual carefree self, until recently. Kerstin wanted to flee, to reject this woman who obviously knew Bennett better than she did, but against her will she hungered for every morsel of information about the woman who'd thrown her life into chaos.

"And for the record, my wife would be mightily pissed if I fooled around."

"Your wife?" Kerstin's angry spiral slowed a notch. "Why didn't you say so sooner…I wouldn't…you know?"

"Sometimes you need to risk losing something, or someone, to realize what you really have. Trust me, Ben is a keeper."

The wooden gate behind them squeaked, and Bennett walked slowly toward them, one arm curled tightly across her stomach, holding her side. "What's going on?" She looked at Kerstin, her dark eyes sleepy but full of concern. "Are you okay?"

Kerstin nodded.

"I'm leaving," Jen said. "Check on you tomorrow. If you need anything, let me know."

"How about a doctor's note releasing me for regular duty?"

"No can do, pal. You wanted to play hero. Now you pay the price."

"Thanks." Bennett waved to Jen before turning her attention to Kerstin. "You're not going too, are you?"

The disappointment in her voice almost changed Kerstin's mind, but she needed space and time to think. "Yeah. I only heard about your injury today. Sorry I'm so late."

"No biggie. I've been pretty rotten company anyway, groggy and half-asleep most of the time. Everybody's conspired to keep me drugged so I won't do anything stupid, like go back to work too soon."

"Drugs don't sound like a bad idea if you're already considering returning."

"Would you come in for a while?" She motioned toward the cottage.

"I really should go. Jen updated me pretty thoroughly."

Bennett breathed deeply and winced, placing both hands over her right side. "Did you need something else?" Kerstin must've looked as confused as she felt because Bennett added, "Work, maybe? Is everything all right at the site?"

What was happening to her? She didn't let personal situations interfere with work and her career, but she also didn't usually let a fling rattle her. Bennett stared at her. Damn, she'd asked a question. "Oh, yes, everything's fine."

"Are you sure?"

"Definitely." Her news wasn't good, and she couldn't face another emotional conversation tonight. "I'll swing by soon and fill you in, after we're both rested."

"And maybe we can talk about what happened tonight too?"

"Tonight?"

"What you saw just now, with me and Jen. This isn't the time for either of us right now." Bennett opened the car door and waited while she settled in. "I hope to be back on desk duty next week. Thank you for stopping by. It's good to see you."

She rested her hand on top of Kerstin's before closing the door, and desire sprouted so rapidly she jerked away. "You…too." She stomped the gas pedal too hard, and her tires barked as she left the curb. "Really mature, Anthony."

Chapter Eighteen

Bennett paced back and forth in the cottage and drank coffee before sunrise, waiting for Dylan to stop by. She'd discovered getting up early wasn't difficult if she didn't sleep. The hard part turned out to be showering and dressing with a painful gash in her side.

"You look perky. Too much coffee or pain?" Dylan quipped, closing the door behind her.

"Cabin fever. I'm ready to get back to work."

"Soon, my impatient patient."

"I'm not kidding, Dylan."

"I know, but a few more days. Humor me." She dug a pill from the bottle on the nightstand and offered it to Bennett.

"No more pain pills. I need to be myself again, not the zombie version."

Dylan rested on a barstool and studied Bennett's worried pacing. "What's wrong, sis? You seem more agitated than usual this morning."

Bennett stopped suddenly, sloshing lukewarm coffee on her hand. "Damn it. What's wrong? You mean other than being housebound for a week, coddled by my family, stuffed with my favorite fattening foods, and plied with drugs by my baby sister?" Dylan's smile was warm and genuine, and Bennett regretted being so sarcastic, sort of.

"Yeah, other than those few minor details. Have anything to do with the steady stream of women outside your place last night?" Dylan didn't flinch as she waited for the truth.

After a short debate with herself, Bennett said, "Kerstin dropped by."

Dylan's smile grew bigger. "Good. Right?"

"It might've been if Jen wasn't changing my bandage." Dylan's mouth twisted sideways, her sign of confusion. "I was half dressed and, from her viewpoint, probably not so good."

"Oh."

"She bolted before I got off the sofa. Jen went after her, and I have no idea what they talked about before I pulled my shirt on and got out there, but Kerstin didn't look happy."

Dylan's mouth still had a quirky twist. Bennett had given too much away. Her sister didn't miss anything, whether blatant or nuanced.

"So…you're upset Kerstin might think you and Jen are getting busy?"

She'd talked only to Jazz about her feelings for Kerstin, but the whole family had gone through her brokenhearted episode in high school. Might as well own it. "Pretty much."

"Does that mean you're interested in Kerstin again, really interested?"

Bennett slowly lowered herself onto the sofa. "I don't know what it means, Dylan, but I need to see her, soon. Will you *please* help me escape? You write a return-to-duty slip. I go by the hotel and check on Kerstin. I'm in my office this afternoon on desk duty like a good girl."

Dylan raised her hands in the air. "And risk the wrath of G-ma and Mama? You know the old saying 'physician, heal thyself'? I'm not anxious to test the adage."

"*Please*."

Dylan started to leave but paused with her hand on the doorknob. "Under one condition."

"Anything. Seriously."

"Drop a hint to G-ma and Mama about me moving out."

"What?"

"I need my own place, Ben. I want to forge my own way without the family influence."

"Or our overprotectiveness?"

Dylan's reluctance to answer signaled she might regret confiding in her.

"Is this a recent decision?"

"Not really. I've mentioned the subject before, so I'm sure they won't be surprised. But I'm the baby, so there might be some resistance. I'd hate myself if I hurt any of them."

Bennett eased her way out of the sofa and joined Dylan by the door. "I know, sis, really. Besides, living at home definitely puts a kink in your sex life, huh?"

"I mention I still live at home, and women assume something's wrong with me or run the other way. It's embarrassing, Ben, but it's not really about that."

"You need independence, but do you really think moving is the answer? It's not like people won't know you're a Carlyle, unless you change your name too."

"I love our family so much, but sometimes I feel we live our lives by committee. And as wonderfully supportive and helpful as that is most of the time, I need more. I'm a doctor who makes life-and-death decisions every day, but I don't pay my own power bill, cook my own meals, or even have an address that doesn't necessitate sorting mail into five stacks."

Bennett couldn't suppress a chuckle. "Some people would argue those are good things, but I see your point. Not everyone is comfortable living in a family commune. I'll bring it up, soon, but don't push the timeline. Deal?"

Dylan launched herself toward Bennett but settled for a gentle hug. "Deal. I so love you, right now. How about that doctor's note?" She retrieved a pen and piece of paper from a side table and scribbled quickly. "This gives you desk privileges *only* for the time being. No field work at all. Agreed?"

"Agreed." She snatched the note and kissed Dylan on the cheek. "Now out. I have things to do, places to go, and a woman to see. And by the way, I love you too."

"Good luck."

Thirty minutes later, she stood in front of Kerstin's room at the Proximity Hotel, unsure if she should knock. What would she say to a woman she'd had sex with once who might be upset about her having sex with another woman? Did the status of her and Kerstin's relationship, whatever that was, even require an explanation?

Before she had a chance to decide, the door opened and Kerstin stood in front of her wearing a plush white bathrobe that exposed a hint of cleavage and shapely legs. Her blond hair was sleep-tossed and her face free of makeup. She'd never looked more beautiful. The image plucked at something deep inside Bennett. She'd carry this vision of Kerstin as her favorite until another took its place. She fought an urge to take her hand, lead her to the bedroom, and—

"Ben?"

"Huh?

"Bennett, what are you doing here at this hour? Are you okay?"

"This hour?" She checked her watch. Not yet seven. Crap. "Sorry. I needed to see you. I didn't realize. Um…yeah. I'm fine. Can we talk?"

Kerstin picked up the complimentary copy of *USA Today* but remained in the doorway, clutching the neck of her robe, as if considering the request. A few excruciating seconds passed before she stepped aside and motioned her in. "What's so urgent before breakfast?"

Bennett slid her sweaty hands into her back jeans pockets to hide her nervous shaking. Now what? Had Kerstin assumed she and Jen were together? Did it matter? She second-guessed her decision to come here, so what to say now? "Can we talk about what happened last night?"

Kerstin still stood in the open doorway. "Could we possibly have this chat after I've gotten dressed, maybe over breakfast? We have business to discuss as well."

Bennett walked back to her, closed the door, and took Kerstin's hands in hers, tossing the paper aside. "What I have to say can't wait, and I'd rather talk in private."

"You don't need to explain anything about last night." Kerstin squared her shoulders and glanced around the room, looking everywhere but at her.

Bennett stepped closer, forcing eye contact. "Jen and I are not together, or dating, or even having sex…in case you wondered."

"I didn't."

Kerstin's blue eyes sparkled, suddenly full of light and a hint of humor. "Because she changed my—wait. What did you say?"

"She explained everything, which wasn't really necessary. As I've said before, your personal life is none of my business, even though I seem to keep bullying my way in."

"What if I want it to be…your business?"

"Bennett, don't."

"I'm being honest." The anxiety Bennett had nursed on the drive evaporated, and she let out a long sigh. "Do I even want to know Jen's definition of everything? What did she say?"

"She clarified some things."

Bennett's stomach curled into an uncomfortable jumble of nerves. She took a deep breath and pressed on. "Good, because I want to date you. Only you."

Kerstin's head snapped back as if she'd been struck. "What?"

"I apologize for the unromantic delivery, but those are my intentions. I'd like us to go out, get to know each other again, see if we have a future. And I'm not asking because we…you know…had sex. It's not really about sex, though it was pretty intense…I mean… good intense, but still not totally about sex. I better stop talking." She stopped breathing too and just waited.

Kerstin released the grasp on her robe and stepped back, the light dimming in her eyes. "One of the things I've always adored about you is your honesty. But I can't."

Bennett finally took a breath and straightened until the muscles under her skin pulled against the stitches on her right side, creating enough discomfort to distract her from the pain of Kerstin's response. "Oh. Do you maybe want to think about it a little?"

Kerstin just stared, conflict swirling in her blue eyes, but she didn't answer immediately. Bennett took the opening. "I know this is sudden, but I'd like to show you who I am now and find out about you. We could take it slow."

"I really can't, Ben."

I can't wasn't no, but without further explanation, it felt like no when she stood in front of the woman she loved with her heart in her hands. "I see."

"Let me explain."

"No need." She had to get out of this room. The walls closed in, smothering her. No matter Kerstin's excuse—her mother, career, the substation project, their socioeconomic differences, or the simple fact she wasn't serious about Bennett—nothing could mitigate her deep disappointment. She should've expected rejection. Maybe it was time to admit the only real relationship she and Kerstin had was work. "Do you still need to talk about the project?"

"It can wait."

Kerstin reached for her, but Bennett backed away, unable to bear the pitying look in her eyes. "Let's do it now," Bennett managed to say.

"I can meet you downstairs in fifteen minutes?"

Bennett nodded and let herself out.

Kerstin pressed her palms against the door and bowed her head, the last five minutes playing over and over in her mind. Her body still tingled from Bennett's nearness and the desire to have her again. Her terry-cloth robe rubbed and aroused places where she craved Bennett's touch. She'd arrived with an obvious agenda, and Kerstin should've pulled her into the bedroom and quieted her before those words spilled out. But once released, the weight of their expectations overpowered her physical longing.

"I want to date you. Only you."

The moment was inevitable, but she wasn't prepared for Bennett's candid expression of interest. Kerstin had certainly imagined it, even encouraged it in her own warped way, but not prepared for it. The minute she moved their relationship in a sexual direction, she'd offered hope for more. Bennett's expectation was obvious in those brown eyes from the first day, and in everything she did after—talking about the past, dinner with the family, fiery glances, inadvertent touches, and her total sexual surrender. Kerstin planned for every possible contingency in her work but avoided the personal.

She pushed away from the door and walked slowly to the bathroom. While showering, she tried to erase the hurt she'd seen in Bennett's eyes, but it persisted. She toweled off and reached for her mascara brush, but her hand shook so badly she lowered it again. Tears ran down her cheeks, and she roughly brushed at them. Reaching into the closet, she pulled out the first thing she found—a pair of faded jeans and a black, button-front blouse. She dressed perfunctorily, focused on keeping her composure when she saw Bennett again. She stared at her reflection in the mirror, one question churning through her mind. "Why did you say no?"

Bennett's honesty and optimism had nearly undone her. And she offered Kerstin the closest thing to a commitment possible, considering their circumstances. But Kerstin was—she'd never said the words aloud. "I'm deathly afraid of intimacy." She wanted what Bennett offered more than she cared to admit, but more involvement equaled potential pain. The circuitous conflict swirled round and round with only one possible conclusion. Focus on business. No possibility of intimacy.

After grabbing her tote, she trudged down the hallway toward the elevator, rolling her shoulders to relieve the tension that had started the minute she refused Bennett. Could she sit across from the woman she desperately wanted but couldn't have and carry on a normal business conversation? She was about to find out.

She entered Print Works Bistro and scanned the room, spotting Bennett's red cashmere sweater she'd wanted to rip off her earlier. The garment outlined her broad shoulders, clung to her compact breasts, and skimmed the muscles of her rib cage before brushing the waistband of her low-cut jeans. The tug of something strong, almost primal gripped her, and she faltered. Her self-discipline, usually free of emotions, always turned shaky around Bennett.

Bennett stood and held out her chair, her expression bland, impassive, but her eyes told the truth. Buried in their depths Kerstin saw plainly the hurt and rejection she'd caused only minutes earlier.

"I've ordered coffee. Wasn't sure what else you might like. Are you okay?"

"Am *I* okay?" Bennett was the one who'd been so callously rejected, yet she was still concerned about Kerstin. "I'm fine. You?"

"Hard to argue with the truth. You were honest. Really all I can ask. Let's not make things awkward. We still have work problems, if the look on your face is any indication."

As Bennett started back to her chair, a young child ran screaming past their table. He nearly knocked a waiter over, creating a chain reaction. The waiter stumbled sideways, dropped a tray of drinks on another guest, lurched backward, and jammed his elbow into Bennett's right side. She winced, closed her eyes momentarily, and paled as she pulled for breath.

"Watch what you're doing." Kerstin rose from her chair, her tone sharp.

The young waiter, trying desperately to placate the drenched diner, turned toward them. "I'm so sorry, ma'am. Please forgive me."

"It's okay," Bennett said to the waiter, gracious in spite of her obvious pain.

"It most certainly is *not* okay." Kerstin started to say more, but Bennett's hand on her arm stopped her.

"I'm fine, Kerst."

"You're hurt, again."

"It was an accident. No harm done, really. Sit."

Bennett coaxed her back to her seat as the waiter cleaned up the mess and hurried away. "Should you even be here?"

Bennett's smile erased any hint of discomfort. "I have to be somewhere. I was going stir-crazy at home. I sort of bribed Dylan into giving me a doctor's release."

Kerstin finally relaxed, watching Bennett's face light up at the mention of her sister. "She can't deny you anything."

"And vice versa."

"What did you barter?" Kerstin was procrastinating, but hearing Bennett talk so lovingly about her baby sister was relaxing in a way she didn't entirely understand. "Or can you say?"

"She wants to move out." She rolled her cup in her hands and swallowed hard.

"That was difficult for you, wasn't it?"

Bennett nodded.

"She's a young woman, Ben. An intelligent, accomplished, independent woman like the rest of the Carlyle women, and she probably wants to prove herself without the family's help. I'm sure you understand. Making your own way is hard if you're the baby…or only child."

"Exactly what she said. She asked me to talk to the family, let them know she's serious. The children in our family always stay at, or at least near, home until we meet the right person, and then we move down the street to another family property, always close."

She placed her hand over Bennett's but immediately withdrew it, the gesture too intimate and evocative in public. "I'm sure they'll understand. After all, your parents raised all of their children to think for themselves and to become their own person."

Bennett stared out the windows facing the sparsely wooded creek bed, a faraway look in her eyes.

"Bennett, are you okay?"

"I wonder if the cottage would be enough distance for her."

"Your place?"

"Yeah. I moved out back while I was dating someone…special. We'd planned to relocate to a house the following spring. I'd have to talk with Jazz because she's up for the cottage next."

Kerstin's stomach roiled, imagining Bennett with another woman, setting up house with her, permanently. She fought down a foul taste, struggling not to ask, but having to know. "What happened, with your special someone?"

"She had an opportunity for a once-in-a-lifetime job overseas and accepted without even discussing it with me. I would've supported her no matter what, but she didn't want the challenges of a long-distance relationship starting out."

The next question hung in Kerstin's throat, but she forced it out. "Do you…are you still in…love with her?"

Bennett waited until Kerstin looked at her and then delivered her answer. "No."

Kerstin controlled the relieved breath escaping her lips. "That's good…I mean…okay then. Should we order breakfast or get straight to work?"

"Whatever you want." Bennett's eyes sparkled, and her sexy lips quirked into a smile.

They shifted easily from emotionally charged conversations to business and back again, thanks to Bennett's capacity for empathy and vulnerability. Without having Bennett's courage, Kerstin automatically retreated to the shallows of business.

"I'm not really hungry, but feel free to order if you want." She pushed her coffee cup aside, pulled the project cost assessments from her bag, and placed them on the table between them. "I don't have good news. The changes we agreed on will run over budget, considerably over. You should probably inform the chief, since we have a full committee meeting in a few days. I don't want to ambush him or the manager."

"Anything specific cause the overages?"

"If you recall, we divided several open spaces into rooms, which require walls, which cost more. The security doors, bullet-resistant glass, the specialized outdoor lettering and lighting, and landscaping are expensive."

"What specialized lettering and lighting and landscaping?"

"Those items fall under form, not function. How the building appears from the outside says as much about the architect and the occupant as the inside."

"I don't care about the outside. We can cut all that as far as I'm concerned."

Kerstin straightened in her chair. "No, we can't."

"Why? Because it won't be pretty enough for your portfolio?"

The question sounded like an attack. "My portfolio has nothing to do with it." Was she being honest with Bennett, with herself? "Both of our names will be associated with Fairview Station. Don't you want the building to be attractive and functional?"

"All I care about is a workable space for my officers. Don't start pulling punches with me now. What's so important about a few bushes and a sign?"

Kerstin rolled her first drafting pen between her fingers, staring at the figures on the page. "The exterior of the facility represents my style, integrity, and work ethic as much so as the interior, and I won't allow either to be compromised. I started the project with someone else's design, an inferior design in my opinion, but I've tried to make it my own as well as what you wanted." Her eyes burned with tears as the heartfelt sentiment tumbled out. Damn it. Her emotions were all over the place with this woman. She had to hold it together a few more weeks, and then she could…what—go back to New York to a mother who didn't really need her anymore?

"Kerstin, did you hear me?"

"Sorry. What?"

"Why don't we go over your figures and the drawings one more time and see where we can cut costs? I'm willing to concede a few items so you can have your pretty exterior." She tapped Kerstin's foot under the table and smiled. "Sound fair?"

Kerstin nodded. "When do we start?"

"How about right now?" She stood quickly and nearly doubled over, a grimace etched across her face.

"What's wrong?" She scanned Bennett's body and stopped on a large patch of deep scarlet on the right side of her red sweater. "Oh my god, Ben. You're bleeding."

Chapter Nineteen

Don't cut my sweater. It's one of my favorites," Bennett said.

Dylan just stared at her with an expression that was all business. "This is the thanks I get for letting you go back to work, and you didn't even make it to the office." She gingerly slipped the sweater over Bennett's head, and Kerstin stepped back as far as possible from the ER gurney. The white bandage on her side was soaked in blood, and Kerstin almost lost her coffee. Hospitals made her uneasy enough, but the crimson color and coppery smell of blood set her stomach tumbling.

"Damn it. I shouldn't have let you out of the house so soon." Dylan removed the bandage from Bennett's side and inspected the injury. "You've popped a couple of stitches. What have you two been doing?" She glanced from Bennett to Kerstin suspiciously.

"Having breakfast." Bennett smiled.

Kerstin replayed the incident at the restaurant and became more agitated with each word. "But you know your sister."

"Pretended she was fine?" Dylan accepted a needle from the nurse and pointed it at Bennett's side.

Kerstin suddenly found a copy of *People* magazine totally irresistible.

"You can wait outside if you want," Bennett said.

The sick feeling in her stomach wasn't enough to drive her from Bennett's bedside. She wanted to be with her here, at the hotel, her cottage, or the substation, wherever. She grabbed the back of a nearby chair, her thoughts unexpected and sobering. Earlier she'd declined a simple dating offer, and now she wouldn't leave Bennett's side?

This back-and-forth, wishy-washy, ambivalent inability to decide was exactly the reason she didn't do emotions.

"Maybe you should step out," Dylan said. "Now you're pale, and I can't handle two patients at once. I'll call you when I'm finished."

Kerstin shook her head and finally spoke. "I'm…fine…staying." She settled into the chair. When had her feelings for Bennett become so intense? She didn't want to be around any other woman constantly after sex. Quite the opposite. Maybe her mother's recent good news had flipped a switch allowing her to think and feel more optimistically about the future. Bennett Carlyle and the future—the two seemed incongruous.

After several minutes of intense concentration, Dylan stepped away from the gurney. "Well, that should hold until your next round, but I'm afraid this sweater is done for. I have a sweatshirt in my locker you can wear until you get home."

"I'm not going home, yet. Kerstin and I have work that can't wait."

"Oh, yes, it can," Kerstin said as she rose and moved toward Ben. "It can wait as long as necessary. Your health comes first. Listen to your sister, the doctor." She smiled at Dylan, who gave her an appreciative nod.

"What happened this morning was a freakish accident. We'll be in a hotel room going over numbers. How dangerous can that be?"

Kerstin shrugged. "She's right about the low activity."

"If you two promise nothing physical." Dylan placed her hand on Kerstin's arm. "I'm putting you in charge."

Kerstin's face grew hot as she picked up her bag. "I'll do my best."

"Wait here, and I'll get the sweatshirt." Dylan and the nurse left the examining bay, and she turned to Bennett.

"Are you sure about this? We can wait a couple of days to work over the budget."

"I'm sure. We've had too many delays already. Besides, I'll sit in a chair and watch you work. How hard can it be? And maybe later we'll order room service, on the company."

"Bennett—"

"Don't worry, just business, but you know me and food. As long as you promise to feed me at some point, I'm good."

"Promise." Jeez, thirty seconds ago she wanted to be with Bennett all the time, and now she'd brought up the professional boundary again. She made herself dizzy. How could Bennett possibly know what to expect?

"Here you go." Dylan offered her shirt to Bennett.

"Pink? Really?"

"It's a spare. Beggars can't be choosers." Bennett reached for the sweatshirt, but Dylan held it for a second. "One more thing. If you breathe a word about this to the family, I'm a dead woman. Understand?"

"Totally, sis. I got your back."

Dylan, her brown eyes so much like Bennett's it was disconcerting, looked to Kerstin for agreement. "I'm certainly not going to tell."

A few minutes later, with Bennett squeezed into Dylan's small pink sweatshirt, they were back at the Proximity with the design drawings and cost sheets spread across the bed. "Okay, Captain, start cutting."

Bennett eased her roller chair to the side of the bed and took the pages Kerstin offered. Her brown eyes shifted between the numbers and the plans, an adorable look of concentration on her face. She occasionally worried her bottom lip between her teeth or raked her fingers unconsciously through her short, gray-streaked hair. The simple things she noticed about Bennett, but not with anyone else, stirred her feelings again. She wanted to claim her full lips, to kiss her deeply until she begged for breath. Maybe working in her hotel room, on her bed, had been a bad decision.

"I've got a starting pla—" Bennett said, but stopped when she looked up at Kerstin. "Are you all right?"

"Sure. Why?"

"You're flushed and your eyes are, I don't know, sort of glazed over. Bored?"

Bennett's stare and the slight tilt of her head told Kerstin she had no chance of lying her way out of daydreaming. "Guess my mind wandered a bit. What were you saying?"

"I'd rather know what you were thinking. It looked far more interesting than number crunching."

"Maybe another time." And surprisingly, she meant it. She could hardly keep her hands off Bennett when they were so close, and Bennett was far too adept at reading women's nonverbal cues. "About the costs?"

Bennett pointed to one of the line items. "I think we can definitely cut the price of the locks. We don't need the biometric type you've budgeted. A keypad entry system would work fine. It's not Fort Knox."

"How about a card-swipe system? They're more secure, and if someone loses a card, we deactivate it and issue another."

"Cops are notorious for losing things, and the cost of cards will add up over time."

Kerstin considered the idea, ran a few calculations, and nodded. "Okay. Keypad it is. Good. What else?"

"Is there a less expensive option for the interior doors?"

"We could replace the more expensive fiberglass interior doors with 24-gauge metal at the security points. It's not quite as sturdy, but with cops on either side, if someone unauthorized is coming through, you guys can probably stop him." She grinned at Bennett.

"Can we leave the heavy metal exterior doors?"

"Sure." She made notes as they talked, pleased with their progress, and then studied her exterior plan again. "I can nix the fancy up-lighting for a simple spotlight focused on the name. And the letters don't have to be quite so thick. They'll stand out fine." She scribbled more changes in red ink in the margins.

"Did you include the cost differences between the canteen and the cafeteria on the original plans?"

Kerstin shook her head. "Good catch. I'd forgotten about that." She looked up again, and Bennett had taken her shoes off, propped her feet on the side of the bed, and had a smug grin on her face. "What?"

"You obviously love what you do. It's like I'm not even here."

The words washed over Kerstin, a wave of affirmation and acceptance. "Thank you. I think that's the indication you've found your passion, getting lost in it for hours, oblivious to the world around you. I do love it." She closed her notebook, rolled the drawings up, and placed them both in her bag. "Enough for tonight."

"Are we back on budget?"

"Probably not, but we won't be as far over. I'll check the landscaping totals tomorrow and make a few adjustments, which will help even more. I'm pleased with what we've done. And now, I think you've earned the dinner I promised. Do you want to go back to the hotel restaurant, out to another place, or…"

"I'm good with room service, if you are. I hate to admit it, but I'm a bit tired, and the less moving I have to do, the better."

"Room service it is." They negotiated their order, and Kerstin called it in. "They said it might take a while. There's a big conference here this week."

"I'm in no hurry, unless you want me to leave."

"Of course not. A promise is a promise."

Bennett's long legs were still perched on the side of her bed, her hands wrapped around her sides as if protecting her injury. Dylan's tight sweatshirt crept up her abdomen, exposing a small glimpse of flesh that teased Kerstin. She couldn't look away. The memory of her hands roaming over Bennett's skin, skimming below her waistband and lower, raised heat between her legs.

"If you don't stop looking at me like that…"

"I'm sorry."

"Seriously, Kerst?"

"Not at all. You can't blame a woman for admiring something beautiful." Kerstin grinned, and Bennett's face colored bright pink. "Are you embarrassed?"

"Maybe. I don't think of myself as beautiful, but I like that you do."

She debated going to Bennett, finally gave in, and knelt beside her chair, resting a hand on her leg. "I realize I'm giving you so many mixed messages, cold one minute and hot the next, but I can't keep my hands off you."

"You don't hear me complaining."

She rose on her knees and kissed the side of Bennett's mouth. "Maybe you should."

"Why?"

"Because this fling, tryst, whatever can't go anywhere, and you deserve more."

"I'm a big girl, and you've been honest. It's only sex." Bennett shifted from the chair to the bed, guiding Kerstin with her. "I'll take whatever you offer with no complaints."

"Should you be—"

"Enough *should*s. I want you, and I don't care if I pop every stitch. Just one thing."

"Name it." Kerstin swung her leg over Bennett and straddled her on the bed. She'd give Bennett whatever she wanted this time, and Bennett knew it.

Bennett cupped Kerstin's ass and urged her closer. "I'm in charge. My side. We might have to take things a bit slower."

A tinge of something uncomfortable swelled into recognizable panic, but Kerstin nodded. Relinquishing even small decisions about her life practically gave her hives. Could she be vulnerable enough with Bennett to give up control? Did she want to try? Her urgent need for Bennett minutes earlier cooled a bit, something akin to performance anxiety gripping her. She hoped Bennett couldn't feel her apprehension. "Should I undress?"

"Let me take care of you. Relax. Can you do that for me?" Her voice dropped to a husky timbre, sending goose bumps across Kerstin's skin. Bennett placed her hands—once rough from volleyball and the outdoors but now gentle and soft with the patience of a woman used to giving pleasure—on either side of Kerstin's face and forced eye contact. "I've got you."

Bennett raised her hands inches above the surface of the skin and moved her fingers, slowly tracing the contours of her face, so close Kerstin felt their warmth and ached for their physical touch. Bennett raked her fingers in front of Kerstin's eyes, across her nose, and stopped at her mouth. Kerstin moistened her lips, praying for Bennett's mouth on hers.

"Your breath is so hot and fast. Do you like this?"

She swallowed hard. Did she like being teased, controlled, and wound up until she exploded? "I'm…not sure."

"Maybe you need more convincing. I'm going to kiss you now."

She didn't like kissing during sex. Kissing implied intimacy she didn't feel, but before she could say no, Bennett's mouth settled on hers and her objections vanished. Bennett traced the tip of her tongue lightly across Kerstin's lips, bringing a new level of heat. Kerstin opened to her, and Bennett's tongue entered gradually, explored her mouth, and toyed with her tongue before finally claiming her completely. A flash of desire spread from her center so quickly the force shocked Kerstin, and she released a soft cry.

Bennett pulled back, and Kerstin cupped her head, desperate to kiss her again. "Don't stop. I liked that…very much." The admission surprised her, but she was too aroused to analyze why. "More of that."

"Easy. Remember, I'm injured." Bennett kissed her lightly several times and each time pulled back. She fisted Kerstin's hair, tugged gently, licked a path along her throat and released, and then repeated the sequence until the tugs registered in her crotch and she grew wetter.

"Ben, please." She didn't beg during sex. Ever. Another light kiss. "Please."

Bennett traced her face again, moaning quietly as if they were already joined. "You're so wired I can feel you vibrating without touching you. So sexy."

"Ben…what are you doing to me?"

"Loving you." Bennett unbuttoned her blouse, one button a time, careful not to touch skin. She blew her breath across each patch of exposed flesh, driving Kerstin wild.

She rocked forward in Bennett's lap, signaling her need, but Bennett carefully peeled her blouse off her shoulders. The ambient air hit her skin and she shivered, surprised by the coolness. "Touch me?"

"Soon." Sliding her index fingers between Kerstin's bra straps and the dip of her shoulders, Bennett eased each down. "Slip your arms out." Kerstin started to jerk her arms free, but Bennett said, "Slowly. We're not in a hurry."

"You might not be, but I'm dying here."

"Unfasten your bra for me."

She did as instructed and cupped her exposed breasts, offering them to Bennett. Instead, she blew her hot breath against each breast and then sucked in the air around it, cooling her nipple and making it pucker and ache.

"Oh…my…God, Ben."

"Do you like that?"

She nodded.

"Tell me."

"I *really* like it, but I need to be touched." Imagining Bennett's skillful hands replacing her perfectly executed breaths turned her insides liquid. She was so wet she was certain Bennett could feel it through her clothes. How was it possible to be so turned on by someone breathing on her? Was she simply excited by a new experience or by

Bennett? She rolled her pelvis forward, desperate for contact, but Bennett pulled back.

"Are you ready, Kerst?"

"So ready."

"Unzip your jeans for me."

Kerstin was quick and started to work her body out of the confining clothes.

"Leave them on."

"But I want to feel you."

"You will." Bennett folded Kerstin's jeans aside, twisted her finger in the band of her bikinis, and pulled up.

"Ohhhh, yes." She rocked back and forth, enjoying the pressure of the fabric against her. "Good."

"I'm going to touch you now, Kerst."

"Yes."

Bennett slid her hand into Kerstin's jeans and stroked her. "You really are wet."

"I want you, now."

"Right now?"

Kerstin opened her eyes and stared at Bennett's smiling lips. "This second." She grabbed Bennett's wrist and shoved it farther into her jeans.

Bennett entered her and pressed the heel of her palm against Kerstin's clit. She rose on her knees and stretched backward, giving Bennett as much room as possible to maneuver. "That's it. Like that." She pumped up and down on Bennett's hand, the sensation almost driving her to immediate orgasm.

"Slow down, Kerst. I want to enjoy this as long as possible."

"Can't…slow…down." She panted each word, unable to stop her building climax. "Let me…go. *Please*, Ben."

Bennett leaned forward and captured Kerstin's breast between her lips, sucking her nipple in time with her thrusting fingers. Kerstin lost it. She pulled Bennett deeper as she trembled and her insides turned molten. Continuous waves of pleasure swept through her until she could barely breathe. The spiraling slowed, but Bennett wound her up again, sending her to another screaming orgasm.

They completely undressed and went several more rounds before she finally whispered, "St…op."

"You actually want me to stop?" Bennett slowly slid up Kerstin's body and pulled her into a hug. She kissed Kerstin's forehead and brushed a few strands of damp hair off her face.

"I need to breathe."

"Relax." Bennett wrapped her arms tighter around her. "And thank you."

"For what?"

"Giving yourself to me."

Kerstin was still gasping for breath, her heart pounding hard against her chest. Was that what she'd done? No, she'd had sex, great sex, but still only sex, right? She didn't have such intense or prolonged orgasms with others, nor did she feel so satisfied or such a sense of belonging. She wanted to examine why, to understand what made this encounter different, what Bennett's words meant, but she resisted, content in her pleasure and the feel of Bennett's arms around her.

CHAPTER TWENTY

Before daybreak the next morning, Bennett eased out of Kerstin's arms and gently covered her with a blanket. She sat on the bed watching the delicate rise and fall of Kerstin's chest and listening to the steady cadence of her breathing. Her blond hair cascaded around her head on the pillow, a halo highlighting a satisfied face. She wouldn't forget the way Kerstin's fingers threaded through her hair when they kissed, the subtle darkening of her blue eyes when aroused, or the way she arched backward and flushed as she came. The image of Kerstin climaxing, her body first tense and then in release, replaced the bathrobe vision as Bennett's favorite.

Kerstin's skin was so silky. She responded to Bennett's kisses urgently, hungrily seeking more. Kerstin's touch and scent still lingered on Bennett's body and in her nostrils. Though her injury limited vigorous activities, she'd enjoyed making love to Kerstin more than she imagined possible. She carefully studied Kerstin's nude body, memorizing every detail, unsure if she'd have the opportunity again.

She dressed and debated writing a note, but what would she say? *Thanks for the sex. Let's do it again sometime. See you at work. I don't want this to be casual.* Nothing made sense until the last possibility. She didn't want her night with Kerstin to be just a spontaneous romp. Their relationship didn't feel casual before, and after having sex with her again, it certainly didn't now.

Leaving without saying anything wasn't her style and didn't feel right either, but Kerstin had left her asleep the first time. Maybe that was her way of keeping things simple, so she followed Kerstin's example. As she walked toward the door, part of her remained with Kerstin, where she belonged. Only one thing was powerful enough to pull her away.

Bennett stopped on the street outside the Green Hill Cemetery behind the Ma Rolls van. Two stone pillars connected by an arched wrought-iron sign marked the entrance to the fifty-one-acre garden-style cemetery. Her grandfather and father were buried here in a circular family plot with enough space for the entire family. She got out of her car, and G-ma and Mama exited the van.

"Morning, Ben." Mama gave her a big hug and looked her over. "Everything all right?"

"Cheeks are a bit rosy," G-ma said and grinned. "Sweatshirt's a little small for you."

"I'm fine. Where's everybody else?" Picnic breakfast at the cemetery on the anniversary of the deaths of Garrett and Bryce Carlyle was another family tradition. Today they'd honor her grandfather, killed so many years ago that Bennett barely remembered him.

"They'll be along." Mama opened the back of the van and handed her the familiar checked tablecloth. "That's heavy enough for you today. The others can help with the rest."

As she walked toward the entrance, Simon, Stephanie, and the kids drove up, followed by Jazz and Dylan. "Help Mama with the folding chairs and baskets?" The family pitched in, and a few minutes later, breakfast sandwiches, coffee, juice, and fruit adorned the tablecloth.

Dylan handed her a coffee and whispered, "How's the side?"

"I'm good. Thanks. I owe you."

"No problem." She leaned in closer and whispered, "FYI, everybody knows you didn't come home last night. See what I mean about needing space?"

"Great."

G-ma stretched her arms out to the side, and they joined hands around the food in front of G-pa's headstone. "Dylan, I believe it's your turn to say a few words, if you will."

Dylan nodded and looked around at the family for a few seconds before speaking. "Papa died before I was born, but I feel like I know him through the stories you guys tell. I know he loved his family, his job, and his community. He left a legacy of dedication and commitment we live by still. We love you and miss you, Papa."

G-ma wiped a tear from the corner of her eye, kissed her fingers, and pressed them against the stone. "Love you, honey."

"Let's eat." Simon grabbed two paper plates and placed a sandwich and some chopped fruit on each before passing one to Ryan and Riley.

They ate for the next hour and told stories of Papa's shenanigans while wooing G-ma, the birth of their son, and his adventures on the force. They laughed more often than cried, and that was the way Garrett would've wanted it, according to G-ma.

Jazz helped Bennett pack the van for Mama and waved as she drove away. "I love this family so much, Ben. I'd probably be dead if Mama and Pa hadn't taken me in."

They bumped shoulders and walked toward their cars. "And we wouldn't be complete without you. Some jealous lover would've probably killed me years ago if you hadn't had my back. You've always been a good fit."

"Speaking of lovers, where were you last night? Your car wasn't out front when I came in from work around two and wasn't there this morning. Something you need to tell me?"

"Not a thing." Her big smile was all Jazz needed to reach her own conclusion.

"I see how it is. You finally sleep with the woman you've been hot for—exactly how long has it been—and you don't want to share? It's okay for you to set me up and pry into my love life, but I can't do the same?" Jazz's kidding told Bennett she cared without seriously prying.

Bennett propped against the side of Jazz's car and shrugged. "You know how it is." They occasionally shared vague tidbits about a tryst, but not specifics. They were both too principled. And if the *right* woman came along, everything was off-limits unless shared in the strictest confidence while seeking advice.

"Yeah, I do, and I'm happy for you. I hope things work out." She gave Bennett a hug. "See you at the station later?"

"You bet." She watched Jazz drive down Wharton Street toward Battleground and hoped the same thing.

❖

Kerstin stretched her arms and legs languidly across the big bed, enjoying the loose feel of her muscles and the sense of peace inside.

She'd slept soundly, woke relaxed and something else, happy perhaps. Bennett had made love to her, intimately, sensually, completely, and she'd melted in a series of powerful orgasms. She turned toward the last spot she'd seen Bennett. Kerstin hungered for her again, but the only evidence of Bennett was an impression of her head in the pillow. Kerstin's stomach seized and she was suddenly tense again.

"Ben?" She glanced toward the bathroom, the open door and dark room confirming what she suspected. She checked the nightstand for a note. Why had Bennett left without a word? Hypocrite, but she was more upset about being deserted than she cared to admit.

Now she understood how other women felt after she bolted from their beds like a freed animal. She shook her head. She'd been honest with those other women going in that she only wanted sex, and Bennett knew as well. Didn't she? Why shouldn't she leave and avoid the awkward morning-after? Kerstin accepted the logic, but Bennett's departure still stung, and her body still ached. Grabbing Bennett's pillow, she inhaled her distinctive scent combined with sweat and sex, and the ache worsened. Did she simply crave sex, or had Bennett somehow weakened her and touched a part she'd kept inviolate for years?

Kerstin flung the pillow and bolted from the comfortable nest of sheets and blankets Bennett had tucked around her, suddenly feeling too domestic and tame. She glanced at the clock as she approached the coffeepot and diverted to the bathroom. In her sexually sated daze, she'd overslept and completely missed the alarm. "Snap out of it, Anthony. It was *just* sex."

She took a quick shower, but the washing reminded her of Bennett's hands on her body. Switching the temperature between hot and cold, she tried shock treatment to zap her back into work mode. No luck. "This is not happening to me." She wasn't ready to examine the specific definition of *this*.

She donned a pair of sweats and settled at the corner desk, determined to finish the cost estimates. She pounded the calculator, made computer adjustments, and printed a clean copy of the changes. With her feet propped on the desk, she read over everything, pleased she and Bennett had reduced the overages to only two thousand dollars. Good enough. She reached for her phone to share the news, but before she could dial, it vibrated in her hand.

"Hello?"

"Ms. Anthony?"

"Yes."

"This is Chief Ashton's office. He asked me to notify you the meeting scheduled for tomorrow with the full building committee has been rescheduled for Monday at the same time. Chief Ashton and Chip Armstrong have been called away on a budget retreat."

Kerstin dropped the papers on the table. Another damn delay, city government at its finest. "Thank you for the call." Now what? Five days to do nothing. If she stayed in Greensboro, she'd go stir-crazy in her hotel room or give in and eventually have sex with Bennett again. Neither option was a good one. She needed a break from the slow pace of this town and a return to the familiar, to the places and things that made her feel in charge of her life again. She fired up her computer and booked an afternoon flight back to New York.

She quickly packed her bag and tapped out a text to Bennett.

Budget revised. Looks good. Going home. C U at meeting Monday.

❖

At the airport bathroom in New York, Kerstin changed into black jeans, boots, and a white silk blouse. Nothing said prowling lesbian like black and white, especially at her favorite hangout, Cubbyhole. Slipping into her black jacket, she inhaled the deep, rich smell of leather she associated with recklessness and danger. She slid her hands over the soft buttery finish and checked the pockets for her club kit: two condoms and a dental dam. After hailing a cab, she stopped by her mother's building and dropped off her bag, securing the concierge's silence with a couple of crisp twenty-dollar bills, and then headed to the West End. She wouldn't make it in time for happy hour, but Wednesday was whiskey night, and though she wasn't a big whiskey drinker, with enough mixers she could manage, and she'd get a quick buzz.

The taxi dropped her a block from the building, and she walked across the cobblestones to the green corner building, its paint peeling from trapped summer heat and bitter winter storms. People were already overflowing into the street, and she found the anonymity of the crowd comforting. Loud voices and the smell of spilled beer and cigarettes wafted in the air as she got closer. When she entered, the small space closed around her, making her feel welcome. The ceiling decor, which included everything from paper lanterns, rainbow flags, and lights to leftover decorations from St. Patrick's Day, the Fourth of July, Easter, and Thanksgiving, added a cheerful element.

She squeezed in beside two young women and shouted to the bartender, "Whiskey and Coke with a lime, heavy on the Coke, please." Her drink arrived, and she slid a ten across the counter for the five-dollar drink and faced the crowd. Cubby had a reputation as a trendy, intimate hangout for the area's diverse population, welcoming gay, straight, and everything in between and beyond.

Oldies from the jukebox and singing patrons made conversation difficult, but she wasn't here to talk. She found security among the throng of people searching for the same things—closeness without intimacy, connection without commitment—mosquito lovers, she called them, one taste and release. Here, she expected superficiality and got what she wanted. She took a swig of her drink, forced the bitter liquid down, and scanned the room. On the second pass, she spotted a dark-haired, sporty baby dyke in the corner staring back at her. She finished her whiskey and raised the empty glass in the woman's direction.

As her target walked toward her, Kerstin admired the way she elbowed a path confidently but gently through the crowd. Black hair shaved close on the sides with a longer swath falling across her forehead topped her stocky build. The woman stopped in front of her, and Kerstin boldly finished her inspection: muscular chest and arms, small breasts with no bra, tight T-shirt, low-rise jeans, and a jean jacket. Yummy.

"I'm Dale. Can I buy you another drink?"

Her voice was higher than she'd expected, nothing like Bennett's husky one. "Stop it."

"Sorry?"

"Nothing."

"Good, because I thought you said stop, and I haven't even started yet." She gave Kerstin a slow visual from head to toe and settled on her breasts. "You're hot."

"Thanks." Not a great conversationalist, but again, not here to talk. This was going better and much faster than she'd hoped. One more drink. "Whiskey and Coke with lime, please."

Dale ordered two drinks, paid, and nodded toward the back of the club. Kerstin was content to let her lead for the time being, hoping they wanted the same thing. Dale cocked her leg against the wall and leaned back, and Kerstin straddled it and slid up.

"Nice. Come here often?" Dale asked.

Kerstin shook her head. "I'm not that girl."

Dale smiled, and her dark eyes sought Kerstin's mouth. "So there's no misunderstanding, what girl?"

"The one who needs small talk."

"What about foreplay?"

"Seriously overrated." Kerstin slid her crotch along Dale's leg again.

"Kissing?"

"Not the first time."

Dale encircled Kerstin's waist and pulled her close. "How about fucking?"

"Perfect. Do you live nearby?" The scene playing out in her mind teemed with dominance, getting off, and walking away, and her body vibrated.

"No, but I have an SUV parked down the street. Is that too high school?"

"It'll do, but not another word about high school. Got it?" She hadn't had sex in a vehicle ever, but she wasn't letting location interfere with her plan. Besides, people in the city didn't care what you did on the street as long as you didn't block their front stoop or the door of their favorite coffee shop.

She ran her hand up Dale's leg, producing a needy moan she craved. "One more drink for the road?" She wanted to be a tad drunker so she wouldn't notice the slight similarities between Dale and Bennett's appearances. Her goal was to forget, not to fuck a surrogate.

They finished their third round, and Kerstin grabbed Dale's belt and pulled her out the door and into the street. "Which way?"

Dale pointed down Twelfth Street. "Red Escalade ESV."

The power of control layered with sexual arousal ignited inside Kerstin. She was in charge for the first time since—nope, not going there. She stopped beside the vehicle Dale indicated. "This thing is huge."

"Bought it for the extra-long body and tinted windows. I put the seats down, and it's party central in there." She climbed in, and a few seconds later the entire back of the vehicle was an adult play space.

"Impressive. Get in and take your clothes off." The inside reeked with the cloying scent of lemon air freshener, but Kerstin focused on the prize.

Dale eyed her before complying. "You weren't kidding about foreplay."

"I'm sort of a control freak."

"Figured that out already, and you don't hear me complaining."

"*You don't hear me complaining.*" Bennett had said the same thing before she scooped Kerstin up and settled her across her lap in bed. *Get out of my head, Bennett Carlyle.* Kerstin climbed into the back of Dale's vehicle and closed the door, determined to return to the familiar. This woman wouldn't tell her what to do, restrict her actions, bring her to multiple orgasms, or rock her into a satisfied sleep in the comfort of her arms. *She* would control this scenario, and *she* would decide when or if she came. End of story.

"Hey, you still with me?" Dale was on her knees in front of Kerstin, her torso bare and her jeans pushed around her ankles behind her.

"I'm so with you." She needed exactly this, a woman with no connection to the past, raging hormones, willing to be dominated, and no agenda other than to get laid.

Dale crawled closer and touched the side of Kerstin's face. "You really are beautiful."

Kerstin slapped her hand away. "No touching unless I tell you. Understand?"

Dale raised her hands and waited.

"Down on all fours." Dale's response was immediate, and Kerstin thrilled at the power and safety from confusing emotions and worries about intimacy. None required. Dale's smooth back and the swell of her ass beckoned, awaited whatever whim Kerstin chose.

And suddenly a flash of memory stopped Kerstin—Bennett in the same position, moaning her pleasure. Kerstin draped over her back, fingers buried inside her. She couldn't do the same thing to another woman that she'd enjoyed with Bennett. She considered other variations but got the same result. Kerstin shivered from a combination of fiery anger and cold sweat. Her go-to attitude adjustment failed, and she was pissed. "I can't do this."

Dale turned and looked over her shoulder. "What?"

"I'm sorry." She opened the back door, jumped out, and ran.

The next night Kerstin returned to the Cubbyhole, determined to regain control of her life and her favorite pastime. She spotted a tall, busty, femme blonde, the physical opposite of Bennett, in the crowd and winked at her. That's all it took.

The woman weaved a slow, deliberately evocative path through the crowd, lightly touching patrons with her hands or brushing up against them until she stopped in front of Kerstin. "Hi. I'm Candy."

"Of course you are."

Candy's white designer dress dipped low on her large breasts and rose high on her shapely thighs. The package didn't really turn Kerstin on like a hot butch would've, but she could do variety. "Want a drink?"

"I'm good. Had a little something earlier." Candy touched the side of her nose with her forefinger, the sign for snorting cocaine. "Let's get comfortable."

"Sure." Kerstin followed Candy to the back of the bar into a quieter room with low, cushioned benches.

Kerstin dropped onto the soft surface with her back against the wall and motioned for Candy to sit beside her.

Instead Candy spread her legs and made a show of inching the hem of her dress higher, exposing flesh all the way up. She straddled Kerstin's lap and hooked her hands behind Kerstin's neck. "I've got something for you, lover."

Kerstin's clit twitched, and she was immediately wet, her sexual responses automatic. But tonight she yearned for something else—different but the same—more tenderness, but controlled. "Why don't we talk for a bit first?"

"Who needs talk when you've got these babies? And they're real, not silicone." Candy grabbed her breasts and squeezed before scooting closer and grinding her pelvis into Kerstin's crotch.

"Wait." What was wrong with her? *Wait? Talk?* Those weren't part of her sexual vocabulary until…Bennett had ruined her. Having sex with a stranger wouldn't feel the same now. *She* wouldn't feel the same. Kerstin slid from under Candy. "This isn't going to work." She rushed to the door, Candy's angry voice gradually absorbed by the music.

Kerstin stood on the sidewalk outside the Cubbyhole and waited for a taxi. What was happening to her? She never turned down sex, until recently, and now twice in as many days. She returned to the same answer—Bennett Carlyle.

After thirty minutes with no cab in sight, she started walking. A couple of blocks over was a busier street with a better chance of hailing a ride, but still no luck. She'd forgotten about the large tech security conference in the city and strolled three more blocks to the subway entrance, but it looked like a hobo convention. She kept walking, trying to flag down a cab until she was back at Central Park in front of her mother's building.

She dropped onto her bed without getting undressed and fell asleep immediately. When she woke the next morning before daylight, she was rested, clearheaded, and not hungover. She'd slept all night for the first time since Bennett had held her after sex.

As she dressed for her early flight back to Greensboro, she stopped in front of her bathroom mirror and stared at her reflection. Pick-up sex didn't work for her any longer. It didn't get her high, make her forget, or make her feel powerful or safe. But if pick-up sex didn't work, how was she going to control her stress, her life?

Chapter Twenty-one

Bennett rolled the lint brush up the front of her uniform, across her back, and down her arms for the second time, finally satisfied with the result. The full building-committee meeting started in half an hour, and she'd finally see Kerstin again. Four days since she'd left her stretched across her hotel room bed, a sated look on her sleeping face. Four days that seemed like months. She'd played the casual lover, but leaving went against her grain. As she drove downtown to the city building, she mentally chanted, sex, sex, only sex, but the words magnified her desire for something more meaningful and enduring with Kerstin.

She entered the lobby, and Kerstin stood in front of the information desk wearing a burgundy skirt, which brushed her knees, a matching jacket with stand-up collar, and a cream-colored scoop-neck shell. Bennett almost tripped over a magazine rack as she approached her. Kerstin's shoulders were rigid, her posture square, and she kneaded her neck with her fingers. Bennett took a deep breath. "Good morning. Are you ready for this?"

Kerstin slowly glanced up but didn't make eye contact. The pulse point at her neck pounded rapidly. "Yes. Are you?"

"I'm always ready." Bennett noticed dark circles under Kerstin's blue eyes and a washed-out pallor to her skin. "You look tired. Are you okay?"

"I'm fine."

Kerstin was unsettled and restless in a way Bennett hadn't seen. Something significant gnawed at her, even if she wasn't willing to admit it. "Your mother?"

"She's good too." Kerstin's lips pressed together in a tight line. "I think we did a great job with the cost cuts. The committee should be pleased, and once we get the go-ahead, the full work crews can return."

Bennett wanted to talk, to ask all her questions, but Kerstin had shifted to business mode. Nothing she said would change things between them anyway. Kerstin made the rules, and she abided by them, like it or not. "Shall we go in?" She held the door, and Kerstin passed, sucking in a breath as she brushed her in the doorway. Her flowery-citrus perfume coaxed a moan up Bennett's throat that she released as a choked cough.

They walked into the chief's conference room, and the five men huddled around a coffeepot quieted as they approached. Chief Ashton joined the usual committee consisting of the city architect, planner, public works, and Chip Armstrong, the manager's rep.

Armstrong shook hands with Bennett, then touched Kerstin's elbow and escorted her to a seat. "Can I get you coffee, Ms. Anthony?" He didn't offer any to Bennett.

"No thanks."

Chief Ashton nodded to Bennett. "Let's get started. I'm sure everybody has other things on their agenda this morning. Captain Carlyle, will you or Ms. Anthony be updating us?"

"I will," Kerstin said before Bennett could answer. "Since the focus is primarily architectural changes that affect the budget." She passed a stack of papers to her left and waited until everyone had a copy before starting her briefing.

Bennett watched, her chest puffed out, as Kerstin outlined the new items on their budget proposal, her voice strong and confident. She made eye contact with each committee member as she talked, except Bennett.

"I'll let Captain Carlyle field that question," Kerstin said.

"I'm sorry?" At least she was staring down at the papers when Kerstin called on her. "Repeat the question."

Chip Armstrong pointed to an item. "Why gun lockers in a noncustodial facility?"

"Safety. We don't have the luxury of arresting only one suspect at a time, and the entryway into the interrogation rooms is quite narrow. We don't want armed officers interacting with suspects in such a confined space. If the officers secure their weapons in the lockers, they're safer and so are the suspects and other officers calling in reports or turning in evidence nearby."

"Makes sense." Armstrong glanced across the table at Kerstin. "Good job."

Chief Ashton smiled at Bennett and addressed Kerstin. "And you're confident these changes represent your final figures?"

"Unless we encounter something entirely unexpected."

"Where is the construction process right now?" the chief asked.

"Framing for the new walls is in place, and the builders start electrical and drywall this week. We should still finish on time."

"Excellent, because we absolutely can't afford any more problems or delays."

"A two-thousand-dollar overage isn't bad, Chief," Armstrong said. "I'm sure you'll find that in your discretionary budget."

"No doubt. So, we agree the project can move forward?" Chief Ashton looked around the table as the other committee members gave their consent. "Okay. Let's get going. Thanks for your hard work, Ms. Anthony and Captain Carlyle. We're adjourned."

Bennett spoke to the chief for a few minutes and looked around for Kerstin. Chip Armstrong had her pinned in a corner. Their eyes met for the first time today, and Kerstin pleaded for help. She walked over and offered her hand. "We should get going."

Kerstin accepted her gesture without hesitation, and Bennett felt they became the only two people in the room. Their hands slid together and fingers entwined as if they touched this way every day. Bennett's pulse drummed in her ears, and her breath came in quick bursts. The slow burn of arousal always lingering below the surface for Kerstin flared. She wanted her. Now. As soon as they exited the chief's complex and entered the lobby, Bennett released Kerstin's hand, afraid of what she'd do if they remained connected a minute longer.

"Thanks for backing me up in there and for the save," Kerstin said.

"We're a team." She couldn't look at Kerstin without blurting her feelings. "Now I have to go." If Kerstin wanted her to stay, Bennett wouldn't be able to go. If she wanted her to leave, Bennett would be devastated. She made the only choice that would respect Kerstin's boundaries and maintain her own dignity. She fast-walked toward the door.

❖

Kerstin stared as Bennett retreated, shocked by how viscerally she'd responded to her touch and relieved she didn't have to explain. But why was Bennett so eager to leave? Bennett Carlyle didn't shy away from challenges. Kerstin was the runner. She ran from conflict, from commitment, and most of all from intimacy and the possibility of love. She'd spent five days in New York hiding and avoiding. A third visit to the bar had produced the same result as the first two. When she wasn't thinking about how thoroughly Bennett satisfied her, she puzzled over the state of her life if her mother continued to improve and eventually moved to Florida. She'd barely eaten and slept little, until last night after she walked over two miles. The only productive thing she'd done was plan for this meeting. Now what?

The future she'd designed so perfectly blurred in her mind, complicated by factors out of her control—her mother's health, completion of the substation, Bennett, and now her own conflicted feelings. Kerstin pored over the potential of a relationship with Bennett like a spreadsheet she could analyze and reach a logical conclusion. She'd returned to Greensboro after her self-imposed exile only slightly less confused about her next step than when she left. She made her way to the parking deck, pleased with the outcome of the meeting and determined to concentrate on her job instead of things she couldn't control.

She drove by the Parks and Recreation building slowly to make sure Bennett's car wasn't there before parking in the substation lot. At least Bennett wouldn't be around stirring up traitorous emotions while Kerstin steered the project back on track. As she walked through the building looking for Henry, she inspected the framing for the new walls, satisfied the spaces appeared roomy for the intended purposes.

"Henry, are you here?" Several flashes of light from the canteen area guided her to where he stood with two other workers. "Good morning, everyone. The committee approved the new budget, so we're good to go."

The two men with Henry looked at the floor but didn't speak. Henry removed his hard hat and scratched his head. "Maybe not so good to go."

"What now?" The look on Henry's face was like a vise squeezing the breath out of her, draining her of her purpose and future.

"We removed these windows and found some wiring not up to spec." He directed a large work light on the exposed studs and wiring. "See?"

She leaned closer and examined the new wires running through the studs to an outlet box. "What? Looks fine to me."

"Not according to your draft specifications. Guidelines for the use of federal funds on construction projects require American products only. These wires are not only a lower gauge than you specified, but they're also foreign made."

"Oh, God." Kerstin placed a hand against the wall, her body suddenly hot and weak. She'd assured the committee of the project's soundness and timeliness less than an hour ago. An image of the substation and her career flushing down a huge toilet with Made in China stamped on the side played through her mind. Had Gilbert Early known about the inferior wiring? Somebody had ordered the subpar items. Maybe she'd just quit too, but being like Gilbert Early in any respect was so distasteful she rejected the idea immediately.

The three men were staring at her, obviously waiting for direction.

"Does this affect the old wiring?" She needed confirmation.

"If the current system is up to code, only the new subpar wiring is a problem. But if we uncover wiring that isn't up to current code, the whole system has to be updated."

"Is the wiring all? I mean is everything else up to par?"

"I honestly don't know," Henry said. "We just found this. We'll have to stop work, go through your plans, and double-check every item already installed."

"How long will the check take?" Her nausea worsened and she needed fresh air.

"A couple of days should be enough." Henry didn't need to remind her that a violation of federal building codes was a criminal offense. "We can't work until we've cleared this up."

"And I wouldn't ask you to, Henry. I couldn't condone putting people's lives at risk because of faulty wiring or violating federal regulations." Her mind whirled with other necessary changes. "I'll need new estimates on all the electrics, at least three. The new supplies will cost more. Could you suggest a few names since you're local?"

"I'll get the estimates, if you want me to. It'll keep me busy while the guys check the specs."

"I'd appreciate that. Thanks, Henry. If you need me, call." She kept her voice steady. These men depended on her to know what she was doing and to keep her shit together.

Her mind whirling, she forced herself to walk casually toward the front of the building. How would she tell Bennett and the committee about this latest setback? New electrical work meant more money. The financial situation could make or break the project, but using foreign-made products in a government contract could destroy the firm and her reputation. Who knew about the subpar products, and when? The list of consequences stacked up in her mind, a guillotine about to decapitate her dreams. She could be barred from federally funded projects, charged with filing false claims for payment, and possibly even embezzlement.

She burst through the outside door and ran to the picnic table, clinging to the top to steady herself. Roaring in her head blocked all sound except the thunderous pounding of her pulse. Her emotions had been raw for days, and this discovery doused them with vinegar. She closed her eyes and fought rising panic, forcing herself to breathe evenly. Her pulse slowly returned to normal, and the roaring stopped. She opened her eyes and sat down at the table.

She had faced professional challenges before, but not with her personal life in such turmoil. She needed stability and security, not chaos and emotional upheaval. "I can do this." She attempted to reassure herself.

"I'm sure of it." Bennett's husky voice was unmistakable.

Kerstin wiped her face, realizing for the first time she'd been crying. Giving herself a few extra seconds to regain her composure, she grabbed the seat on either side of her and squeezed. She finally looked up into Bennett's eyes, and tears threatened again. "Go away."

Bennett knelt beside her on the grass. "What's wrong, Kerst?"

"Plea—se, leave…me alone."

"I…can't." Her voice cracked. "I can't leave you upset. Let me help."

"Nothing you can do."

"I'm willing to die trying."

The sincerity of Bennett's words released another round of tears. "Don't say that."

"Why not? It's true." She urged Kerstin's hands from the bench. "Come with me."

"Where?"

"Let's get away for a few minutes. See something beautiful."

"I shouldn't leave the site, in case Henry needs me." She should tell Bennett about the wiring issue. They were partners, and she deserved to know, but she couldn't, not right now.

"Henry has your number."

Kerstin rose slowly and walked beside Bennett across the lawn to her car. Their joined hands again produced powerful energy she couldn't deny. Why Bennett's touch and no other? Why now? They pulled away from the station, and Kerstin asked, "Where are we going?"

"You'll see." Bennett drove in silence down Cornwallis Drive to Lawndale and north toward the city limits. She turned into the Lake Brandt marina, past the rental shack, and stopped between two trees with a magnificent view of the lake. "Do you remember this spot?"

"We took a joy ride in my parents' car one Sunday afternoon and ended up here. It's as beautiful as I remember. The lake is like glass, reflecting the trees and fall colors on the other side." She turned sideways in her seat. "Why are we here, Ben?"

"You needed a break. Can you tell me why you were so upset?"

She shook her head. Another opportunity for honesty and she balked. Coward.

"When you're ready." Bennett stared at the water and raked her fingers through her hair. "I brought you here for another reason too. I want to talk without interruptions."

Bennett's shoulders were tight and the muscles along her arms rigid from gripping the steering wheel. Whatever she wanted to talk about seemed serious. Did Kerstin want to know? Her answer only took a second. Yes, more than anything. "Talk."

Bennett faced her and held out her hands, an unspoken invitation.

Kerstin took a deep breath and reached out, placing more than her hands in Bennett's care. "I'm listening."

"I'm a coward."

Kerstin winced, the word striking a place full of insecurity and her own weakness. "What? You've never backed away from anything." Bennett's whiskey-brown eyes zeroed in on hers, unwavering.

"I left you in bed, alone, after we had sex. I ran out this morning after the meeting."

"It's okay, Bennett."

"No, it's really not. I've held back so much, afraid to say what I feel, afraid of being honest with you."

Kerstin couldn't stand the anguish in Bennett's voice, knowing her crime was as great, if not greater. "I should probably tell you something too."

Bennett's mouth quirked into a mischievous grin. "Remember what we used to do?"

Kerstin nodded.

Bennett squeezed her hands. "I'll count to three, and we blurt it out. Agreed?" She nodded again, and Bennett continued. "One, two, three."

"The substation wiring is fucked up."

"I'm in love with you."

Chapter Twenty-two

"What?" Bennett dropped Kerstin's hands. Her body was numb and her mind fuzzy. *Kerstin is concerned about work.* Why did Bennett always reach for the impossible? She finally summoned the courage to glance at Kerstin, who looked as stunned as Bennett.

"You're…*in love* with me?"

She hesitated, but her heart demanded the truth. "Totally. And I'm tired of playing cool, being casual, or whatever people do who don't really care about each other. Hit-and-run isn't my style. I hated waking up in the cottage without you. And I really hated leaving you alone in your hotel room."

"Why did you?"

"My family. We meet at the cemetery on the dates of my grandfather and father's deaths for a quick breakfast. And I thought you wanted me to leave."

"I see."

She waited for Kerstin to elaborate, but she stared out across the lake. By admitting her love, Bennett had emotionally slit her wrists and was bleeding to death. Her pain and disappointment demanded a retreat to safety. She adopted one of Kerstin's coping tactics—work. "What about the wiring?"

Kerstin's eyes misted, and she brushed a tear with the back of her hand. "Apparently, Gil used subpar supplies, a violation of federal guidelines and a criminal offense." A tear slid down her cheek. "Henry found the problem this morning."

Bennett rolled down her window and sat quietly watching small waves splash against the lakeshore. Kerstin's news mingled with hers and shuffled through her mind in bullet points. She'd declared her love. Another work stoppage. An unhappy chief. Nothing from Kerstin about her declaration. More evaluations. No idea how Kerstin feels. New supplies equal budget increase. All her professional and personal vulnerabilities floated around her, out in the open. She tried to shrug off her feelings, telling herself she couldn't lose something she never had. *Focus on work.* "Any idea about the financial cost for the upgrades?"

"Henry is getting estimates. I didn't know Gil sidestepped the regulations. I should've double-checked his supply list along with the design. My assumptions could cost me this project and have some unpleasant consequences for both our careers. I can't tell you how sorry I am."

Kerstin touched Bennett's arm and she flinched, the connection quicker and sharper than any weapon. "It's not about my career right now, but I don't want the chief, the department, and the officers to be disappointed." She couldn't concentrate on work, but could she risk returning to her feelings? She had to. She needed answers. "What about *us*?"

"This isn't the time for—"

"It's exactly the time, Kerstin. Pretending is not who I am. I'm in love with you."

Kerstin looked at her again, her face twisted in a combination of pain and confusion. "But we don't even know each other anymore. We're not the same people we were in high school. How can you—"

"Life taught me not to bypass what I want if I know it's right. Can you honestly say you don't feel anything for me?"

Kerstin studied her hands before answering. "No, I can't, but this…us…can't work, and you know why."

Had she misheard? She was no longer willing to assume or accept vague responses. "Are you saying you have feelings for me too?"

Kerstin placed her hand over Bennett's where it rested on her thigh. "Of course I do. I've given you mixed messages since I got back because I've denied my feelings and run from them, but I can't really leave them. I also can't turn my back on the commitment I've made to my family. You of all people should understand."

Bennett's heart hammered, and she choked down an urge to shout. Kerstin wasn't offering her a clear path, but there was hope. Looking back, she'd often dreamed of a do-over with Kerstin. "Things change,

Kerst. Don't rule us out yet. We'll face whatever happens with the project and our lives together, like we tag-teamed the committee this morning."

"I don't know if I can. I've been in denial for so long, not just about my feelings for you but feelings in general. Intimacy terrifies me."

"Trust me, and let's take it one day at a time."

"I'll try, but no promises. This whole emotions and trust thing will take some getting used to." Kerstin slid across the seat, rested her head on Bennett's shoulder, and placed her hand across Bennett's heart. "Will you do something for me now?"

"Name it."

"Hold me. Just hold me. I feel like I'm unraveling."

Bennett wrapped her arms around Kerstin and reclined the seat so they could still see the water. "If you do, I'll put you back together." The moment, with Kerstin so close, was right. She still wanted to hear Kerstin say those three words, but it would have to be on her timeline. As she watched the waves lap lazily against the shore, an old insecurity crept in. *Please let me be enough for her this time.*

❖

Kerstin nuzzled closer to Bennett, inhaling the scent of her. "I feel safe with you." The truth of her statement astonished her as much as Bennett's declaration of love. She did feel safe and, more surprisingly, didn't have the slightest urge to run or control what was happening between them. The tension she usually carried in her shoulders faded, and she considered the future, possibilities, and happiness.

She kissed Bennett's cheek and down the side of her neck, savoring the mixture of sweat and tangy perfume, a recipe from the past that comforted her. As she listened to the steady rhythm of Bennett's breathing and the splashing water, her eyelids grew heavy and her worries slowly vanished.

Kerstin jerked awake to her cell phone ringing. She'd fallen asleep in Bennett's arms, the first restful sleep she'd had since they made love days ago. The afternoon sun had settled at the tops of the trees, bringing shadows and cooler temperatures. She punched the answer key, annoyed at the interruption. "Hello."

"What the hell is going on down there, Anthony?" Leonard Parrish's loud voice forced her to hold the phone away from her ear.

"Sorry?"

"Damn right, you're sorry. Why aren't the guys working? And where is my check? I can't run a business on promises."

Kerstin considered her options: tell him the truth and give him a chance to cover his tracks if he was involved in the illegal activity or come up with a plausible excuse. She looked over and Bennett shook her head. "The building committee got our budget updates this morning." As if that really answered his question.

"And?"

"You know how governments operate. A dozen people are probably reviewing every tiny detail. And they're notoriously slow handing out money. Be patient."

Leonard mumbled something under his breath. "So, things are moving along?"

She formed an image of her and Bennett and imagined he'd asked about that. "Things are definitely moving along. I've got it under control, Boss." She didn't usually call him boss because he didn't behave like one, but maybe the address would throw him off.

"Okay, but get my damn check to me ASAP." He hung up without waiting for a response.

She slid her cell back into her pocket. "Pretend you didn't hear that. I lied big-time."

"Hear what?" Bennett kissed her hand. "I assume you have a plan for how to handle the subpar issue with him."

"Not yet, but I'll make one after I receive all the information. Then I'll confront him and find out if he and Gilbert conspired about the substitutions."

"Is this the same guy you said you'd never stood up to?"

"You don't forget much, do you?"

"Not about you."

"I hate to leave, but we should probably get back."

Bennett hugged and kissed her before reluctantly releasing her and starting the car. "Are you okay about earlier?"

"Not really. I'm totally freaked out because I'm not heading for the hills like I normally do. What's that even about?"

"I don't know, but I like it. Please don't run. I meant what I said. I love you, and we'll work things out as we go."

"I'm holding you to that, Carlyle. Now drive."

"Yes, ma'am."

"And one more thing. Don't ever leave me in bed again without saying good-bye. Understood?"

"Totally."

Maybe it was time to stop running in her professional life as well. If Parrish was involved in fraud, she'd have to be careful how she approached him. She wasn't quite ready to start her firm, but she might have to adjust her timetable. Right now, she wanted to keep him in the dark until she had all the facts and pray the city didn't shut the project down completely when she delivered the new delays and costs.

Chapter Twenty-three

Kerstin glanced at her cell beside her on the hotel desk, saw Bennett's ID, and pushed the answer key. Seven a.m., so she was probably on her way home after night shift. They'd communicated only by phone the past two days, and she'd started doubting the feelings Bennett expressed at the lake, thanks to her overactive insecurities. "Hey, stranger. How are you?"

"Missing you like crazy."

"Sure. You declare your love and then desert me."

"I'm really sorry. Night duty will be over as soon as Jazz returns from management training. Weird shifts are a reality of a relationship with a cop."

She smiled at the connection Bennett so easily assumed but couldn't resist kidding her because she missed her so much. "So we have a relationship now?" There was a long pause on the other end. "I'm kidding, Captain. Lighten up."

"You always keep me guessing."

"And you love that I'm not falling at your feet in adoration like other women." She warmed at Bennett's heartfelt laughter. "I miss you, and I need to touch you, soon."

"Sounds good to me. I'll be off this weekend. You going to New York?"

The tug of family responsibility and the specter of confronting her boss dampened her mood. "Actually, I have a flight later today. I need to find out the truth about my boss, and it could end my career."

"You've gotten the estimates?"

"Yeah, and they're not good. I'd like to go over them with you before I leave. Any chance of breakfast this morning?" She needed to look into Bennett's eyes before she left, to see her love one more time, for courage.

"Sure, if we can go around eight. The chief called me in. He's already heard about the problem. Apparently he and Henry go way back."

"Great. Still more problems for the project?"

"I'm not sure yet, but he's scheduled another full committee meeting on Friday with the mayor. We'll need to present a united front."

"I should be back in time, but I'm not sure how Leonard will take the news."

"Do you want me to come with you for backup? Not that you need me, but I'm certainly available and willing."

Bennett's offer startled her for an instant. She wasn't accustomed to this kind of familiarity in her life or career, but it touched her and filled the empty spaces inside. What was happening to her? She cared deeply for Bennett, but this seemed like more. She shook her head, determined to concentrate on one major issue at a time. "Thank you, but I really have to do this on my own. It's time."

"Okay. Give him hell, and remember I'm at your side in spirit. Meet me in the chief's office around eight, and we'll hit Smith Street Diner before you leave."

"Sounds perfect. See you then." Kerstin hung up and gathered the papers she'd studied most of the night. She'd reached some pretty damning conclusions about Gilbert Early and Leonard Parrish, and Bennett's legal perspective would help nail down her tactical approach.

She dressed quickly, packed, and entered the chief's complex a few minutes before eight. She heard voices coming from his office, but his administrative assistant wasn't in yet, so she stepped into the conference room where she and Bennett had collided a month ago. She smiled, remembering how much had happened since that day, how quickly old feelings resurfaced and became new.

Suddenly the voices in the chief's office went up an octave. She started toward the door, but the chief's next comment stopped her.

"This wiring issue, the delays, and associated costs are totally unacceptable."

"I think we should scrap that whole plan," Bennett said.

"Are you serious?"

"Chief, it's clear we have too many problems. If you want, I'll step aside, and you can assign someone else to manage the build. I've failed you too."

"Ben, I admire your willingness to take responsibility, but *you* will be the one to see the project through."

Kerstin's insides quivered and her stomach churned in disbelief. Was Bennett actually recommending the chief fire her and scrap her plan? She pushed off her right foot, starting toward the office to confront them, but pivoted to the left and hurried from the complex. "One crisis at a time," she mumbled as she made her way back to her car. She couldn't face Bennett right now without totally losing control. Her career and her future depended on her meeting with Leonard. She had to hold it together.

Bennett had betrayed her, again—just like her denial of their feelings years ago and her disagreement with Kerstin at the full committee meeting. This time Bennett had denied her for the sake of her own career. She reviewed the conversation she'd overheard. Did she misunderstand? She should've gotten clarification, like any logical professional would, but her insecurities had kicked in. She doubted Bennett's sincerity, her love, and her loyalty, and retreated to the familiar. She'd repeated what she'd done years ago: left Bennett without a good-bye or an explanation.

Kerstin raced to the airport, bought a ticket for the next flight out, and boarded seconds before the doors closed. She settled in her seat and pressed her cheek against the cold window, needing something concrete. Pain burrowed deep, shredding muscle and bone and leaving her bleeding. She brushed away tears before they fell, denying her grief. Her warm feelings for Bennett chilled with each mile between them, and her disbelief morphed into something more sustainable—anger—at what she'd heard, at life, but mostly at herself.

She got off the plane in New York and saw that Bennett had called six times and left three voice-mail messages. She erased them without listening on her way to the penthouse, unable to confront Bennett's feelings or her own. Dinner passed with rote conversation about her trip and Elizabeth's continued progress. After coffee, Elizabeth insisted on going to the building's ground-floor gym by herself, and a mixture of amazement and pride made Kerstin smile as she waved good-bye.

"She's been working out alone for the past two weeks. She's determined to be completely independent again," Valerie said.

"When hasn't she been? Is she okay, really?"

"She's impressive. She still has a few memory challenges, but she does the exercises several times a day and is improving. She uses her notebook for reminders and isn't embarrassed about it anymore."

"Very good news." Her mother's successful recovery gave Kerstin more courage than she'd had in years. If her mother could overcome her debilitating physical challenges, Kerstin could certainly face her boss…and maybe even her emotional fears. She fidgeted with the hem of her blouse, her mind shifting to Bennett, hundreds of miles away.

"You barely spoke during dinner. Woman trouble?"

"Every kind of trouble. The chief of police lost confidence in my work and is replacing me. Leonard Parrish will probably fire me tomorrow. The federal government may criminally indict me. And Bennett threw me under the bus after saying she loved me. If any of the first three things happens, my career is over, forget my own firm and caring for Mother."

"Wait. Back up a second. Bennett said she loves you?"

"Yes, but you're missing the point."

"I don't think so. You've faced more serious work issues with far less anxiety. You're more upset about Bennett."

"Ridiculous, Val. Focus. I could go to *federal prison*."

"How do you feel about Bennett?"

"Seriously? I don't have time to dissect my love life."

"So, you love her?"

The question stopped Kerstin's spiral further down a doom-ridden track. "No. I mean possibly. I have no idea. I'm angry because she sold me out…I think." Damn. Valerie was right. Her feelings were totally out of proportion for only work.

"You *think* she sold you out? You're not sure?"

"I overheard part of a conversation and—"

"You didn't overreact? That would certainly be out of character."

Kerstin nodded and dropped her head. "What am I going to do?"

"Have you told her how you feel?"

Valerie slid an arm around Kerstin's shoulder, and she fought the urge to cry. "No." The word was barely audible. She'd only told Bennett she had feelings for her, not that she loved her. What a coward.

"I can't deal with this right now. I have to prep for my meeting with Leonard." She rose quickly and escaped to her old bedroom feeling very much like the lost child who'd occupied it years ago.

❖

Bennett glanced at her cell phone again—still nothing after ten hours. An off-duty officer working at the airport confirmed that Kerstin had taken a morning flight to New York. Bennett shifted in her seat, her small office growing more claustrophobic by the minute.

Jazz waved a heavy stack of papers at her. "Should we put this off until later?"

"What?"

"CompStat? Tomorrow? The chief drilling us about crime stats? Ring any bells?"

"Sorry, Jazz. Guess I'm distracted."

"Want to talk about it? The *it* being Kerstin Anthony, I'm sure."

Kerstin's departure was reminiscent of seventeen years ago, but this time she knew Bennett loved her and she had still left. "One minute we're planning breakfast, and the next she stands me up. I feel like a circus punk."

"What the hell is a circus punk?"

"Those stuffed toys with weighted bottoms we threw balls at to win a prize. That's how I feel, up and down, over and over. I told her I'm in love with her, and we talked about working things out."

"You're in love?"

"Surely that's not a surprise to you, the good twin." Bennett smiled and told Jazz about the conversation at the lake and her hopes for the future. "I have no idea what happened this morning to change her mind. She hasn't returned any of my calls."

"Congrats on finally saying the words, a first for you, if memory serves." Jazz paused in her casual but intentional way of letting things sink in. "Probably the last thing you want to hear, but my advice on the subject is the same as the first time we talked. Be patient and wait for her to come to you."

"You're right. Your advice sucks. We were so close two days ago. Maybe I was too honest and she felt trapped. Someone gets too close, and she runs. I want to find out what happened and fix it."

"What if you can't? What if her leaving has nothing to do with you?"

"I'm sure it does. And if I can't figure out what happened and make it right, then…"

"Finish your sentence, because *that* thought is part of the problem."

Could she admit the insecurity plaguing her, making her feel unfinished and weak? She swallowed hard against rising emotions. "I'm not…enough for her…again."

Jazz walked around Bennett's desk and perched on the corner, waiting for her to look up. "Which has nothing to do with Kerstin, but you *can* change."

Bennett eventually met her sister's gaze and saw only love and concern. "How did you get so smart?"

"We're twins separated at birth, remember? I know you. And all the money Mama and Pa spent for therapy after they adopted me is probably paying off too." Jazz gripped her shoulder and held it for a few seconds longer than her customary squeeze. "I love you, sis."

"Ditto." Bennett shoved aside the papers in front of her. "I'll worry about CompStat tomorrow. If I don't know what's happening in our district, you do. Let's go home for dinner."

"What about Kerstin?"

As they walked to the parking lot, Bennett said, "I wait and let her make the next move. I've offered her all of me, and I'll either be enough for her or I won't. But, by damn, I will still be enough for myself."

Chapter Twenty-four

Kerstin woke acutely aware of a new sensation, the loneliness of separation from the one she loved. Love. The word rolled around in her mind and then sifted lower, settling in every part of her, perfect and absolute. After her chat with Valerie last evening, she'd wrestled with the concept. In the light of a new day, all of her confusion and struggling with feelings finally boiled down to the same conclusion. Emotionally or logically, the answer remained the same. She was in love with Bennett Carlyle.

She started dialing Bennett's number but stopped. Bennett was special, made her feel special and want things like a relationship and family, things she hadn't considered possible. Bennett was worth fighting for, but Kerstin couldn't tell her over the phone or even apologize for her very bad behavior. Bennett deserved to hear her words in person, and she wanted to deliver them eye-to-eye with the woman she loved. If Kerstin was lucky, she'd get another chance, but she had to get her life in order. And the first order of business was Leonard Parrish.

She stared at her reflection in the subway-car window. The charcoal pinstriped suit highlighted her blond hair, and the blue silk blouse accented the clarity of her eyes. She exuded professionalism and confidence, but her looks belied the nervousness of pending battle. She'd dreamed of her father's parting advice. "Have the courage to fight for what you want." Strange advice from a man who hadn't fought for his family; but domestic life never seemed to suit him. She finally understood her father, to a point, because she hadn't found anything worth fighting for or that she couldn't live without either, until now.

Leonard Parrish sprawled behind his oversized desk and glared as she entered his office. The few hairs still on his head were slicked back with perspiration, as if he'd already swiped his pudgy hand over them several times. "You keep showing up here in the middle of the week when you should be on site earning me money."

Kerstin squared her shoulders, reached into her bag for her report, and tapped the record feature on her phone. "I've uncovered a problem, a big one." A flash of panic crossed Leonard's face. He wasn't surprised about the wiring. "Did you really think I wouldn't find out?"

"I don't know what you're talking about." His face flushed, further confirming her suspicions.

"Then you won't mind if I share this information with the building committee and our contact at the Department of Justice. We need to find out who's behind these civil and criminal violations." She had his attention and went for the kill. "Discrepancies such as these reflect poorly on Parrish Designs and could put you out of business entirely." She'd already faxed her findings to the chief's office, along with an apology and her resignation from the project. He could direct the investigation into the criminal aspects of the situation.

Leonard jumped from his seat. "Wait a minute. We don't need to inform anyone about anything. A little tweak in the cost of wiring is no big deal. Everybody does it."

"I don't." Now she was certain he'd either directed Gilbert to use the substandard supplies or at least been complicit.

"Because you're perfect." Leonard's face was so red she feared he might have a stroke.

"No, because I have integrity and want my work to be above reproach. Reputation is everything, but you've effectively destroyed Parrish Designs with your greed and deception."

"I don't need you preaching to me about ethics."

"You're right. It's too late for that lesson."

He pointed toward the door. "Get out and don't bother coming back."

Her legs trembled, her first instinct to escape, but this was her chance to right so many wrongs and to stand firm like she had failed to in the past. "Not until we reach an agreement."

"Agreement about what?"

"The police substation."

"And if I'm not inclined to agree to your terms?"

"I'll take great pleasure in reporting you to the feds."

Leonard crumpled into his chair, pulling at his tie as if it were a noose. He glared, probably trying to intimidate her. It didn't work, and he asked, "What do you want?"

"Every cent of federal money returned since their regulations haven't been followed. And you agree to fund the substation, all of it, according to these specs." She placed the new figures on the edge of his desk and slid them toward him.

He flipped through the papers, a gurgling sound coming from deep in his throat. "I can't do all that. It'll bankrupt the company and me as well."

"Take it or leave it." Realization dawned, his red-blotched face turned pasty white, and she smothered a grin. "Do you agree?"

"You realize this is blackmail. I could report you as the culprit and be done with this whole business. Gil would back me up."

"I'm sure he would, but I have witnesses, documentation, and the truth on my side."

"What do I get out of this?"

She measured her words carefully before answering. If the case went to court, her recording could be used. "I won't initiate criminal charges against you."

"And you agree not to send your *evidence* to anyone else?"

"I completely agree, but I want everything in writing, signed, before I leave."

He nodded. "When did you grow a set of balls, Anthony?"

She answered from the heart. "When I realized some things really are worth fighting for."

He slouched in his chair, a defeated man but, after a few quiet moments, suddenly stood again. "What I said earlier still goes. You're fired."

She had expected the firing, but the words still shocked her. "There's a full committee meeting about the substation with the mayor tomorrow."

"Not your concern anymore. I'll go and present them with a big fat…ch—check."

Kerstin was more than a little pleased by his apparent discomfort. "How do I know you won't back out?"

"Because, unfortunately, you hold all the cards. I hope I never see you again."

"I'll clear my desk and type our agreement. Once you sign it, you'll get your wish."

An hour later, she was back on the subway headed home again, savoring a sense of accomplishment. She had stood up to Parrish for the first time and not only for herself but also for everyone who had a stake in the substation project and all the clients he'd swindled. The police department would get their facility, she'd be free to start her firm, her mother was more independent, Parrish would go to jail, and Bennett—the list of wins ended abruptly. What about Bennett? She tabled the nagging question as she entered the penthouse.

Valerie and Elizabeth were having lunch on the balcony overlooking the park enjoying the unusually balmy weather. "Enough for one more?"

"Of course, dear," her mother said. "Bring a plate."

Kerstin filled her dish with green and pasta salads and joined them. "Looks great, Val."

Elizabeth gave her a slow appraisal, and a smile spread across her face. "You're almost radiant. What sparked such a change in my daughter?"

"She's right," Valerie added. "You're practically glowing."

Kerstin placed her knife on the side of her plate and made eye contact with each of them. These two women were family and the foundation of her newfound strength. They deserved the truth. "I have something to tell you." She took a slow breath to calm her nerves. "Leonard fired me today and—"

"What?" Elizabeth stared at her, mouth twisted in a grimace. "I will blackball Leonard Parrish in New York City and the entire state. He can't mistreat my daughter. Don't worry."

"Mother, it's all good."

"It most certainly is not."

"Elizabeth, I think Kerstin's happy," Valerie said.

"Leonard cheated on a government contract, and I suspect he's done the same to other clients. I refuse to work in a company without integrity. I'm sorry, Mother."

Her mother leaned forward and placed her hand gently over Kerstin's. "No need to be sorry. You did exactly the right thing, and

I'm very proud. You weren't happy working for him. I thought I was helping when I got you an interview with the firm." The smooth skin of her mother's forehead creased, and her smile dissolved.

"I gained experience at Parrish for my future, so I'm very grateful to you. Which brings me to another issue. I'm finally going to launch my business…and I might be moving." She prepared herself, fearing her mother's reaction, afraid she'd hurt her, but she couldn't let current or past circumstances dictate her future. "I'll take care of you, but it might be in another place."

"Because of Bennett Carlyle?"

"Elizabeth, please."

Valerie moved to intervene, but Kerstin waved her off. "Not entirely. The time is finally right to open my firm. I do hope Bennett will be part of my future because I'm in love with her, Mother." The words spilled out, creating more confidence, peace, and certainty. "I think I've loved her for a very long time."

"Yes!" Valerie pumped her fist in the air but abruptly stopped when Elizabeth eyed her.

"I see." Elizabeth slowly dabbed the corners of her mouth, then folded and placed the napkin beside her plate.

The thick tension weighed on Kerstin, threatening to tarnish her dreams. "Mother—"

"Stop." Elizabeth rolled her chair closer. "Why this particular woman?"

Not the question Kerstin expected, but the answer was easy. "She's worth the risk."

Elizabeth captured Kerstin's hands and studied her closely. "In that case, I'm very happy for you, my dear."

Kerstin was stunned. "You're happy for me?"

"Absolutely. My fondest desire is for you to love and be loved. It's the greatest gift. I've pushed men in your path in the past, but I thought that was what you wanted. If Bennett makes you happy, I couldn't be more pleased."

She was so proud of her mother and of the difficult times they'd weathered. She'd surprised her again, and she deserved to know everything. "Bennett and I have some issues. There was a mix-up before I left. No, that's not entirely accurate. I overreacted to a conversation I heard. It scared me and—"

"You ran. It's how you cope, dear. I'm afraid I taught you to avoid your problems or gloss over them with other things." Her mother, who still held her hands, gripped them tighter. "But you're learning. You and Bennett will figure things out together. And don't worry about me as you make plans." She glanced over at Valerie. "Should we tell her now?"

"Seems like the perfect time."

"Tell me what? You two have been scheming again, and it freaks me out."

"I'm selling the penthouse and joining my friends in Florida to soak up the sun, enjoy a few cocktails, and explore my own possibilities."

"I…I'm excited for you." Kerstin's vision blurred with tears. The successful recovery opened the door to a new life for her mother, but had Kerstin rushed her with this news? Was she capable of living on her own again? And could Kerstin move forward without constantly worrying about her? Elizabeth's expectant face brought her back to the conversation. "But are you sure? Are you ready?"

"Never more sure or more ready for anything in my life. Both of us need to fly the familial nest. I can't possibly repay you and Valerie for your care and kindness these past months, but I'm going to try." She nodded to Valerie, who disappeared briefly and returned with an envelope and handed it to Kerstin. "This will help with your new venture."

"Open the envelope," Valerie said, excitement making her voice quiver.

Kerstin slid her finger under the flap and pulled out a piece of paper with a long number and a dollar amount. "What's this, Mother?"

"A bank account, in your name only, and the current balance. You wouldn't let me pay for your education, Miss Independence, so I put it all into savings. The total represents your college fund plus interest. I hope it's enough."

The figure was staggeringly generous. Kerstin knelt beside her mother's chair and hugged her, tears falling freely. She had started this day with such anxiety, but her life was falling into place. "Thank you so much. I can start my firm debt-free. I love you, and I want you to be as happy as I am right now." She rested her head in her mother's lap, something she hadn't done since childhood. As her mother's fingers raked through her hair, another question occurred.

"What about Val?" She read her aunt's expression. She needn't worry.

"I'm dividing the remainder of the family trust and a percentage of the sale of the penthouse with Valerie. I won't need as much to live comfortably in Florida."

"But where will you go?"

"My friends live in an independent retirement facility with an adjacent assisted-living component. If I eventually need care, I'll move to another unit on the grounds. I'll be looked after, and you won't have to fret. But I would appreciate you finding a home with enough room for me to visit occasionally."

"Absolutely."

"Now, if you two will excuse me, I'm exhausted from all the excitement." Elizabeth kissed Kerstin's cheek and walked carefully, using her cane, toward her bedroom.

Kerstin flopped into her seat, also a bit drained by a day of emotional ups and downs. Her aunt wore a sneaky grin. "You knew about this, didn't you?"

"Not everything. She shared her plan for you but surprised me with the rest last night. I didn't expect anything so generous, not even close."

"Any idea where you'll go or what you want to do?"

"The world is my oyster, corny, but true. The flight attendant and I are planning to travel and get to know each other better. Nothing like time in confined spaces to learn about someone."

"Val, that's fantastic. I didn't know you'd gotten so serious."

"A recent development."

"And you're happy?"

"Ecstatic. Looks like things are working out for both of us. Ditto what Elizabeth said about room for visitors."

"Definitely. I have to give my stamp of approval, and so do you."

"Are you going back to Greensboro tonight?" She wiggled her eyebrows in the Groucho Marx way she did when they discussed women or sex.

Kerstin laughed and expelled some of her pent-up excitement. "Tomorrow afternoon. I wasn't sure how mother would take my news, and I have a few things to wrap up before I leave."

"Like your condo?"

"Yeah. I'm considering using it for rental income, in case."

"You're going to do great. Trust me."

"*Trust me.*" Bennett had said those words when she pledged her love, but Kerstin hadn't trusted Bennett. She prayed she wasn't too late.

Chapter Twenty-five

"This might be rough, Ben. Tough questions need honest answers," Chief Ashton said when Bennett joined him outside the council chambers where the building committee was scheduled to meet.

She nodded. She was prepared for the grilling she and Kerstin were certain to receive from the members, the chief, and the mayor, but she worried more about seeing Kerstin after almost a week of no contact.

As everyone filed into the room, she searched for Kerstin. A squatty man with a red face and balding head resembling a ripe pimple stood beside the conference table.

The mayor rushed in and checked his watch before moving to the head of the table. "Everyone grab a seat, and we'll begin. I have a hectic schedule this afternoon."

"We can't start yet, sir," Bennett said. "Our architect, Ms. Anthony, isn't here." She didn't really care about the meeting right now. She wanted, no, she needed, to see Kerstin, to understand why she'd run back to New York. Bennett had grown tired of being patient, tired of wanting someone she couldn't have, and beyond tired of guessing why.

The balding man, his face now the color of a red pepper, stepped closer to the mayor. "She's not coming. I fired her."

"You what?" Bennett rose and started toward the man, but the chief grabbed her arm. "Where is she? And who the hell are you?"

The man grinned, an expression she immediately disliked. "Leonard Parrish of Parrish Designs, and I'm the man about to make your day, Mr. Mayor." He slid a piece of paper with a check attached across the table.

"What is this?"

"The answer to your budgetary prayers. The check covers your substation project entirely. You're free to employ another architect of your choosing. If the funds don't cover his fee, contact me. My details are on the letterhead."

The mayor's wide eyes matched the stunned expressions on everyone else's faces. "I don't understand."

"I'm doing the…right thing." He stumbled over the words, and his face distorted like he'd swallowed something foul. He turned and left the room before anyone could ask more questions.

"Are we done here?" Bennett addressed the mayor, but she was already following Parrish. He'd spoken with Kerstin recently and was her best source of information.

"It appears so. Meeting adjourned."

She caught up to Parrish at the elevator door and spun him around. "Where is Kerstin?"

"Somewhere in the city of New York, I'd guess. Beyond that I don't know and don't care." He pulled away, stepped on the elevator, and the doors slid together.

She turned, and Chief Ashton was approaching, a look of concern and compassion on his face. "Boss, I need a few days off, personal reasons."

"Figured you might. Go find your architect so we can get our substation finished."

"Roger that." She dialed Jazz while taking the back way home to skirt red lights. "Can you meet me at the cottage ASAP?"

"You hurt?"

"No. Just need backup."

"Be there in five."

Even though she wasn't born into the family and didn't carry the surname, Jazz represented everything the Carlyle family stood for—honesty, responsibility, dedication, and love. Jazz always came through for her, no questions asked. Bennett trusted this time would be no different. Before she fulfilled her promise to Kerstin, another promise she'd made closer to home required attention.

She was throwing clothes into her rucksack when Jazz arrived. "What's up, sis?"

"Going out of town. Not sure how long. We need to talk."

"About?" Jazz stood at parade rest, hands clasped behind her back, as if waiting to receive an order from her supervisor.

"I have to find Kerstin and bring her back, if I can. In the not too distant future, I hope we'll move into one of the family homes, which means—"

"The cottage will be available, and I'm next in line. I don't want it."

"Why? You deserve it as much as any of us," Bennett said.

"It's not about that, really. I like the big house with the rest of the family underfoot. I spent enough time alone as a kid. Pass my turn to Dylan."

"Are you sure?"

"Hard pass."

Bennett hugged her tightly and didn't let go even when she squirmed. "I love you. You're the best sister in the world. You tell Dylan. She'll be stoked."

"Okay, okay." Jazz wiggled out of her arms and pointed to her bag beside the door. "Let's find Kerstin so you'll stop trying to smother me."

❖

Kerstin grabbed her carry-on from the overhead compartment when the seat-belt light turned off and pushed her way to the exit, apologizing as she went. Her new life waited outside those doors. She hadn't fallen in love with anyone else, settled down, or started her own business because she belonged here with Bennett. Her roller bag spun behind her as she walked faster and faster past each gate toward the exit.

"Kerstin?"

She ignored the voice in her head trying to slow her down.

"*Kerstin!*" Not her voice.

She stopped abruptly, and a fellow passenger narrowly swerved around her. Scanning the people gathered at each gate, she turned in a slow circle until she spotted Bennett. The same excitement every time she saw her, but magnified. She released the handle of her suitcase and ran, her arms wide and her heart full. Their collision almost knocked them both over, but Jazz steadied them.

"You're here." And then she kissed her, baring her soul, praying Bennett felt the same. "I'm sorry I left without talking to you. I got things so wrong. I acted like a scared teenager again. I'm so sorry about everything. Please forgive me. And please tell me I'm not too late." Kerstin kissed her again as people around them stared. Bennett hadn't spoken, but her lips said plenty. "Ben?" After a deep kiss, Kerstin finally looked into her eyes, fearing what she might see. "Ben, can you forgive me?"

"I was coming to find you."

"You were?"

Bennett took her hand and led her to a vehicle outside the entrance but stopped before opening the door. "One very important thing."

"Name it." She repeated Bennett's answer from days ago.

"I'm not chasing you anymore, Kerstin Anthony."

"Good, because I'm not running anymore." Something about Bennett made her weak in the most delicious way, and she wanted to be alone with her, to really make love to her for the first time. "Can we go home now?"

"Home, huh?"

"Your place works for the moment."

Jazz stood curbside, giving them some space, and Bennett waved her over. "Kerstin would like to go home. Think we can accommodate her?"

"Definitely." She snagged the keys Bennett tossed and opened the doors while Bennett stowed their bags in the trunk. "Why don't you two sit in the back?" Jazz turned the radio speakers up front and raised the volume so they could talk without being overheard.

Kerstin snuggled into Bennett's side and waited for her questions.

"Why did you leave?"

Kerstin winced at the hurt in Bennett's voice. "I heard you talking to the chief about getting a new design plan and assumed you recommended he get rid of me as well. In retrospect, that doesn't make sense, but I was emotionally stressed and more than a little scared. You told me you love me, and I was expecting everything to blow up in my face."

Bennett pulled her closer. "Have you figured out that's not going to happen with me?"

"Maybe, finally."

"And FYI, he was looking at Gilbert's old plan, not the new one we submitted. You obviously didn't hear the rest. I told him your plan was perfect and you were the only architect to deliver what we need."

"You said all that…about me?"

"Of course. You're very talented, and for the record, I love you."

"I. Love. You. Ben." She climbed onto Bennett's lap and kissed her until she had to breathe again.

"Hey, could you guys tone it down a notch?" Jazz asked. "Someone might call in about me chauffeuring two teenagers in my police car while they make out."

She and Bennett broke another kiss and laughed at the worried look on Jazz's face.

"That's my dedicated sister and second-in-command. Love her attention to rules and regs, most of the time. Right now, not so much."

"Speaking of breaking the rules, did the chief get the fax I sent the day after I left?" Kerstin wanted to wrap up all the loose ends from the past and focus entirely on the future.

"He didn't mention a fax."

"I sent the details outlining Leonard's theft, a copy of the original plans he signed, and the checks he cashed. Part of our agreement was I wouldn't initiate criminal charges against him, but I didn't mention the police department already had my documentation and either they or the feds probably would."

"I'll look into it when I get back to work."

Jazz turned the music down and parked on the side street closest to the cottage. "Why don't I check on the fax? Who knows if the two of you will ever surface again? And if the rest of the family knows you're here, you might not get much privacy." She helped them unload their bags and dropped them at the door. "See you at dinner?"

Bennett's grin said it wasn't likely.

"But it's only three in the afternoon."

Bennett patted her on the shoulder. "One day you'll understand, sis. And I'm counting on you to make sure we're not disturbed. We'll show up eventually."

The door closed behind them, and Kerstin was suddenly shy, uncertain what to do. She'd had sex hundreds of times but hadn't really made love when she was in love. She glanced up at Bennett's smiling face, and her brown eyes darkened. "I'm a little nervous."

"Me too. I want you so much, and I want this to be perfect, not like before."

She stroked the side of Bennett's face and detected a slight tremble. "It can't be like before because I'm in love with you. It can only be better."

Bennett grabbed her around the waist and swung her around. "Perfect answer. Anywhere special you'd like to start?"

Kerstin pointed to the sofa. "I have an unpleasant memory of that particular piece of furniture that I'd like to erase." She kissed Bennett's neck, rimmed her ear with her tongue, and whispered, "Please."

Bennett's grip loosened slightly as she maneuvered them toward the sofa. "Don't do that while I'm carrying precious cargo." She lowered Kerstin and stood looking down at her. "Do you want me to undress you?"

Kerstin shook her head timidly. "I'd like to start where we left off." Bennett's puzzled expression made Kerstin take pity on her. "Seventeen years ago, fully clothed, and necking like the hormonal animals we were. Is that too weird?"

"I enjoyed our awkward teenage groping." Bennett's mouth quirked into a smile, and the dimples on either side of her mouth blossomed. "Necking in clothes is totally hot." She dropped beside Kerstin. "Like you."

Kerstin captured her lips and tried to eradicate all the frustration, anxiety, and uncertainty of the past in one passionate kiss. She claimed her lover, licked her lips, sucked her tongue, and felt her desire reciprocated. She rolled Bennett on top of her as she stretched out on the sofa, maintaining contact.

Bennett slowed the kiss and reluctantly pulled back. "Who's in charge this time?"

"We are." She shifted so Bennett was on her side facing her, enjoying the march of pain and pleasure across her face as Kerstin touched her breasts and tugged on the waistband of her jeans. "Do you like that?"

"I…like everything…you do to me." Bennett's breathing was labored.

"You're mine."

Bennett moaned and pressed her crotch against Kerstin's leg. "I need you."

"Say it."

"I'm totally…yours, Kerst. Always have been."

Bennett's words released another surge of adrenaline and desire. She squeezed Bennett's sex through her jeans and was rewarded with an urgent groan. "Do you need to come already?"

"All the time when I'm with you."

Kerstin pulled Bennett into another searing kiss that melted her completely. She could no longer tell where her desires and Bennett's diverged. This was the real power, feeling loved and needed. They matched each other breath for panting breath, stroke for stroke, excitement building with every movement like a sexual orchestra growing to an exploding crescendo.

Kerstin's clothes rubbed and teased, arousing her simultaneously. She ached to feel Bennett's skin against hers again but reveled in the heat burning between them even fully clothed. "I'm going to make you come now, Ben."

"Please." Bennett unzipped her jeans and guided Kerstin's hand inside. "I'm so ready."

She slid a finger through Bennett's hot wetness, and Kerstin's clit twitched. She was just as wet and ready. "I want us to come together. Will you wait for me?" She stroked again, and Bennett arched against her hand.

"I've waited for you my entire life. I might be out of patience."

Kerstin pulled Bennett's leg between hers and settled against her firm thigh, the connection creating an involuntary shiver. They worked in tandem, up and down, press and release. She lowered herself against Bennett, her hand trapped between them pumping as she whispered in time. "I've. Never. Been. In. Love. Before. This. Is. The. Best. Thing. Ever." She quickened her pace as something inside her broke loose. "Come for me now, Ben." Bennett's low, tortuous growl turned into a contented moan as she released into her hand.

"Oh God, Kerst. So good."

Kerstin followed immediately, a series of tiny orgasms building into a cosmic climax—boneless, liquid, soft, and more satisfied than she'd imagined possible. She collapsed against Bennett, the feeling of safety and security she'd chased all her life settling around them. "I love you so much, Bennett Carlyle, and I'm totally yours."

"You have no idea how happy you make me." Bennett ran her

fingers through Kerstin's hair, feathering the layers back into place. "I don't know about you, but I feel sort of like a teenager again but not as sexually frustrated."

Kerstin laughed. "Definitely not as frustrated, but we have a lot of catching up to do."

Bennett hugged her close again, the energy between them shifted, and Kerstin started worrying. "What are you thinking, Ben? Weird. I haven't asked that question of anyone before. Guess the answer didn't matter until now."

"Nothing really. I'm getting ahead of myself."

"Tell me, Ben. I need us to be honest with each other."

"I'm thinking what happens now? How will this work with you in New York and me here?"

She cupped the side of Bennett's face and traced her slightly swollen lips with her thumb. "I have some options we could discuss."

Bennett chuckled. "Of course you do."

She filled Bennett in on her plans for the condo, her mother's move to Florida, and suddenly stopped. "I'm homeless." A few days ago those words would've thrown her into a full-blown panic, but now they opened the door to possibilities.

Bennett sat up and dragged Kerstin into her lap. "You're welcome to live here, if you want, or we'll take it slow and talk more later. The cottage is small, but eventually I'd like a bigger place."

"I'll need an in-home office or a separate facility to work with clients. Hold up. We're definitely out in the twilight zone now. Let's not spend time thinking about the past or worrying about the future. I want to enjoy every second with you, and I have unfinished business right here at the moment." She kissed Bennett lightly, but the kiss quickly heated. "Take me to bed."

Bennett rolled Kerstin gently off her lap, rose from the sofa, and reached for her hand. "And that's your last bossy command of the night, because I'm about to demonstrate the things we didn't get to do as teenagers."

"Oh yeah?" The question sounded just as needy as Kerstin felt.

"Ohhh, yeah." Bennett took her hand and led her into the bedroom.

EPILOGUE

Eight months later

Bennett stood at attention outside the Fairview Street Station with a group of officers and saluted while a young community woman sang the national anthem. Seeing her entire family, including Kerstin, at the front of the crowd made the August heat almost bearable. Kerstin's red, sleeveless dress brushed the top of her knees, and the thin straps accented her creamy shoulders and décolletage. Bennett subtly shifted to accommodate a flush of desire.

Their eyes met, and Kerstin smiled in her sexy way, arousing Bennett even more. She knew exactly what Bennett was thinking, their connection more symbiotic every day. Kerstin's wink promised she'd answer Bennett's need soon. After eight months together, they still spent most nights making love in their new home, down the street from the family. Kerstin blended with the Carlyle clan as easily as if she'd been born into it, and Bennett had never been happier. Kerstin's bright-blue eyes suddenly shifted to the building as the singer hung onto the final notes of the anthem.

Chief Ashton moved from the formation to a makeshift podium at the front of the gathering. "Thank you for celebrating with us today. This very special National Night Out marks the opening of Greensboro Police Department's flagship substation. The facility represents our commitment to the community and our hope that you will utilize the space for neighborhood events or celebrations. So, don't be shy. The building will also be available twenty-four seven for normal police operations, if you need us. Now, if I can get a couple of volunteers, we'll uncover the entrance and go inside where it's cooler and refreshments await."

Two officers flanked the front door and grabbed the ropes attached to the fabric covering the building name.

The chief called out, "Here we go. One, two, three."

The covering fell away, and several members of her family echoed Bennett's shocked gasp. The large copper lettering over the front door read Carlyle Building. She looked across at Kerstin, certain she knew about the surprise. Bennett mouthed *I love you* and joined the family in a group hug.

"Why didn't you tell us," G-ma asked her.

"I had no idea, but *someone* did." She nodded at Kerstin and pulled her into the circle. "How did you keep it from me?"

"The chief swore me to secrecy. It wasn't easy because we promised no secrets."

Mama smiled at Kerstin and said, "I think she'll forgive you this one time." Then she kissed Bennett's cheek. "Your father and grandfather would be as proud of you as I am right now. This is a tribute not only to their lives and deaths in service, but to all of us as a family. I only wish they could be with us now."

"They are, Mama. They are." Bennett placed her hand over her heart and felt the shell casing under her fingers.

"Mind if I cut in for a second," Chief Ashton asked as he approached Bennett and Kerstin. "I wanted to say congratulations to the whole family and to thank these two for all their hard work. If it hadn't been for Kerstin, we would've scrapped the renovations, but instead we got a fully funded substation."

Kerstin shook his hand. "You're welcome, Chief. I enjoyed the process quite a lot. Speaking of scrap, what happened to Leonard?"

"I forwarded your information, along with documentation of our payments, to the feds. Last I heard he was awaiting trial on several federal counts."

"Serves him right," G-ma said. "I can't stand a thief or a liar. And I couldn't be prouder of our two girls." She nodded at Bennett and Kerstin. "Quite a team."

Bennett's cheeks flushed. "Thanks, G-ma."

Kerstin entwined her fingers through Bennett's and gave a light squeeze. She couldn't wait much longer to reveal her other surprise to her lover. *Her lover.* Her heartbeat quickened. She finally felt a part of Bennett and needed to be alone with her. "Will you excuse us, please? I want to show Ben something inside."

"Sure. We'll see you around the food later," Simon answered.

"What are you up to?" Bennett asked as she followed Kerstin through the secured door and into her office.

"As I said, I have something to show you." Kerstin backed her against the closed door and turned the lock. She captured Bennett's hand and slid it between her legs and up.

"Oh, my God, Kerst. You're not wearing any…and you're so wet."

"It was rather hot out there."

"Not that kind of wet." Bennett moaned deep in her throat, her fingers already worrying Kerstin's flesh. "You might have to pay for deceiving me, young lady." Her mouth covered Kerstin's, and she poured the excitement and surprise of the day into her. When they pulled apart, they were both breathless. "I love you so much, Kerst. Can I make you come?"

"I'll just let you think about how wet and horny I am all afternoon. So close yet so far. Maybe when we get home, I'll let you."

"Jeez, Kerst. I'm hurting."

Kerstin slowly unzipped Bennett's uniform pants. "Why don't I punish you for the smoldering look you gave me in front of everyone?"

"Here? Now?" Bennett placed her hand over Kerstin's, already inside her briefs.

"Unless you want to wait until later too." Kerstin raked her fingernails through Bennett's pubic hair, and she rose on her tiptoes.

"Baby, please."

Bennett's breath came in short bursts. She couldn't wait, and Kerstin loved her even more.

"Stop…I should be helping the chief greet people."

"Please stop or please don't stop? If we christen your office, the memory will inspire you to hurry home every day." Kerstin flattened her hand against Bennett's stomach and slowly started pulling out, but Bennett stopped her.

"Tick tock, tick tock." Kerstin slid her hand back into Bennett's briefs and rubbed the heel of her palm against her pubic mound. "Decision time, Captain."

"It feels so good. Maybe…if I'm quick…"

Kerstin easily slid two fingers inside her lover. "You will be."

About the Author

A thirty-year veteran of a midsized police department, VK was a police officer by necessity (it paid the bills) and a writer by desire (it didn't). Her career spanned numerous positions including beat officer, homicide detective, vice/narcotics lieutenant, and assistant chief of police. Now retired, she devotes her time to writing, traveling, home decorating, and volunteer work.

Books Available From Bold Strokes Books

A More Perfect Union by Carsen Taite. Major Zoey Granger and DC fixer Rook Daniels risk their reputations for a chance at true love while dealing with a scandal that threatens to rock the military. (978-162639-754-5)

Arrival by Gun Brooke. The spaceship *Pathfinder* reaches its passengers' new homeworld where danger lurks in the shadows while Pamas Seclan disembarks and finds unexpected love in young science genius Darmiya Do Voy. (978-162639-859-7)

Captain's Choice by VK Powell. Architect Kerstin Anthony's life is going to plan until Bennett Carlyle, the first girl she ever kissed, is assigned to her latest and most important project, a police district substation. (978-162639-997-6)

Falling Into Her by Erin Zak. Pam Phillips, widow at the age of forty, meets Kathryn Hawthorne, local Chicago celebrity, and it changes her life forever—in ways she hadn't even considered possible. (978-163555-092-4)

Hookin' Up by MJ Williamz. Will Leah get what she needs from casual hookups or will she see the love she desires right in front of her? (978-163555-051-1)

King of Thieves by Shea Godfrey. When art thief Casey Marinos meets bounty hunter Finnegan Starkweather, the crimes of the past just might set the stage for a payoff worth more than she ever dreamed possible. (978-163555-007-8)

Lucy's Chance by Jackie D. As a serial killer haunts the streets, Lucy tries to stitch up old wounds with her first love in the wake of a small town's rapid descent into chaos. (978-163555-027-6)

Right Here, Right Now by Georgia Beers. When Alicia Wright moves into the office next door to Lacey Chamberlain's accounting firm, Lacey is about to find out that sometimes the last person you want is exactly the person you need. (978-163555-154-9)

Strictly Need to Know by MB Austin. Covert operator Maji Rios will do whatever she must to complete her mission, but saving a gorgeous stranger from Russian mobsters was not in her plans. (978-163555-114-3)

Tailor-Made by Yolanda Wallace. Tailor Grace Henderson doesn't date clients, but when she meets gender-bending model Dakota Lane, she's tempted to throw all the rules out the window. (978-163555-081-8)

Time Will Tell by M. Ullrich. With the ability to time travel, Eva Caldwell will have to decide between having it all and erasing it all. (978-163555-088-7)

Change in Time by Robyn Nyx. Working in the past is hell on your future. The Extractor series: Book Two. (978-162639-880-1)

Love After Hours by Radclyffe. When Gina Antonelli agrees to renovate Carrie Longmire's new house, she doesn't welcome Carrie's overtures at friendship or her own unexpected attraction. A Rivers Community Novel. (978-163555-090-0)

Nantucket Rose by CF Frizzell. Maggie Jordan can't wait to convert a historic Nantucket home into a B&B, but doesn't expect to fall for mariner Ellis Chilton, who has more claim to the house than Maggie realizes. (978-163555-056-6)

Picture Perfect by Lisa Moreau. Falling in love wasn't supposed to be part of the stakes for Olive and Gabby, rival photographers in the competition of a lifetime. (978-162639-975-4)

Set the Stage by Karis Walsh. Actress Emilie Danvers takes the stage again in Ashland, Oregon, little realizing that landscaper Arden Philips is about to offer her a very personal romantic lead role. (978-163555-087-0)

Strike a Match by Fiona Riley. When their attempts at matchmaking fizzle out, firefighter Sasha and reluctant millionairess Abby find themselves turning to each other to strike a perfect match. (978-162639-999-0)

The Price of Cash by Ashley Bartlett. Cash Braddock is doing her best to keep her business afloat, stay out of jail, and avoid Detective Kallen. It's not working. (978-162639-708-8)

Under Her Wing by Ronica Black. At Angel's Wings Rescue, dogs are usually the ones saved, but when quiet Kassandra Haden meets outspoken owner Jayden Beaumont, the two stubborn women just might end up saving each other. (978-163555-077-1)

Underwater Vibes by Mickey Brent. When Hélène, a translator in Brussels, Belgium, meets Sylvie, a young Greek photographer and swim coach, unsettling feelings hijack Hélène's mind and body—even her poems. (978-163555-002-3)

A Date to Die by Anne Laughlin. Someone is killing people close to Detective Kay Adler, who must look to her own troubled past for a suspect. There she finds more than one person seeking revenge against her. (978-163555-023-8)

Captured Soul by Laydin Michaels. Can Kadence Munroe save the woman she loves from a twisted killer, or will she lose her to a collector of souls? (978-162639-915-0)

Dawn's New Day by TJ Thomas. Can Dawn Oliver and Cam Cooper, two women who have loved and lost, open their hearts to love again? (978-163555-072-6)

Definite Possibility by Maggie Cummings. Sam Miller is just out for good times, but Lucy Weston makes her realize happily ever after is a definite possibility. (978-162639-909-9)

Eyes Like Those by Melissa Brayden. Isabel Chase and Taylor Andrews struggle between love and ambition from the writers' room on one of Hollywood's hottest TV shows. (978-163555-012-2)

Heart's Orders by Jaycie Morrison. Helen Tucker and Tee Owens escape hardscrabble lives to careers in the Women's Army Corps, but more than their hearts are at risk as friendship blossoms into love. (978-163555-073-3)

Hiding Out by Kay Bigelow. Treat Dandridge is unaware that her life is in danger from the murderer who is hunting the woman she's falling in love with, Mickey Heiden. (978-162639-983-9)

Omnipotence Enough by Sophia Kell Hagin. Can the tiny tool that abducted war veteran Jamie Gwynmorgan accidentally acquires help her escape an unknown enemy to reclaim her stolen life and the woman she deeply loves? (978-163555-037-5)

Summer's Cove by Aurora Rey. Emerson Lange moved to Provincetown to live in the moment, but when she meets Darcy Belo and her son Liam, her quest for summer romance becomes a family affair. (978-162639-971-6)

The Road to Wings by Julie Tizard. Lt. Casey Tompkins, air force student pilot, has to fly with the toughest instructor, Captain Kathryn "Hard Ass" Hardesty, fly a supersonic jet and deal with a growing forbidden attraction. (978-162639-988-4)

Beauty and the Boss by Ali Vali. Ellis Renois is at the top of the fashion world, but she never expects her summer assistant Charlotte Hamner to tear her heart and her business apart like sharp scissors through cheap material. (978-162639-919-8)

Take Me There by Julie Cannon. Adrienne and Sloan know it would be career suicide to mix business with pleasure, however tempting it is. But what's the harm? They're both consenting adults. Who would know? (978-162639-917-4)

Fury's Choice by Brey Willows. When gods walk amongst humans, can two women find a balance between love and faith? (978-162639-869-6)

Lessons in Desire by MJ Williamz. Can a summer love stand a four-month hiatus and still burn hot? (978-163555-019-1)

Lightning Chasers by Cass Sellars. For Sydney and Parker, being a couple was never what they had planned. Now they have to fight corruption, murder, and enemies hiding in plain sight just to hold on to each other. Lightning Series, Book Two. (978-162639-965-5)